THE SILENT

PARALYZER

A decade of life disrupted

By Natasha Chai

ABOUT THE AUTHOR

Natasha Chai was born an Aussie and grew up in Alberta, Canada, where she has spent over 20 years working in the public sector. She is also a chronic migraineur who suffers from hemiplegic migraine - a rare and specific subtype of this invisible disease that renders her temporarily paralyzed. Being diagnosed with such an ailment at 33 years of age, Natasha is set to voice her personal story in *The Silent Paralyzer* to raise awareness of this debilitating condition to erase the stigma many migraine sufferers have endured for so long. Natasha lives with her husband, Luc; and together, they have two children, Dennis and Isaac, who are their everything.

DEDICATION

To Luc,

For all the times you've stood guard, protected and held my
hand to lead me back to our home when it got too dark.
From my heart to yours, thank-you for never letting go.

FOREWORD

*"We are stronger in the places we have been broken." –
Ernest Hemingway*

It has taken me a long time to put words onto paper. Even today, after a decade's worth of specialists, ER hospital stays, MRIs, CT scans, lumbar punctures, and countless drugs, I'm still unsure how I am to label what I have. Is it an illness? A disability? Or a condition? What is certain is that my story is cursed.

Because of what I have, I can only remember flashes and hazy facts of when an episode comes. The main recollection of memories only happens in the aftermath, or post-dome, of an attack. Sometimes, it may even be based on how others remembered things, and I often question if what I experienced really was what happened or if it was a hallucination disguised by my brain as an actual event. All the self-doubt collected through the years because of this curse has led me on a journey trying to reclaim a self that many a time has been on the brink of being lost into an abyss. I am neither a writer nor a journalist, but logic suggests that I leverage whatever evidence I do have that includes testimonials from family and friends, medical information shared by doctors and nurses, credible online sources that cite research findings, and pages of monthly diary entries written to my dear child housing certain events, sentiments and events that are supposed to be a recount of what happened. Still, despite my best efforts in retelling facts, I would be the first to admit that I am unreliable. It doesn't matter how vigilant I am to seek out the truth because, in the instance of being dragged and assaulted through the hurt, the essence that gives the shell of my body life would never be present during an attack.

For a long time, I had thought that because of my lack of presence, this story would not be worthy - and for many, it still might not be. But perhaps for the few in this world who, like me, have also been chosen to carry this burden, they will, if nothing else, find comfort knowing they are not alone. Though most names and characters of my recount have been changed, the story I share is real. The voice that tells this story is real. It has been real not only for me but for my closest family and friends, who have watched helplessly on the sidelines. It certainly has been real for many others who have been struggling to find their sense of self in the face of this cruel fate.

Call this whatever you deem fit – a memoir, personal essay, a work of nonfiction, or a blend of everything in between. There will be things unresolved and events likely remembered wrong. But in the end, labels, and categories aside, this is a recount of just one person's journey. It is the retelling of *my* story, a long-awaited attempt to pick up the scattered pieces of whatever that has been left in a tattered memory bank in hopes that there is still a future for me to live in.

Table of Contents

CHAPTER 1

LIFE

I found out I was pregnant with the love of my life in June 2010. It was such a joyous time – especially when, years ago, my doctor had said because of my endometriosis, the chances of getting pregnant would likely not be an easy feat. Though my husband Luc and I never thoroughly discussed it, there was a silent mutual understanding between us that if we couldn't conceive naturally, then it wasn't meant to be. Married for a little over a year and a half, we already had an adult son from Luc's previous relationship and had joked that if we couldn't have a second, it would be alright, as it would have only been our *'spare'* kid anyway.

But nothing could have prepared me for the euphoria that filled my heart that Monday afternoon when I saw the two lines on that stick. While I already had my suspicions weeks before - with my missed cycle, swollen breasts, and the sensation that whatever I ate or smelled was going to double down in my gut and be thwarted out in a violent gag. Still, all that could have just been stress or the onset of a bad summer cold or flu. I didn't want to be disappointed. When Luc came home later that night from work and was told the news, like the stoic guy I fell in love with, he simply gave me a hug as if to signal that this was the beginning of our life's next chapter. It was a kind of happiness I never knew existed until then.

*****

But the joke was on me. The happiness and comfort I thought that had descended upon our home left as quickly as it came. Call it a mother's intuition or a sixth sense, but days after the baby news, the dull ache and cramps in the abdomen began to set in, triggering a sense of dread that something was wrong. Another pee test was taken, and what I saw (or couldn't really see) made my heart drop to the depths of no end.

While they were still there, I had to squint to make out the double lines on the stick that were now so very faint. With heart pounding and anxious thoughts, I called my doctor to explain the situation, hoping that she would, in turn, tell me I was overthinking things. But instead, she told me to come to the clinic as soon as I could.

Driving to Dr. W's office was the longest drive I had to make. Countless horror stories rushed through my mind as I kept within the speed limit while trying to convince myself that all would be well, that what was happening was a normal course of early pregnancy symptoms, and that Dr. W was a thorough doctor (which was why I would forever be her patient) and was just being extra cautious as all good doctors should be. There was nothing wrong and nothing to be worried about. Everything was fine.

When Dr. W finally came into the examination room, I recounted my story again of how I went from being elated to a total freak-out in less than a week. In turn, she asked me when my last period was, what the pain was like, if I experienced any spotting - and other questions that I can't recall now, though certain they were all queries to help discern if the life inside me was at risk. The visit was relatively quick, and I was then sent for blood work, primarily to check my HCG hormone levels, which I learned was the key indicator of whether the baby was still with me.

After suffering through the first of many sleepless nights, I got a phone call from the doctor's office. My HCG level, though not super high, seemed alright. It was at least enough to validate that I was indeed still pregnant. I was instructed to take it easy at work and to head to the ER the minute there was spotting or excessive abdominal pain. I was provided with a requisition to do another HCG blood test a few weeks later to make sure the baby was still snug and protected within me. When the results of my second test showed an increase in hormone levels, I was relieved but not fully convinced. It took ingesting gallons more of water and another eight boxes of Clearblue pregnancy test sticks (because the ones at the dollar store were unreliable) to help settle the worry that was haunting my daily existence. It was only after seeing day after day the double lines on those pee sticks get darker and darker, with every bathroom visit, did I begin to feel less anxious.

Less than two months after leaving my doctor's office with fear so intense that it rattled my core, I was scheduled to go back again for my first official prenatal appointment. I was now technically nine weeks pregnant and didn't know what to expect. With Luc by my side this time, the arrival of nurse Cora was like a sign from above that we were finally allowed to move forward despite the initial scare. I remember Cora to be so very helpful, loading us up on brochures and pamphlets, all filled with sage wisdom and advice on how to grow a healthy human.

Then came the highlight of the visit. Just before I was about to get ready to hop out of the hospital gown, Cora asked if we were interested to see if we could hear the baby's heartbeat. She cautioned that at nine weeks, we likely would not be able to detect anything just yet, but it was worth a try. I pounced on the opportunity without a thought while Luc stepped back and let me shriek a *"Yes!"* for the both of us.

Lying down bare and flat with the gel spread across my belly, I was nervous, excited, and anxious, all twisted into one emotional heap. While the doppler kept searching for a heartbeat, I held my breath. Then, from behind muffled static, we heard it. A steady beat, ever so faint, but was solid and true.

"So, you really are pregnant," was the comment the father of my child managed to blurt out. But it didn't matter. At that moment, nothing mattered as I was lost in the beautiful music of my child's heart. I remember Cora saying in awe, "Well, look at that. I wasn't sure if we would get anything today. You're cooking up a strong-willed baby, mama." Little did any of us know that day that Nurse Cora was right. I was destined to have a child who would grow to be determined and stubborn, just like his mama.

***

In the months that followed, pregnancy gifted me daily bouts of headaches, migraines, and backaches that were always supplemented with constant nausea. I felt sick all the time and began to forget the days when I didn't feel like dry heaving. It was like having a hangover every day, but without the youthful fun that used to come with such consequences. As difficult as it was, I continued to charge forward, and the stubborn will within did not relent and forbade me to succumb to the temptation of pills to calm the queasiness. I was convinced that anything to do with ingesting medicine while pregnant, other than folic acid, would harm my baby. For sure, I was stronger than anything for the sake of my child.

My sleep became broken at best, and I would often wake in the middle of the night with a hammering heart and a numbness in my leg or arm that made me second guess if I even had limbs of my own. But no matter how uncomfortable my body was, I would always dismiss them as the usual rite of passage any expectant mother had to endure. Now, looking back, I wonder if it was, in fact, the beginnings of the ailment I would later come head-to-head with a few years later.

In time, we found out that we were having a boy, and at twenty-four weeks, I had another scare when I was rushed to the ER in the middle of the night with abdominal cramps and spotting. The nightmare I thought had passed returned for another round of horror – this time with an even greater vengeance, knowing I had that much more to lose. Like an experimental specimen, I was poked and prodded inside and out before doctors concluded it was a thinning cervix that was the culprit threatening everything. It was deemed already too late to have my cervix plugged or stitched to prevent me from going into early labor, so the next best thing was to be placed on bed rest. But stubbornness got the better of me yet again when I refused to leave work before my scheduled parental leave. The thought of being confined and imprisoned in bed for months was simply something that could not happen. It wasn't part of the plan.

I promised Luc, Dr. W, the nurses, and anyone else who would listen that I would do the bare physical minimum at the office, taking only the elevators (even if it was for one floor), not doing any chores at home, and would no longer work late into the night that was often the case during that time. In all, I would march myself directly into bed the minute I got home from work and stay (mostly) in bed on non-workdays. Despite slowing down my pace, the migraine head pains continued to make periodic visits that compounded the nausea that never left me. At the peak of the pain, the sensation would grow so big in my head that it felt as though I was carrying another baby in my brain.

I couldn't open my eyes, much less move any other part of my body. Whenever these episodes came, everything around me felt so piercingly raw; it was excruciating, even to breathe. Countless times, I was driven into unrelenting submission, where my body learned to freeze all motion until the sea of pain passed, and I was permitted my freedom again. But this was a small price to pay for being blessed with having a child growing and moving every day within me. Perhaps it was the fear of upsetting the status quo or not wanting to jinx something so fragile and precious to begin with, I never told anyone the extent of my pain. Every episode, every attack was endured in private. So long as my baby boy was kept healthy, growing, and kicking up a storm inside me, nobody needed to know. Besides, I was certain that such pain was likely par for the course in entering the world of motherhood and would leave once the baby arrived. I only needed to hold on a little longer.

***

My perseverance finally reaped its reward the day my son Isaac came into our world. The labor was unbearable, and nothing as I had ever experienced. But at 5:50 PM on January 29, 2011, after nearly twelve hours of unfathomable hardship, I became a mother. If I thought hearing a heartbeat through a doppler was magical, then the fierce cries of my own flesh and blood being brought into the embrace of my love was a wonderous marvel. It was nothing short of euphoric. I'll never forget the pair of dark eyes that stared into mine when he was placed on my chest. He weighed less than eight pounds but charged me with the greatest power and responsibility anyone could ever possess. Upon hearing my voice, he looked up at me with such ferocious intensity as I tried to soothe his shock of joining a new world that was to be his home. In the immediate moments after giving birth, I finally knew, and all became clear. Every decision, every action, and every struggle that had ever happened in my life had only one purpose – to lead me to my son. Luc and I were chosen to be the guardians and protectors of this perfect, perfect soul, and I made a promise on that January night to be just that for this child who became my world and reason for existence in an instant.

CHAPTER 2
LIFE LOST

Every life experience has its honeymoon period and parenthood was no different. The first few weeks of being a mother made me feel as though I was in a dream, floating on a cloud, carefree and inspired. I no longer lived in constant trepidation, fearing that there would be something wrong with my child inside of me. Isaac was safe by my side in the world, and I would keep it that way at all costs.

But the dream soon turned into something else. The bodily pain that ensued in the aftermath of childbirth was a pain that rivalled the agony experienced during labor. My stubbornness still stuck with me as it did when I was pregnant and prevented me from taking any medication to help soothe the hurt that was torturing my body, in fear of the potential side-effects that I was convinced would have on the breast milk I was feeding my baby. I soon later found out that during labor, I had dislocated my pelvic bone and suffered a third-degree tear, which likely contributed to my physical misery in those early dark days.

Nothing and nobody had warned me of the physical toll post-labor would have on the body; nor was I prepared of the complexities nursing a baby would entail, where concepts of latching, mastitis, and issues of milk production now became my world and all that I thought about. But the moment I held my child in my arms, everything would be well again in an instant. The peace I found in holding and rocking my baby to sleep at all hours of the day and night made everything right. Isaac was now my every breath and purpose; and so long as I was with him to protect and love, the little discomforts that came post-partum was worth it – all the tears, hurt, pain and everything else in-between.

***

I would say that the honeymoon period for me and Isaac came to an abrupt halt when he decided after four months of life to stop sleeping. Certain that there was something wrong with him and needing every shred of evidence to convince Dr. W of this, I began to log the days and nights of sleepless torture. I was determined to show the good doctor what a demon of a child my once sweet baby had become. Surely, not letting your primary caregiver go without sleep for forty-eight hours straight was not normal. I tried every method in the book and on the internet from going through the 'cry it out method' (which made Luc and me cry even more); to soothers, to using every toy and gadget invented on earth - like using white noise machines and placing garlic and lemons in every corner of the baby room, because I was beyond desperate. But with every doctor visit and with every check-up, I was assured there was nothing wrong with my child. In fact, he was growing faster than most babies his age and was always within the top ten percentile of the growth charts. Isaac was nearing two years old now and continued to wake every couple of hours every night. I was in awe and even more livid of how a human could still grow and eat well without the function of sleep.

I had been back at work from maternity leave for over a year and despite the continued sleepless nights in needing to tend to my child, I still managed the heavy workload that was demanded of me during the day in the office. It was a stressful time that put strain on my work and married life. Because both Luc and I were always sleep-deprived, our patience with each other would also wear thin. While Isaac continued to be the center of our lives, the days became tedious, plagued with a monotonous pattern of work, daycare, taking work home to work some more, rinse, wash, and repeat. The pressures as a corporate program manager in a central human resources department grew to be an extreme pressure-cooker as the organization underwent a series of senseless re-organizations and inserted less than competent leadership teams on rotation, with each leader being worse than the last. A once promising place that offered its employees a full and meaningful career journey soon turned into hell on earth; and it didn't take long before a piece of that hell leaked into my own personal and family life.

The intense pressures of working over twelve-hour days coupled with my son's continued insistence of not sleeping, led to increasing heart palpitations and chest discomfort which in turn led to anxiety that then also gave constant headaches which then prompted migraines to return coupled with daily bouts of nausea and stomach cramps. This time, my will finally broke, as I began taking medication to help with the head pain so that I was able to get through my days.

I still do not know why despite all I was going through; did I not reach out for help then. Perhaps it was the constant self-talk that this was only a 'phase' that would pass in time; or a form of naivety accessed only as a form of self-preservation. Upon reflection, I don't know why I didn't do a lot of things back then – simply that self-care was not a priority, even though it should have been. Perhaps, if I had reached out then and sounded an alarm, many things could have been prevented. But regardless of the should have's and could have's – in the end, I did not.

With the ongoing multiple years of sleep deprivation, constant pressures of getting things done and ongoing guilt that came with being a full-time working mom, a reckoning finally came to confront me.

The month of March in 2013, was a particularly stressful one. At home, Isaac's 'terrible two's' were in full swing; and at work, bosses and clients constantly left me anxious and unsettled. I was worn out and unhinged, always being pulled into numerous impossible directions of which I wasn't able to fully commit to anything. I was alive but wasn't living. And I certainly wasn't well.

Then came *the day*. After having Isaac, my periods had grown to be irregular; and when they did come, it was with cramps that a younger me never used to have. My doctor had explained that it likely was because of my uterus being stretched during pregnancy that now was the reason for my intense cramps during menses.

When the bleeding started that morning, I was reminded that I had gone without a menstrual cycle for almost two months. I was relieved that it finally came to release me from the pre-menstrual woes of unusual snack cravings, swollen breasts and mood swings, that had made Luc walk on eggshells around me too.

While it started out light, by mid-morning, I had already gone through almost a box of pads and the cramping didn't let up. In fact, it got worse. Still, it was only the first day of a process that typically took six to seven days to pass through; and I had to be at work hosting a corporate event. Like everything else, I pushed through and dealt with the inconvenience of frequent bathroom breaks throughout the day to prevent any 'accidents' from seeping through my bottoms.

The end of the workday finally came to fruition. It wasn't until when I drove home and got out of my car, did I realize the pool of bright red substance that had soaked into the driver's seat. More annoyed than shocked, I bolted into the ensuite and stripped the now contaminated clothes off of me before heading into the shower for a full-on cleanse. Not too long after the hot water hit my skin did the piercing pain in my abdomen started again.

But the sensation was different this time. While the cramping I experienced throughout the day was unpleasant, they were at least tolerable and allowed for me to stand upright and move. The throbbing ache within me now seemed to grow exponential by the second; and I was soon diminished to a hovering crouch, having no choice but to let the pain take over my entire body. Still hunched over and panting in short, arduous breaths; muscle memory took me back to two years ago when I was at the hospital going through labor with Isaac. But labor was not possible if you had no child to birth. *What was going on??*

And just in that moment, an urge so great from within charged through as I pushed with all that I had, causing a sack of red within a sea of red plop near the shower drain. I collapsed to my knees then, scrutinizing this foreign object of a tumor that just came out of me. It looked like a collection of blood clots bulged together forming an imperfect circle that was smaller than a ping-pong ball, but most definitely larger than your regular blood clot from a discharge of a menstrual cycle. With this mystery substance now outside of me, the pain seemed to have subsided a bit and I naturally pushed some more, forcing out all the rest of the remnants of red clots and blood-stained water drops, to be forever drained away, before shutting off the water. It was likely the longest shower I ever took.

After that surreal moment, I went about the rest of the night as I did every other night - cooking and tending to Isaac when he came home from daycare and trying to engage in some small talk with my husband in-between the distractions of parenting a toddler. I remember the embarrassment of admitting to Luc the 'accident' I had in my car, blaming the incident all on an especially painful heavy period month. My humiliation grew even larger when I disclosed that I hadn't yet cleaned up the mess that happened hours ago; and asked if he could help disinfect my vehicle, so that I could drive it the next day.

Despite the grumbling and annoyance, my husband dutifully did what I asked and, on the surface, the day ended like any other day, uneventful and normal. I never told Luc about the blood ball that came out of me in the shower, only that I was exhausted and shaky, likely from the mass exodus of blood that I had excreted throughout the day. But while on the surface, everything was fine, something began to eat at me and wouldn't relent until I silently promised myself that I would go see the doctor the next day.

***

I kept true to my word and made an appointment the very next morning to find myself in Dr. W's clinic later that afternoon. I remember her practicum student was the first to greet me and asked a whole lot of routine questions about my issue. The regular queries of when my last period was before this cycle happened, what was the pain like, and did I eat or do anything different than before, were all met with regular responses. Then, finally came the part where I came clean and described the experience of pushing through a blood clot that didn't feel like a normal clot. The student paused for a bit in her notetaking when I was describing this part of my story and she asked me again when my last cycle was and confirmed if my husband and I were trying to conceive. Even then, I was completely clueless as to what she was trying to get at, until she asked, "Have you taken a pregnancy test yet?".

It seemed like such a random and irrelevant question, but I answered, "No".

"Why would I need to take a test if my period was here?"

"Hmmm… your periods have been coming irregularly?"

"Yes…"

"And the last time you had a period was over eight weeks ago?"

"About that time, I think so, yes…"

"It's true that you may have just been going through a really heavy cycle, or it could have been something else. "

"Like what?"

"Judging by what you told me, it could have been an early miscarriage."

And just like that, my world came to an abrupt and violent halt as I tried to calibrate what was just said. She mentioned it so casually, like it was just a simple flu or cold. Before I was even able to react, an offer was made to write up a lab requisition.

"I think we should have you go for some blood work. If it was a miscarriage and because it happened so recently, there may still be traces of hormones in your system and we should monitor your hormone levels during this week to see its fluctuations."

What happened afterwards was a blur of subsequent blood tests confirming low HCG levels that declined by each passing day and an ultrasound to confirm all bodily tissue was passed. Never did I think I would ever be concerned with HCG levels again; and here I was once more, obsessed with its numbers. Only this time, it was for the purpose of confirming that life was lost and could never be saved. Doctors and nurses upon validating the results, tried comforting me saying that at least what happened had happened in the early stages of the process – six to eight weeks at most. They used the word "process" like it was a cold, sterile transaction without any meaningful impact to anything or anyone.

If having a child changes your outlook on life, I would argue that miscarriages equally do the same thing for women. When I told Luc about the news, while shocked and sympathetic in the moment; he was able to recover and carry on with life, head-strong and unphased by the loss.

For me, there hasn't been a day that goes by where I don't think about the life I failed to carry and bring into this world. It's as though to forget, would be to discount a miracle that had every right to live, but was denied life, because of some sick joke.

While my head knows there wasn't anyone to blame; and the science proves it is a common reality, my heart will forever carry a regret that Isaac will never get to know the sibling he could have had, and I question what I should have done to save my child but didn't. Science suggests that because it happened early, my loss was minor, almost inconsequential. But science doesn't regard that a life is still a life – no matter how small or premature its seed. It doesn't acknowledge the love that could have been or a responsibility that should have been fulfilled. What is left after such loss is an emptiness within an emptiness that goes on for eternity. While my wound today is no longer as open and raw as it was ten years ago, it has turned into a deep scar of a marking that can never be erased, forever deeply etched inside until the end of my days. It is with this haunting that I pay tribute to my unborn child who had every right to live, grow and be loved; but only ended up as a *what could have been*.

I often wonder now if this loss was the beginning of my body showing signs of dysfunction as it was no longer capable to support life. Or perhaps it was because of this sorrow eating at my soul that was the trigger in setting off the beginnings of a cursed journey.

CHAPTER 3

NIGHTMARE'S PREQUEL

The summer of 2013 was an especially hectic one. Work was not letting up, and while Isaac continued to be the center of my world, the battle with his sleepless nights continued to be my nemesis. By now, I was still averaging only two to three hours of slumber per night while working over ten-hour days. My reality resembled more and more like Zombieland as I went through life's motions, but in a state of stupor that I couldn't escape from.

Then came the day in August of what started as a typical day in the office and ended up being anything but. I remember making several calls that morning, connecting with colleagues and clients on an initiative I was working on. I was in a rush to get this task done so that I could get to start the next thing on my 'to-do' list. It was one of those work weeks where the list of items kept growing while the hours in the day that were left kept shrinking. Time was flying at warp speed so quickly that there wasn't even a chance to take a bathroom break..

Over lunch, when I finally had a window of opportunity, I bolted to the ladies' room while making a mental note to ease off on the water for the rest of the day so that I wouldn't have to make such an inconvenient trip. I remember leaving the bathroom and swiping my access card to get back into my work area, and then – nothing.

Nobody knew exactly how long it was from the time I entered my work area to when I was found sprawled on the carpeted floor – breathing but unconscious. I came to with a handful of colleagues surrounding and hovering over me, fretting about making calls to 9-1-1 emergency and helping me sit up so that the designated first aider on the floor could inspect me to make sure I didn't injure myself from seemingly doing a face-plant on the ground. Initial inspection concluded that I was still intact but understandably shaken and in shock. Before I knew it, the paramedics arrived on scene and came to my aid with rescue gear in tow.

Questions were asked, and preliminary tests were also conducted, from measuring my blood pressure to having me take a few aspirin pills in case it was my heart that was giving way. My rescue team didn't think it wise to opt out of being seen by a doctor right away, and I was whisked off into the ambulance, destined for the closest ER hospital, while my colleagues called my husband to tell him what had happened.

By the time I arrived at the hospital, Luc was already there waiting. If he was frantic or worried, he didn't show it. Like the rock he always was, he came to my side and patiently stood by the gurney I was lying on until someone came to us asking for my information to admit me. Once transitioned to a bed and curtains drawn around us, the real marathon of waiting began.

A rotation of random interns and doctors came to my station through sporadic visits, each with their own mission of the types of tests they were assigned to do. Some came to take my blood, others placed electrodes on my chest to conduct an ECG, and then some more people came to simply hear me recount my experience. I lost count of the number of times I retold my dramatic tale or to how many people I had to speak to again and again. This pattern kept up for at least a few more hours, and in between waiting for the next rotation of doctors and nurses to come, Luc and I managed to call my parents so that they could help pick up Isaac. As calm and collected Luc was on the outside, he couldn't find the courage to leave my side at the mercy of ER doctors, and for that, I was so very grateful.

After another round of being poked and prodded, a cardiologist came for a visit and asked for my story again. But this time, she added another question.

"Have there been previous experiences you've had with syncope (or fainting)?"

"Actually, there were a few times that I remember passing out. Probably the most recent was a little over a year ago when my son was a few months old. But I think it was just because I was really sleep-deprived and was so busy that I didn't get a chance to eat anything for most of the day. But I remember after taking in some food and water, I felt alright."

"Hmm… right…"

I went on to explain another moment in my recollection that happened on an even earlier timeline - before I became a mother or was married. I was doing laundry, and with the hamper in hand, I was going down the stairs when I simply just blacked out and took a fall, suffering some minor rug burns and a load full of clothes needing to be refolded and placed back into the hamper. I was young then and refused to see a doctor when urged to do so, dismissing it as a symptom of low blood pressure, which I already knew I was a victim of.

The retelling of these past events, followed by a second round of ECGs, prompted the cardiologist to admit me for a few days for observation as she took my case for consultation with her supervisor and other colleagues. We weren't really explained what the concern was, only that I was to be transferred to cardiology and wait for further tests as there were seemingly some anomalies discovered from my last ECG readings. Anyone would have thought panic was to set in by now, but I remember only feeling anxious that I wasn't home giving Isaac a bath or cooking dinner for him, as I normally would at that time.

In the meantime, I was immediately hooked up onto an IV and another machine that monitored my heart rate around the clock. I wasn't allowed to leave the cardiology floor and, though permitted to enjoy the comforts of my electronics and visits from family members, was left to wait until doctors were able to tend to me. I eventually convinced Luc to leave for the night, knowing that Isaac would likely be unhinged with being forced out of routine, and it was better for him to at least have one parent with him at home for bedtime. I suppose the one silver lining through all this drama was that I was finally able to have a night's rest without needing to get up every couple of hours to tend to a child wanting his mother. In theory, I was finally able to get the sleep I had so very much coveted since before motherhood. But in the moment of being all alone in the quiet of a hospital room, devoid of anything familiar, I instead spent much of the night wide-eyed and awake, yearning for my baby's whimpers that I normally dreaded.

As the morning set in the next day, the lead cardiologist paid a visit to check my chart and detailed the reason for my extended hospital stay.

"Ms. Chai, there were some abnormalities detected from your ECG readings that could suggest a condition that we call Brugada Syndrome. This is basically where your heart gets to beating too fast that it becomes life-threatening."

Met with stunned silence from Luc and me, the doctor took it as a sign to continue.

"Now, because when we did the ECGs yesterday, the readings weren't all that consistent for us to conclude definitively that what you have is, in fact, Brugada Syndrome. We're gonna have to put you through another set of tests to confirm for sure. The good news is that we have the equipment, and you are in line to undergo the testing. The bad news is that the lab is backed up now, and we will have to wait a few more days before you get tested. Given your past history of syncope and the potential that you have this condition, we will need for you to stay here for observation until your test, which is scheduled in three days."

This news set in motion a number of phone calls and emails to work and family members that I was going to be out of commission for the remainder of the week. My parents eventually brought Isaac for a visit, and while a little terrified at first, he was able to find his mommy buried under all the wires and electrodes that had become extensions of her.

Other family members and friends also came for visits during the week that offered well-needed distractions. I recall that it was also in that same week when a good friend gave birth to her first-born at the same hospital I was in, and because I wasn't allowed to leave my floor, Luc and my friends made a concerted effort to convince the nurses that I was only going up a level for a quick visit. After many a plea, the nurses conceded, and I was temporarily freed from my prison for a few hours to celebrate a new life. It was such a win in my books and a good demonstration of the power of teamwork.

That one week in the hospital, while there were moments of concern about what my future would hold, I can't say I was ever fearful of what would become of me – even as I later discovered in talking to some of the nurses that a common nickname for Brugada Syndrome was that it was coined the 'drop-dead syndrome' – as it was a condition where your heart could beat so quickly, you would literally "drop-dead". There was enough commotion throughout my days between routine blood work and ECG readings that distracted me enough from dwelling too much on the negatives of why I was still staying where I was at. I secretly enjoyed having meals served to me - literally on a platter; and it made the hospital stay a little easier to endure, with Luc also bringing me snacks from places we normally wouldn't visit. The most difficult was still being away from Isaac, and while I didn't think too much in the moment, there was always a shadow looming over, as though taunting us that something very wrong was waiting for me in the very near future. When those dark thoughts came, I would silence them with snacks and entertained myself with YouTube videos.

The day finally came for the long-awaited test. I remember it to be a Tuesday morning after a long weekend, and no less than ten doctors, interns, nurses, and technicians all piled into my room with equipment, wires, and more electrodes in tow. I was once again stripped of my top and hooked onto a machine. A needle was then inserted to infuse my body with sodium channel blockers. These substances were meant to purposely stress out my heart to observe any premature arrhythmia. If the monitor detected any irregularities as a result of these channel blockers, I would be deemed "positive" and confirmed to have Brugada Syndrome, in which case I would immediately be transported into surgery to have an ICD implantation – or in other words, my own internal defibrillator for my heart, in case I ever needed a literal shock to reset any abnormal heartbeat back to normal. Before the hour was up, I was declared to have tested "negative." Almost immediately, I was discharged and instructed to go back and visit my family doctor. While the tests at the hospital showed I was fine physically, I still needed an explanation of my fainting spells and was advised to look to neurologists for any dysfunction inside my head.

But the doctor's visit was for another time. We took the day's win, and I was reunited with my boy and husband back at home – all in one piece.

***

After the hospital ordeal, I went back to work pretty much right away, but I followed orders and visited Dr. W, who in turn immediately referred me to a local neurologist. I was told that in Edmonton, where I lived, the city really didn't have that many neurologists at its disposal. So, when I was told there was a waitlist and that I wouldn't be able to see the specialist until three weeks later, I wasn't entirely surprised.

My appointment date to see a Dr. Kerr came, and as a good patient would, I arrived at the clinic a few minutes earlier to fill out the paperwork before seeing the specialist. I was greeted by the practicum student first to verify my responses to the form and other coordinates before meeting Dr. Kerr in person.

The visit must have lasted no more than fifteen minutes. But within that time, the woman had the talent to incite shame, humiliation, and self-doubt – solely by a judgmental stare supplemented by her harsh and critical tone.

Upon explaining the recent key events that led up to my visit, she never once showed concern or interest in my case. I don't even recall her taking any substantial notes. I will never forget the condescending way she looked at me from head to toe as she offered up the explanation that what I had gone through was because of a headache or migraine.

"I might have been able to give you more information if you didn't wait three weeks to see me," was the best she could offer.

"It looks like you did all the tests you could do when you were in the hospital, so I don't think there's anything more you need. Again, you shouldn't have waited so long to see me."

"But I went to see my family doctor right after being discharged, and she referred me to you immediately. I would have wanted to see you sooner but was told you had a three-week waitlist."

"Well, unfortunately, there's nothing I can do."

And just like that, I was excused, dismissed, and deemed an irrelevant case for her portfolio.

I didn't know it then, but this encounter would be the first of many that I would have had to face for years to come. Doctors, who I assume, chose to go into their profession because of a desire to help and heal others, but instead, have grown so jaded that they look to their patients' cries for help and understanding as something to be spat upon and condemned. It was the first time where I left a doctor's office feeling hurt and emotionally assaulted in the most unfair way. Sadly, it wouldn't be the last time of such a sorrowful experience.

CHAPTER 4
NIGHTMARE'S BEGINNING

After licking my emotional wounds and reflecting on what had gone wrong and whether there was something more I could have done for a more meaningful and constructive experience, I resolved to go back to Dr. W to ask for another referral. This time, I wanted a different neurologist for a second opinion. If previous doctors and specialists found something in my ECG readings that warranted a reason for a hospital stay, surely, I deserved more than a casual diagnosis of "it was just a migraine headache." After all, I was a Canadian with a public healthcare system. I had a right to expect more to come from my tax dollars, especially when it came to my health and wellness.

The latter days of the summer months were upon us, and I made a mental note to call Dr. W after our trip to Las Vegas in early September of 2013. The vacation to Sin City was a surprisingly enjoyable one and a lot more manageable than previous trips. We attributed that with Isaac now growing to the ripe old age of almost three; perhaps life, including family trips, would only get better as we continued to escape the torturous grip of the *terrible twos*. The trip was so great that we even contemplated extending our stay in Vegas for an extra couple of days towards the end of our week-long holiday.

Even though it was barely a few weeks ago, the unpleasant visit with Dr. Kerr, was already like a distant memory. Health-wise, I was feeling fine. Despite having a few bouts of migraine headaches, they were never enough to stop me from going through my daily routine – whether it was at work or at home. It was as though the health scare that dominated our attention before had been funneled and concentrated all into that one intense week at the hospital. While I still had plans to see Dr. W again, I didn't feel the urgency I felt a few months before. I even began to wonder whether what happened earlier that summer was just a variance for an otherwise healthy person. Still sleep-deprived and likely overworked, but healthy enough all the same.

By now, my son was sleeping on a mattress on the floor, sandwiched between his pillows and snuggled up close and warm with his beloved stuffies. A few months ago, we made a serendipitous discovery that our two-year-old slept better and longer on the floor than in a crib. I remember getting some subtle, strange looks when we told people about this. Surely, it wasn't *proper* to banish a toddler to sleep on the floor. I'm sure it seemed almost barbaric to many, but for me, it was a eureka moment. Even though he still couldn't sleep through the night, getting up four or five times in between slumber was exponentially better for everyone's health and well-being than being called awake over ten times in the night.

One night, Isaac did his regular call-out, and like clockwork, I migrated over to his room to fulfill my motherly duties. As with every night, I laid beside him on his mattress, patted and rubbed his back for what seemed like an eternity, and left his room when he fell back to sleep.

In a trance, I wandered back to my bedroom with eyes half-closed, but not before making a mental note that it was almost 4 AM, and I only had a couple more hours before needing to start the workday again.

I woke up again, but not to Isaac's whimpers. To this day, I'm still not quite sure what nudged me awake, only that something was *off*. Something was not right and was very wrong. Lying on my back in bed, it seemed like only the right half of me was attached. As for the rest, it felt like my body had been sliced in half, with the left side abandoned to rot in the abyss of darkness where sensation and feeling did not exist. I could not move my left hand, arm, or leg. It was as though someone had severed all nerve connections that would normally be linked to my brain, and as a result, my brain could not communicate with the left side of my limbs because they no longer spoke the same language.

My immediate instinct was to wake Luc, who was still in slumber, lying ever so far away on the other end of our bed. *How could a queen-size bed be so large?* I struggled to maneuver my torso in every way, but it refused to make any meaningful movements. The only limbs I could control were on my right side, but even then, I didn't have the strength to sling-shot sideways to make a 180-degree flip to get the attention of my sleeping husband. Unable to make any substantial moves, I resorted to using my voice in a frantic cry for help.

But the words I knew to use only spilled out in a heap of messed-up gibberish that even I couldn't understand. While my talking made no sense, I was still able to push out a desperate "Ahhhh…" with one thrashing arm waving in the darkness as though signaling my left side to return so that I could be made whole again. My distress call finally succeeded in jolting Luc up from sleep. It took another few seconds for him to realize something was terribly wrong. Immediately, he jumped out from his side of the bed and flicked on the lights, only to witness his wife in a savage fury of panic. I will never forget the look on his face as he tried to keep calm while making sense of everything that was happening to me right before his very eyes.

The man who had always been my pillar and the calmer second half became someone thrust into a chasm of fear so great that you could smell the horror radiating from him a mile away. Later in the years that followed, when the frenzy was over, Luc would tell me that he had thought my life was finished that night. He described seeing such a twisted face, so "distorted" I was beyond recognition. Every inch of my face on the left side had been dragged so low that my eye looked as though it had sealed itself shut. The left side of my mouth had relinquished all control and had let a flood of saliva seep through, making my pillow and parts of our bed wet. This loss of control was something never experienced and felt like it was out of this world. I didn't know what else to do but continue with my violent thrashing and jerks with the one able side of my body while screaming out barbaric, mangled noises in desperate hopes of breaking free from whatever was holding me captive. But all efforts were in vain. It was of no use, and I stayed trapped.

Luc's calm returned as fast as when the terror set in moments before. A call to 9-1-1 happened, and a second call was made to my parents to help us look after Isaac while I was in transit to the emergency. I can't say for sure, as it was all a blur. But I do remember paramedics entering our bedroom, likely expecting a stroke victim.

And then, a miracle was gifted. After Luc gave the summary of what he witnessed, paramedics turned their attention to me and started asking questions. My words started to flow, and sentences began to take shape, and I found myself speaking again. While the left side of my body felt like it was weighed down by a ton of bricks, I began to feel tingling and a sensation that my limbs were returning to their rightful owner. The prickles extended everywhere on my left side, including my lips.

I was able to communicate in slurred speech, as I felt my sense of feeling return. I heard someone comment that my face still seemed rather "lopsided," and I was then immediately whisked onto a gurney and out of my house enroute to the nearest ER. By the time I arrived and was in the line-up for an immediate MRI and CT scan, a wave of warmth had gushed over my left side. It was as though a pail of warm water was injected into my system and was now making its way inside every vessel of my body. While the part of my brain that was supposed to connect with my limbs was still shaky, I managed to move ever so slightly a few fingers and toes with the greatest of all effort. I remember while waiting to be wheeled into the room, I glanced up at the clock and saw that it was 4:45 AM. How very fickle things were in this world. In a span of barely forty-five minutes, we had gone from everyday mundane routine to being at the cusp of losing it all.

I was queued up to do both a CT scan and MRI almost back-to-back. And by the time I was done with both, it seemed that the hospital had run out of physical space to store me. I was wheeled alongside the edge of a hallway and propped up against a wall to wait for the verdict that would direct the very fate of my future. I spent the better part of that day watching all the commotion that went on in an ER ward while re-training my brain to talk to my left arm and leg on the basic motions of up, down, left, and right. By this time, my facial features were all back in the positions they were supposed to be, and my speech had pretty much reverted back to normal. I could only imagine what my test results would say.

It was nearly six hours later when a neurologist by the name of Dr. S came to see me. While he had a gentle bedside manner about him, you could also tell that he was one who was proper, thorough, and rather thoughtful. After exchanging formalities, Luc and I held our breath as we braced ourselves for what could come next.

"Ms. Chai, the good news is that both MRI and CT scans have come out normal. There is no sign that you had gone through a stroke."

With that news, about half a ton of weight lifted from our shoulders, with still a lingering worry clinging to our psyche as the mystery of what had happened remained unresolved. We still needed to find out what was the matter with me, if not for the images captured by the scans.

But it seemed the doctor still had a few more tests of his own to go through. Before divulging anymore, he asked me to follow with my eyes the motion of his index finger that was moving in all sorts of directions in front of me. He then checked my reflexes with a small hammer, asked me to stand, hop on one leg, and walk a straight line up and down the hospital hallway as though I was on the cusp of being charged for drinking and driving. And as if for good added measure, my coordination was further tested when I was asked to move my left finger to my nose and once again with my right side. My muscle strength was tested as I followed instructions to push against the doctor's hands with my arms extended out towards his. *Just what exactly was he trying to uncover? What was he trying to find? Did I pass his tests?* It seemed all very bizarre to me.

Being allowed to sit back up on the hospital bed, Dr. S asked more questions.

"Have you been in a car accident recently?"

"I had one over ten years ago. But it was nothing too serious, except for some whiplash and soreness for a few days afterward."

"Did you have X-rays and scans done after the accident – especially on your neck area?"

"Yes, I think I did, and I think they all came back normal."

With an approving nod, Dr. S continued. "Ms. Chai, are you aware of any family history of stroke?

"No, none that I'm aware of."

"Do you smoke or drink alcohol regularly? Recreational drug use? Do you have any pre-existing health conditions before today's incident?

"No… I definitely don't do drugs. I'm not a smoker and don't drink, except in some social settings, but never a lot. I was admitted to the Royal Alex a little over a month ago because of passing out at work. They thought I had Brugada Syndrome, but the tests came out negative. Otherwise, I'm usually pretty healthy. I have migraines and headaches sometimes, but that's about it."

"Hmm… that's good to know. Your chart does suggest you are pretty good, health-wise. I think we can likely rule out transient ischemic attack then."

"What is that?"

"A transient ischemic attack or TIA is like a stroke but is temporary in nature and usually lasts for a very short period of time. Because it doesn't usually cause permanent damage, if you had had a TIA and took the CT scan or MRI, the images should have also come out normal. Some folks think of it as the 'ministroke' warning before the real one comes. But based on your history and background, I don't believe that is what you had."

"Then what do you think I have?"

Looking past me while stroking his chin as though deep in though, Dr. S answered, "I think you had a migraine."

Not again. Were all neurologists in this city the same? I had just told him that I have had migraines and headaches before. As someone afflicted with it, I *knew* exactly what migraines were about. In that instance, I had another 'life is fickle' moment where I went from being hopeful to skeptical. I was utterly insulted and wasn't shy to show it.

"I really don't think so. I've had migraines before and know that it usually involves a lot of pain on one side of your head and maybe nausea; but you don't get stroke symptoms like I did earlier. I didn't even get any head pain today, so how could it be just a migraine?"

"Depending on the literature you read, there are at least ten to twelve types of migraines a person could have. Some people go through what we call a migraine without aura. That's the most common type where you get what you just described – the intense, throbbing pain on one side of your head that can last for a few hours or, at most, a few days."

With this initial explanation, my internal annoyance calmed slightly, but I wasn't yet entirely convinced. To pin the most traumatizing experience I have ever had in my life on a mere headache was something I couldn't accept, no matter what.

"What I think you experienced, Ms. Chai, is what is called a hemiplegic migraine. This is by far not a headache and isn't your typical migraine. It is actually a very rare and severe type of migraine attack that causes one side of the body to go into paralysis."

At this point, I had nothing to respond back with. A migraine that brought along temporary paralysis was the first I had heard of. I needed to learn more.

"So, what do I have to do next?"

"Well, hemiplegic migraine is my initial suspicion, but we have to make sure that there isn't anything else that caused the paralysis and stroke symptoms. Once those tests are done and if they come out normal, we can then conclude that you do have this condition and can talk about the next steps from there."

At least there was a plan to tackle this.

"But to start, while I'm pretty sure you didn't suffer a stroke, I'll still have you go on some blood thinners first, just to be safe. We'll schedule you for some regular visits to our stroke clinic in these next few weeks, do up a job requisition for some blood work, and go from there. Does that sound good?"

No. None of what he said or suggested sounded '*good.*' But what choice did I have? While still not free from the threat of a stroke and still unsure exactly of what I had, the next steps Dr. S outlined were likely my best offers. At that moment, I only knew that I had to look up more information on this mysterious hemiplegic migraine issue and that I wanted to go home.

Not too long after my first encounter with Dr. S, I was given a prescription for one week's worth of blood thinners, some scheduled dates to visit his stroke clinic, and strict instructions that if symptoms returned or changed, I was to go directly back to the ER. I left the hospital that day, battered and limp, with more questions than answers, being only able to see a path ahead forged with more unsettling worry.

CHAPTER 5

FINDING MY BEARINGS

I made my first visit to Dr. S's stroke clinic as an outpatient a few days after being discharged from the hospital. It was interesting that even as an outpatient, I was still provided a wrist bracelet, was weighed and measured for my height and blood pressure – all things seemingly unrelated to why I was actually at the facility.

Not long after the nurse left me in the examination room, Dr. S made his appearance as tranquil and collected as the last time I saw him. He already had my chart in hand and settled in the chair across from mine, ready to diagnose (or at least I hoped).

"Hello, Ms. Chai. How have you been doing?"

"I've been doing okay. Still more tired than normal and been getting some headaches here and there, but nothing that isn't tolerable."

"Ahh… were you having headaches before your last paralysis?"

"Not so much headaches, but more like full-on migraines, with the one-sided head pain."

"How often do you get migraines, and does it come with the onset of aura – like nausea, sensitivity to light, and any other discomforts?"

I mentally chuckled at his usage of the term 'discomfort.' Through my recent hospital stays and more frequent interactions with doctors, nurses, and even paramedics, it seemed that healthcare providers all had different definitions of 'discomfort' as compared with the general public. 'Discomfort' meant being afflicted with something that could be a little uncomfortable but tolerable. The key differential was *a little*. 'Pain,' on the other hand, meant infinitely more than just *a bit*. In fact, I don't think I had ever heard a doctor or medical practitioner use the work 'painful' in any context. Perhaps it's something that is taught in medical school under the topic of 'terms to avoid' in efforts to curb patient anxiety. Afterall, going ballistic in anticipation of pain isn't helpful to anyone when a needle is being inserted into your body.

My attention focused back on the questions being asked, and I reflected on the countless times that I suffered from bouts of migraine pain (not discomfort).

"When I get the head pain from migraines, I usually get nauseous and am severely sensitive to light. Sometimes I throw up, and other times it feels like a really bad hangover."

"How long do these migraines last?"

"It varies. Sometimes a few hours and other times even a full day. I notice that I usually get them when I'm really exhausted."

"What's making you so exhausted?"

"Mostly my son. He's two this year and has never really been a good sleeper. He normally wakes up at least four or five times a night, and I may average, at best, two to three hours of sleep for myself before I go to work. I'm getting used to this sleep pattern, though, since it's coming on three years already with his broken sleep."

"Work… you work fulltime?"

"I took a couple of weeks off as sick days because of last week's incident, but I normally work fulltime – yes."

"What do you do at work?"

"I work in human resources. I pretty much have a desk job with most of the time being on the computer and lots of meetings with people."

"Hmm…" were the thoughtful sounds of Dr. S as he jotted down notes in response to what I shared. I was getting more and more intrigued with each passing minute, wanting to know what he was thinking.

"Ms. Chai, I don't think you have enough sleep to help support you during the day. If you weren't working, then at least you potentially could make up for it with daytime naps. But seeing as you're only functioning on less than a handful of hours of sleep every day, you are, in essence, running on fumes. In other words, a lack of sleep could contribute to your migraines as your brain gets stressed from having no rest. It may very well be that last week's episode was a greater exacerbation of this root cause because your body was exhausted and was acting out."

I suppose I had always known intuitively that I wasn't doing my body any favors by not getting enough rest. But I never thought of it in terms of harming my brain to the point of stressing it out. It was a new perspective for me.

Seemingly agreeable so far to his comments, the doctor continued.

"The blood work you did all came back with no flags, and I think the next step is to schedule you for a lumbar puncture as a last step to conclusively rule out that you have anything else. While we're waiting for that to happen, I believe it prudent for us to start on some preventative medications to prevent the migraine from returning."

"But what if I end up testing positive for another condition? Will the medications you prescribe to me now be harmful?"

"No, they won't be. Migraines, unfortunately, aren't like other conditions where there's a targeted pill for you to take. In fact, a lot of the medications used for migraines are actually used to help with other ailments like depression, heart conditions, or seizures. But when used in very small dosages, there has been evidence to suggest that they do help with prevention. The trick is to find the right dosage and the right type of medication since there are numerous choices. There are medications to take as well in acute cases at the onset of an attack, but what we want to do first is to prevent the migraine from happening in the first place."

Pausing to gauge my reaction, as I was still digesting the information, I nodded my head, prompting him to continue.

"So, to start, we will put you on the smallest dosage of Amitriptyline along with Zofran and Metoclopramide. The

Amitriptyline should help prevent the migraine from coming, and the Zofran and Metoclopramide will prevent the nausea. If the paralysis comes along again, you can try taking Tylenol as an abortive measure and let it pass. Try taking these for about four weeks, and we'll see you again in a month. In the meantime, my office will contact you for your lumbar puncture when they have scheduled you and will also call to confirm your next clinic appointment with me."

Like a good patient, I took the prescriptions and went about my way, only to realize too late I had wanted to ask about lumbar punctures and what that procedure was about. Knowing I had missed the chance to go back to Dr. S and ask, I remembered that we lived in the 21st century and resolved to do some of my own research with my trusty phone and 4G network.

I did the same sort of investigative work not long after my last hospital stay to search out more about what exactly hemiplegic migraine was. There wasn't a lot of information that surfaced upon searching the topic, but what I did uncover was consistent with what Dr. S had shared with us. Hemiplegic migraine is a rare subtype of migraine that often comes with 'aura' symptoms causing motor weakness typically affecting one side of the body, speech and/or sensation impairment, nausea, one-sided numbness, confusion, and trouble with muscle control. These auras can come on gradually and last for hours and, in severe cases – days but usually revert to normal on their own accord afterwards.

At the time of looking up this new topic of interest, the medical community had been able to identify a set of genes linked to the disorder. Any defects or mutations in these genes have been found to be the cause of preventing the body from making certain proteins, which in turn causes nerve cells to have issues sending out or taking in signals that go between them. It was confirmed that there were no direct tests or scans to diagnosis the condition. CT scans, MRIs, and blood tests don't usually show migraine attacks and could only help rule out other conditions. It was indeed a diagnosis of 'exclusion.'

There were mainly two types of hemiplegic migraines: Familial hemiplegic migraine (FHM), where the disorder runs in the family, and Sporadic hemiplegic migraine (SHM), where there was no history of such a condition and if genetic testing were to be done, there wouldn't be found to have any defects in the genes linked to hemiplegic migraine. I later confirmed with Dr. S that given there were no other family members who had experienced what I did, I likely had SHM. There would then be a fifty-percent chance that Isaac, being my offspring, would have inherited the genes that also caused hemiplegic migraine.

The best part of all this information was that it was reported that while migraines, in general, were common (about one billion people worldwide suffered from them), hemiplegic migraine was found to be so rare that out of the billion-person figure, only one in 10,000 or 0.01% of the population had it. Females had been found to be affected more frequently, but with the onset of the disorder to occur usually from the teenage years to early adulthood – but rarely beyond the age of thirty. What were the chances that out of a billion people, I had been chosen to join the elite group of

0.01%? I was well into my thirties by this time, the supposed age where this migraine should have bypassed me altogether to hunt for someone else with younger genes. What was so special about me that made the hemiplegia barge through my door? I was never one to gamble, but in that moment, I made another mental note to buy myself a lottery ticket in hopes that the money fortune would also think I was special and come through my doorway. Sadly, I had no such luck.

***

Within a few days of seeing Dr. S and on the onset of taking the medications that were instructed, I had another attack and then another and then another – all within a few days from each other. Each episode was different, and I didn't go through a week without having at least an attack or two come for a visit. Sometimes, I only had numbness on a leg or an arm, but no speech impairment. Other times, my face would be impacted, but my limbs would be fine. Still, there were also days when it was decided we would go old-school with the typical one-sided throbbing migraine headache that was just as excruciating as paralysis and numbness. The variations of the symptoms always kept me and my family on our toes.

While no episode was the same, one thing that stayed consistent was that the paralysis was always on my left side. As frightening as the attacks were, my recovery period in those early days had a rather quick turnaround time. Whether it was full-on paralysis of my entire left side or just a part of my body, it always took no more than seventy-two hours to return to normal, short for some exhaustion that took a few more days to shake off. But I would at least be functional enough in three days or less. For that, I was thankful. Isaac was still so young, and while Luc was always by my side, I knew it was taking a toll on him too. Whenever an attack passed, leaving me depleted and near lifeless, my stoic husband would huff in frustration the disbelief that there wasn't anything more 'concrete' that was diagnosed. He was convinced that something had been missed because what I was going through couldn't be normal; and became even more enraged that we were seemingly left to our own defenses against such a thing. His moments of frustration left me feeling even more helpless than when the actual paralysis set in. Not only being incapable of managing myself but also forcing those closest and most precious to me now to carry this burden was wrong and unfair.

But at least we were successful in keeping it away from our child. As powerless as I was with the condition, I would not allow Isaac witness the devastation that manifested within his mother during an attack. No child that young should ever see their parent break at the mercy of something so evil. The attacks miraculously stayed away from my workplace and even at family and social gatherings in the early days. When it did come, it would only haunt us in the evenings or over the weekend when we were at home, away from the public eye. Friends, colleagues at work, and even my stepson, parents, and sisters had not yet seen the hemiplegia's might and the poison it unleashed during an attack. As twisted as it was, there were times I was silently thankful that at least I had Luc to be my witness so that he could validate first-hand that I really had such a disorder. On the outside, when I was free from the episodes, I appeared physically and mentally capable as any other healthy person.

It was understandable then that there were people skeptical of what I claimed I had, especially when it was something so uncommon. I may have also been one of those skeptics myself, had the hemiplegia not made a believer out of me.

***

At my next doctor's visit, I recounted the episodes I had and admitted I likely was only able to recount the most recent instances as my memory could only hold so much. He suggested that I start a log on my phone or in a journal that noted the frequency of my attacks as it could help inform whether a change in medication or treatment was needed.

Upon hearing about the attacks, I was able to remember, Dr. S made some further changes that included upping my dosage of the tricyclic antidepressants I was on. Given the frequency of attacks, I was provided a medical note to work part-time three days a week for a month so that I would be able to use the extra couple of days in that week to sleep and rest. It was figured that I likely needed it for my upcoming lumbar puncture.

Making up for the missed opportunity from last time, I asked about my impending procedure now, mentally comparing his response to the information I found online.

"A lumbar puncture is also called a spinal tap," he began. "The procedure will be done by me where I'll use a needle to insert into the area that is around your spinal column in your lower back to draw out your cerebrospinal fluid."

"What is cerebrospinal fluid?"

"It's a fluid that normally acts to cushion your brain and spinal cord. Your body continuously makes this fluid so that it gets reabsorbed in your brain to maintain balance in your nervous system."

He then explained that once the fluid was extracted, it would be tested for any presence of bacteria, viruses, or other abnormal cells based on the red and white blood cells, proteins, and sugars from the fluid.

"If you were healthy, the fluid is usually clear when extracted. The murkier the fluid, the greater the indication that something is wrong, like if you have encephalitis (inflammation of the brain), meningitis, or certain cancers. So, it's a procedure that can tell us a lot once the fluid is extracted."

"Will I be going under for the procedure?"

"No, you'll be awake the entire process. You'll be given a local anesthetic so that it'll be less uncomfortable when I insert the needle. The needle will be hollow, and I'll have a test tube ready at the base of your spine so that once the needle is in, the fluid should begin to drip out of it and into the test tube. I won't need more than a tablespoon full of it for testing."

The day came for Luc to drive me to the hospital for the puncture. As promised, Dr. S had me lie on the examination table on my side in a fetal position with knees pushed to my abdomen and chin tucked to my chest so my back was arched, ready for the poke.

It was comforting to hear Dr. S describe his every move on what he was doing literally, behind my back. The anesthetic injection was uneventful, and I felt the slightest pressure in my back from where the hollow needle was officially inserted. I was entirely focused on following instructions to stay absolutely still. Before I knew it, I felt a release in my back and was told to stay as flat as I could for a few minutes, ensuring my head wasn't elevated to prevent subsequent headaches *(oh, the irony!)*.

"Ms. Chai, you are a trooper," proclaimed Dr. S as he finished with the process and asked that I stay on my back for about a half hour before being allowed to go home. I was warned that if some fluid leaked from the needle insertion site, I would experience severe headaches but that the pain should subside once the fluids balanced themselves out, usually within a few hours. If the head pain persisted for an extended period of time or if there were other abnormalities like numbness, bleeding, or pain at the injection area, we were to immediately go to the ER for observation.

A half-hour later, I was helped off the bed, changed back into my clothes, and was homeward bound. As we made our way out the door, my eyes darted over to the needles and apparatus used for the procedure I had just gone through. There was a small vial in the pan on the table. Inside the vial was about a tablespoon of fluid that was unblemished and clear as the light of day.

***

The potential side effect of head pain never came - proving how skilled Dr. S was with operational procedures.

No more than a few days later, his office called to share that lab tests of my cerebral fluids all came back negative. I was officially a healthy person. I remember the conflicted emotions that went through my thoughts as I received the news. On the one hand, so very relieved that everything came back normal, and on the other hand, disappointed that nothing definitive was found, forcing me to continue to treat something that I was beginning to realize nobody knew much about, never mind a cure. As if to challenge the science that claimed there was nothing wrong with me, the hemiplegia came again that very night. It settled into my left arms and legs, making me trapped within the very depths of my own flesh. While the paralysis of my limbs could have been classified as a mild one, it later evolved into throbs of pain and conducted a full-on invasion of the right side of my head. Lying in bed being suffocated within a pool of agony, every sliver of light and echo of a whisper was amplified to the extreme. There was no escape.

The hemiplegia kept taunting me without mercy. Its attacks would retreat as quickly as they came. Lighter episodes would have me recover in a few hours, whereas the more serious instances had me mobile again within a few days. I was still logging my episodes then, but neither myself nor my neurologist could detect any pattern that suggested a rationale for why I would be a target of this curse. I would always be offered different reasons for why a particular month was worse than the previous one for the frequency of attacks. Some months, it was rationalized that it could have been something I had eaten, like cheese or chocolate. The next month, it was likely the stress from work or red wine I had ingested. When these explanations failed to satisfy my query, we would always revert to the fact that it likely may have been the hormones during pregnancy, followed by lack of sleep while nursing a child that caused my disorder of the present day. What nobody was ever able to explain was why these trigger foods and substances - things I had always eaten or been exposed to for the better part of my life – were now suddenly the cause of my misery. If I was prone with a constitution to be sensitive to cheeses and wines, one would think I would have reacted to such triggers a long time ago and not wait until I was in my thirties for such a revelation. Surely, my body would not have waited this long to let me know it did not appreciate what I ingested. It wasn't that I didn't believe my doctor, but I started to wonder if the limited literature on this condition used by the medical community was enough. I started to question why there wasn't more research, more awareness, and more attention placed on something so many people knew so little about. And what was worse, I was beginning to feel that even my own neurologist was losing patience with me.

It would have been the ninth or tenth visit to his clinic when I continued to let him know that my frequency of attacks was not subsiding. While the paralysis that invaded always seemed to set me free after it had its moment with my limbs or face, each attack threatened a different set of fears that I wasn't sure whether my husband or I would be able to handle more of. Dr. S began to offer the same counsel of asking if I was getting more hours of sleep these days. *No. I have a toddler that needs me throughout the night.* If I was still not getting enough quality sleep, then perhaps I had to consider not working altogether for a while. It would be good for me to take the rest. *I do not have the luxury of not working.* A list of trigger foods was shared with me. *Yes! I was given that list the last time. I have cut off pretty much all of the foods on that list.*

And with every visit, almost in defense, the doctor and even practicum students would protest to say that all the tests that could have been done were done. The best method, then, was to keep with the medications to prevent the attacks, and if one came along anyway, I should just ingest some Tylenol. And because my attacks were still happening, I would then be given more medications (many of them with names I don't even remember anymore), or the dosages of the drugs I was already taking increased by a milligram or two, and I would be sent off on my way, as if I had been cured.

I remember there was a moment in time when I was prescribed a total of eight medications to be taken daily at different intervals throughout the day. Between the anti-depressants, anti-nausea, and anti-epileptic pills, the brain fog that ensued rendered my days blank and listless. On these drugs, I would be at work, unable to concentrate on my tasks. I would sometimes find myself talking to colleagues or being in meetings and forgetting what I had wanted to say in mid-sentence. I would be with my son, who would share exciting stories from daycare, and while I was physically there, I was no longer able to bask in his enthusiasm or zest for life because I no longer felt life anymore. The lens I looked through my world was drained of color and, instead, showered endless pictures of grays, blacks, and whites – all without meaning and hope. I was sandwiched between different dimensions of misery, and all of this was happening because of the drugs I was told were good for prevention, and yet, the hemiplegia kept on coming. Today, as I reflect on those early days, I realize that this was the very act of insanity, and I, like a puppet, willingly obliged because people with multiple medical degrees and academic accolades told me it was the right thing to do.

CHAPTER 6
FROM WEST TO EAST

It had been a little over a year since the first night we all thought I was done for. While there were no signs of the hemiplegic migraine leaving, Luc and I were finally beginning to accept my disorder to now be a part of our reality together. Isaac, at this time, was three years old, and we continued to be successful in not having him see his mother suffer through an attack. On the days or nights when the paralytic poison came for a session, my son would find me lying in bed with a strained smile, wishing him a good day at daycare in the morning and kissing him good night before his dad tucked him to sleep. He would only know that mommy was 'sick' and be none the wiser. What he didn't know couldn't hurt him, as we were determined to keep him a happy toddler.

I had gone to Dr. W for my annual physical earlier in the year, and when she asked how my hemiplegic migraine was fairing, everything spilled out. It was as if all the grief, sorrow, stress, and fears had been waiting for that very moment to be exposed, so long as there was a willing audience. Not one to normally cry, tears were brimming in my eyes as I poured out the frustrations of the neurologist's increasingly abrupt responses to my iterative, desperate pleas to help me with my disorder and how the drugs I was on for over half a year was wreaking havoc on the quality of life – and without making any noticeable difference in preventing the paralysis that was continuously troubling me and my family. I confessed that I had stopped taking most of the medications that Dr. S had prescribed for a few months now. My sister was a pharmacist, and when I described to her the brain fog and how lackluster my mental state was after taking the drugs, she told me to stop ingesting them immediately. It was the first time I realized that perhaps doctors didn't always know what was best.

Fully expecting a lecture from Dr. W that I shouldn't have gone rogue and 'self-prescribe' myself off the pills, I was prepared to defend my actions with what Dr. W had to say. But what came instead, was something unexpected.

"I'm so sorry you've been going through all this on your own. This must have been the most frustrating and scary time for you. Had I known, I would have called you in and discuss a plan on how best to move forward."

"Yeah… There were times I thought to call, but then I thought that since I had Dr. S specifically for this condition, I would have needed to go back to him anyways or go to the ER.

"You absolutely should go to him or the ER for acute emergencies – of course. But Dr. S is a specialist, and a specialist's time is rather limited with their patients, and your condition is anything but short-term. I'm glad he has you on a plan of sorts to treat and prevent, but if something isn't working, I would rather you come here and discuss it with me first, instead of suffering in silence since booking a time with Dr. S's office is always going to be more challenging than coming to me. If you come here first, I can always try expediting your visits to the neurologist's office from my end."

At this time, she turned towards the computer screen, made a few more clicks on the mouse, and continued on. "I'm looking at your file, and it lists out the medications he's been putting you on with no indication that you've been having issues with any side effects. But that's likely because you haven't yet talked to him. So yes – I absolutely think you should let him know the next time you see him. I agree with his approach of needing to focus on prevention rather than dealing with it at the onset of an attack. But since there isn't one set of medications that can be used to target specific migraines, much of the time, doctors are also trying to figure out the medications right for their patients. In your case, if what he's prescribing is disrupting your everyday life, that isn't good either. Even if the medication was working in preventing the migraine but in exchange for you feeling unwell and suffering through your daily life, that would also not be right. And it sounds like all these medications aren't making things better for you anyways."

"So, you think I should be stopping the medications for now until I meet with him again?"

"Yes. If it's causing you more misery than good – then, absolutely."

Such genuine kindness and empathy radiated through every pore of my good doctor's words. Perhaps, even more than a magic pill, *this* was what I was looking for all this time. I didn't need more prescriptions or repeated explanations of things I should or shouldn't do, and I wasn't asking to be coddled or babied, either. I realized then that honesty and recognition of the ongoing damage that this disorder had caused – and continued to do so since the first day it took over my life, was perhaps what I was looking for in helping me fuel a pathway forward. It took one visit to Dr. W for me to realize why I was finding myself increasingly dreading of going to Dr. S. It was because with each visit and with each report back that the medications prescribed to me were not working, I would always be met with disappointment like I had failed the doctor, his practicum students, and his nurses. The looks would always be subtle, maybe something they didn't even realize themselves but were there. The novelty of my condition was wearing off, and since I wasn't a case that could be touted as a success to help boost one's medical portfolio, I wondered if my file was being tossed into the 'hopeless' categories of files where patients of such cases were seen and dealt with only out of obligation – hence the repeated advice and counsel of how to treat my issue, despite being told that none of it was working. That day, it took every ounce of energy I had to restrain myself from hugging Dr. W to keep things professional between us, though my heart felt full and hopeful for the first time in a very long time. Little did Dr. W know, but in one visit, she reminded me that as a patient, I, too, had power and should not ever be at the mercy of doctors, with the assumption that they always knew best. If only all doctors were more like Dr. W.

"When is your next appointment with Dr. S?"

"In a few weeks."

"Good. Since you're already booked to see him, be sure to tell him that the medications aren't working for you. Migraines are such a tricky thing on a good day, and what you have is the rarest of the rare. Honestly, the best doctors in this world haven't figured much out with hemiplegic migraines. So, while Dr. S is a reputable doctor in this field, he won't have all the answers and is also trying different things with you, as different drugs have different effects on people – especially with your condition. So, if something isn't working, he needs to know so that he can adjust things for you right away."

A few weeks later, armed with Dr. W's assurance that there was nothing wrong in speaking up for myself – specialist or no specialist, I walked into his office, so very much more secure and confident of myself.

"Ms. Chai, how have things been?"

"I'm still getting my attacks, and there hasn't been much difference since taking the medications to prevent the hemiplegia from coming."

"Hmm…" was the response garnered. Without another question that followed, I ventured to continue my story a little longer. "To be honest, taking those pills has given me more brain fog, and I usually am left feeling like I'm in a daze. I don't think the drugs, or at least in this combination, are working well for me." And before a response could be rendered, I quickly squeezed in, "And… I have stopped taking the medications for a few weeks now, just so I can function in my daily life."

There. The damage was done, and the only thing left to do was to gauge the doctor's reaction and response.

"Sure. We can stop the medications and have you go back just to the Verapamil you were on before. I think you didn't have much of an issue with it before, right?"

I nodded in agreement.

"Good, then I'll prescribe just the Verapamil this time. If your attacks continue to come, keep using the Tylenol as an acute abortive approach to keep the paralysis from staying too long. My office will give you a call to schedule your next visit."

Without so much of an added ask for my opinion or discussion of alternative approaches for prevention or otherwise, he handed over the prescription and left the room before I was even able to collect my things to go. The visit from beginning to end took no more than ten minutes. His office never phoned me back for an appointment, and I was too tired to follow up.

***

Isaac had now transitioned into a big-boy bed, and while he still wasn't able to sleep entirely through the night, he was going through longer stretches in between his cries for mommy. For us, that was a win, and I cashed in on it for all its worth. Because Dr. S's office never called, my monthly visits to his clinic stopped, though I had kept on with the Verapamil. I was prescribed enough for a three-month supply, and I promised myself to call his office for a refill once I was done with the bottle. It may have been because I was now only on one medication instead of eight different drugs per day, but my mind felt clearer than ever before. It was like some heavy-duty spring cleaning had been done inside my head, and the clutter and fog were cleared of their density, allowing me to live again. Though the shadow of a paralytic attack that could come any time was always hovering in the background, there were moments I caught myself thinking that perhaps the worst was over and the hemiplegia was growing bored of me.

One night, Luc and I were giving Isaac a haircut and a bath. As we finished with his wash, father and son stayed in the bathroom to dry things up while I headed towards my bedroom to grab the child's PJs to get ready for bed.

I was no more than a few steps away from my destination when, in a sudden instance, the world began to spin, and vertigo sent my heart racing before the blackness set in. Reality came back initially with faint echoes and then got louder and louder as I realized a man was clutching the side of my shoulders with the fiercest intensity, shaking me back and forth. It was as if he knew there was treasure stashed within my innards and was shaking it out of me while yelling, "Tash! Tash!" which I could only assume was someone's name. In the distant background, there were thumping noises accompanied by a child's voice, making airplane crashing side effects *(how fitting),* without a care in the world.

But the child's play was getting drowned out by the crazy man's screams of "Tash! Tash! Come back… TASH!!" *Who was this man, and who was this 'Tash'?*

With the panicked cries so intense, I turned my head and stared blankly at the man. I was supposed to be someplace and felt an intense tug to be pulled into something, but I just couldn't place the coordinates I was supposed to land on. Then, all things came back into focus, and I remembered.

I recalled that I was a mother and wife, and, before that, a daughter and sister. I realized the yelling man hovering over me was the father of my child, and 'Tash' was what my closest and most precious people in my life called me. I also felt a sharp pain on the side of my head that I had never felt before and remembered I was not healthy.

Still lying in my husband's arms and unable yet to calm my heart, I panted, "What happened?"

Still frantic, Luc responded, "I don't know. Me and Isaac were waiting for you, and all of a sudden, I heard this loud bang. When I rushed in, you were already on the floor passed out."

Pulling on Luc's arm to help myself into a sitting position now against the base of our bed, I asked, "Where's Isaac?"

"He's fine. He's in his bedroom playing for now."

Relieved that we once again spared him from a lifetime of trauma, I touched my head and felt a bump the size of a hardboiled egg on its side. "I think I hit my head going down. There's a bump here."

Luc then took his turn inspecting the site on the back of my head and said, "Yeah… you probably hit your head on the nightstand when you went down. We should get you the Tylenol and then to the ER."

After taking the Tylenol, I reasoned with Luc that I didn't have to go to the hospital. I didn't want to spend the rest of the night waiting endlessly in a hallway for another doctor, nor did I want to trouble my parents to watch over their grandson while they worried about their daughter's fate yet again. I was met initially with some resistance but settled Luc's protests with a promise that I would take a sick day at work in the morning and call Dr. S's office to let them know what happened. I further reasoned that despite passing out, the paralysis didn't come, so I likely wasn't having a migraine attack. Since I was conscious now, the best thing to do was to just let me rest in bed until the morning. My energy was all but drained, and I needed time to reboot.

As if on cue, my Isaac rushed into our bedroom then, still butt-naked and faithfully waiting for his PJs before story time. He took in the scene that was in front of him where his daddy still had his arms around mommy and threw himself onto both his parents for a monster family hug and cuddle.

"Is mommy sick again?"

"Yes, sweetie, mommy is not feeling well again."

"You have to eat more healthy stuff."

"You are so very right. This is what happens when you eat too much junk food or don't eat enough fruits and vegetables. You are so smart."

And with that, my baby jumped off and went back to his room, yelling for his dad to help him with his PJs, because he wanted to pick out his book for story-time. That was all the medicine I needed to carry me through the night. I never told Luc how, for a moment, I had forgotten him, my son, and all sense of identity that made me whole. In all hopes of hopes, I wished with all my heart that what had been forgotten was an anomaly, a short circuit of sorts, that had corrected itself and would never malfunction again. Such great wishful thinking that I convinced myself it was the truth so that I could fight another day.

***

Still regaining the energy in bed, I kept my word and phoned the neurologist's office the first chance I had the next day. Not too long after leaving a message with the receptionist, Dr. S called me personally himself.

"Ms. Chai, I received your message. How are you doing today?"

"Hi, Dr. S. I'm ok now. My head still hurts a bit, and I'm pretty tired, but okay overall. I think I bumped my head on the headstand when I was going down last night. At least, that's what my husband thought he heard."

"Your husband didn't see this happen?"

"No. He was in a different room when I passed out. When he came to me, I was already on the floor."

"I see. Have you had any feelings of nausea or dizziness?"

"Not really, just some headache – but not a migraine or hemiplegia. I'm just pretty tired."

He asked a few more routine questions and commented, "It sounds like you may have a mild concussion, so you will need more rest for sure. But it's good the paralysis didn't set in. Given your history of syncope, I would like for you to get an EEG. I'll call the center myself, and you can expect to go there later today."

I then went on to ask further about just what this 'EEG' testing was about. The acronym at first sounded familiar, but then I thought that I may have been confusing it with the 'EKG' and 'ECG' tests done before. These acronyms were enough to make your head spin. At least it did for me.

Dr. S explained that an EEG was a test used to detect any abnormal activity in the brain. Specifically, it was used to find whether there was anything unusual going on with the brain waves or electrical activity. He went on to further explain that once I got into the examination lab, electrodes would be placed onto my scalp, and the electrodes would detect the electrical charges that came from my brain cells' activity, which in turn would appear on a graph for him to interpret the results. He never went into further detail beyond that, but I assumed such a test was another process to explore whether I had something other than a hemiplegic migraine. I wondered why I wasn't given this test sooner when I was going through the scans and lumbar punctures. And while I wondered about it, I never ended up asking the doctor. Instead, we ended the call, and less than an hour later, I was given a time and location of where I was to sign in for my EEG appointment.

I was provided with the results of my EEG the very next day. Like with every other test I had done to date, everything had come back normal. And while I should have been elated with having a 'normal, functional' brain, I couldn't deny that a part of me was yet again disappointed that nothing else was found. I wasn't the only one let down, as Luc was also in disbelief after relaying the news to him.

"That's unbelievable," he said, shaking his head. "How can they find nothing wrong with you when so much has happened and gone wrong? It doesn't make any sense."

I had nothing to offer because he was right. From the very beginning, none of this made sense. In moments when I found myself siloed in my own thoughts, I caught myself even questioning whether this was fabricated within my own mind. Could it be possible that all the countless episodes of paralysis, pain, and torture of being trapped in my own body was something I had willingly made up? Did I somehow fake all the turmoil that had plagued me and my family for almost two years now – and without me even knowing what I was doing all this time? If this was real, surely, an abnormality would have surfaced by now with at least *one* test. Yet, time and time again, the science showed that I was a healthy person, in theory. So, if the science was correct and true without refute, what other logic could there be, except that the actual subject of the issue was faking it all along? The only problem with that reasoning was that I, the subject in question, could not in good conscience say that all of what had happened was not real, and I was brought back to square one all over again. But this time, I couldn't just let it simmer in silence.

I made my way back to Dr. S and used my session with him to push for more answers. After showing me the results of my EEG, I asked, "Dr. S, with all these tests that I've done and have been doing, and with nothing coming out that shows much of anything, how could this be right?"

A little puzzled, Dr. S responded with, "How do you mean?"

"I mean, every test I've done from day one is showing up normal, but there is clearly something wrong with me. How could that be possible? I'm not faking this – I couldn't even make up half the things that I've gone through, even if I tried. But still, nothing ever shows up in my results."

Taking in my frustration, Dr. S settled back into his chair and placed his hands together, as I learned he often did when he was thinking of how to phrase his message. Such thoughtfulness made me more anxious in anticipation of what he was going to say next.

"Ms. Chai, I can certainly understand your frustration. Diagnosing migraines, in general, has always been challenging, and hemiplegic migraine is even more difficult. Now, there has been literature that suggests that if you have familial hemiplegic migraine, genetic testing may detect mutations in specific genes, but from what we know about your background, you likely have sporadic hemiplegic migraines, since nobody in your family has had what you have. You can think about going through some genetic testing to definitively conclude the type of migraine you have, but I don't know how much value it would bring. Whether you have familial or sporadic hemiplegic migraine, how we treat the disorder would be the same. It wouldn't change anything, only that you know with certainty that your children would have a fifty-fifty chance of inheriting what you have. But even without the testing, we would be prudent to assume the same with your children anyways if they begin to exhibit similar symptoms."

I kept silent, waiting to hear more.

"In the case of MRIs, EEGs, and CT scans, any abnormalities of the brain detected are dependent on the time of scanning. Unless you are placed under any of these scans and tests literally during a hemiplegic migraine attack, we know you will likely not find anything of significance. In fact, I've seen cases with normal test results even when the scans and tests were done *during* an attack. It goes to show just how challenging this disorder is to treat, and frankly, there aren't very many in this field in the world who know much about this type of migraine. But one thing is for certain: we *know* this is a very real thing for you and others who suffer through this. It is documented, and there continues to be research done."

"Will I be stuck with this forever, then?"

"It's very hard to say. Most people get this in their teenage years or early twenties, and by the time they are in their thirties or forties, it almost becomes non-existent for them. So, hopefully, your case will be like the majority; and in the meantime, we must keep working on the prevention of your attacks. While it has been extremely minimal, there have been instances that people who get frequent attacks have gone into a temporary coma, and while temporary – it's still something, of course, we want to avoid with you."

With that, I knew there was nothing more to be said other than to move forward. The session ended with Dr. S saying that I could think about doing genetic testing if it was something I was interested in. He also asked how I was doing with the Verapamil. I mentioned that I was still experiencing the brain fog, but it wasn't nearly as detrimental as when I was on a multitude of medications all at once. He must have taken that as a good sign by gifting me with another prescription to top up the drug before I left because a doctor's visit would not be a doctor's visit without a prescription. I was none the wiser, leaving his office, but at least, in some indirect way, I was validated by a professional that I wasn't a fake.

***

Despite the latest incident, life stopped for nothing and for nobody. This was true for both work and home. Still fearful that another attack was imminent and feeling that I was in a stalemate with doctors on how I was to treat my condition, I turned to my parents for advice.

Perhaps it was because of our Asian roots, or perhaps it was due to personal experience that had proven to be tried, tested, and true; my mother had always been a huge advocate of Traditional Chinese Medicine or TCM. I never was opposed to TCM with the disclaimer that you had to find a *good* practitioner for your healing journey. In the early years, the industry was tainted with loads of people claiming to be certified, but in reality, were only half-truths or, even worse, were full-on con artists promising already desperate people that their concoctions and methods would be the magic pill they had been seeking for. In fortunate cases, their false claims would cost innocent victims thousands of dollars before the lie was uncovered, and in the worst scenarios, people would have their health seriously compromised – even more damaged than before seeking out an alternative approach to treat their ailment. It wasn't fair to the practitioners who were the real deal, and unfortunately, it made it even more challenging for them to practice their trade as they had to prove to disbelievers that there was legitimacy in TCM.

For me, I remember to be not more than ten years old when I had my first real encounter with TCM. For as long as I could remember, I would always get throat infections that resulted in doctors treating me with antibiotics. These infections became a monthly routine, so much so that our family doctor at the time encouraged my parents to follow the trend of the day in removing my tonsils. In theory, the removal of my tonsils would mean fewer infections, which in turn meant less reliance on antibiotics, as it seemed my body was getting more and more resilient to the drug with each prescription. I recall that every time the idea was raised, my mom would shake her head and say, "No." To her, tonsils were like a body part. To remove it would be equivalent to cutting off an arm or leg just because it had a minor quirk. Unless it was something that was life-threatening, she didn't think it was the right thing to do, and for her, monthly throat infections were not serious enough to consider going under the knife. Gradually, the throat infections turned into fevers, which then wreaked havoc on my lungs, and I found myself getting diagnosed with bronchitis at least once or twice a month. At first, the antibiotics helped, but then once they were continuously prescribed on a regular basis, it came to a point when I cried to my mom, claiming the medicine was no longer helping me breathe. At the height of the misery, I remember being given an inhaler because I couldn't go up a flight of stairs without stopping to catch my breath. At a time when kids my age would have been the most energetic, I was unable to run or speed walk down the sidewalk without my lungs feeling as though they were filled with liters of water, suffocating my every breath.

It was at this time that my dad's business partner witnessed an episode I was having at home one day. I had already suffered through a fever through the better part of the week, and just like previous incidences, the intense wave of pressure had progressively built up in my lungs as though issuing a warning that I would soon be suffocating in my own phlegm. I buckled under the pressure and collapsed on the stairs as all the adults in the household – mom, dad, and business partner – ran to my side. I was clearly having a great deal of trouble breathing, and despite being young, I could have sworn I saw the grim reaper at my doorstep, just waiting for the right moment to whisk me away.

With one look and a quick check of the pulse, my dad's business partner took out a set of acupuncture needles that he had in his baggage and placed a few on my hands and various other points on my body. No more than a few minutes in, the dizziness dissipated, and most importantly, the pressure that was preventing my ability to breathe began to lift, and I was able to inhale freely again. It was like I had been given a second chance to live.

As he was already staying at our place, the business partner treated me the entire time I was sick and then a little while longer after that for 'maintenance.' By the time the venture fell through and my dad's business partner was no longer affiliated with our family, I was also no longer attached to an inhaler and did not find myself suffocating with a dysfunctional set of lungs. Fevers and bronchitis no longer became a regular occurrence, and I still believe to this day that acupuncture saved me from being asthmatic. After that period in my childhood, mom would periodically take me to a Chinese herbalist in Chinatown if my fevers flared up, and she eventually found a local acupuncturist who proved herself to be a trustworthy and skilled professional.

But in time, TCM slowly slipped back to being an afterthought. While I would never argue its effectiveness, I do think that as lives grow to be more hectic and chaotic, our patience for something to happen and to take effect grows increasingly thin. That is the catch with engaging with TCM methodologies in that it takes patience, time, and money – all combined together in one difficult mix. In a world where everything is expected to come to you in an instant, this is one of the many reasons why TCM is overlooked and, at times, even touted to be futile. It was likely the reason why, despite everything, my family still ended up defaulting to the doctor's clinic every time there was a sickness and would forget TCM as another supplement in supporting our well-being.

But give years of multiple failed attempts to find something that relieves you from random paralysis, and you will find yourself becoming more open-minded. The childhood memories of when acupuncture and Asian herbs had helped nurse me back to health all made its way back to me.

"Of course, you should go get acupuncture!" Those were the words of my mother, who had been making comments from the very beginning that I should have gone to acupuncture from the first day I was sent to the ER. So, needless to say, she was over-the-moon satisfied that her daughter finally obeyed her and had made an appointment to see her acupuncturist for treatment. Throughout my adolescent and young adult life, there were periodic instances that I had looked to TCM to help me through other ailments such as a slipped disc and irregular menstrual cycles, and in every instance, I was always 'cured' after being treated by the acupuncturist or herbalist. So, it wasn't like I had completely abandoned TCM from childhood, which made it even more curious why I didn't look into TCM for the hemiplegic migraine sooner. Even today, as I look back, I still don't have a satisfactory explanation, only that I had gotten overwhelmed by everything. From the random paralysis attacks and fainting spells to the advice and information that would subsequently be given – there was only so much that I could process at once. Or perhaps the underlying reason was that I was afraid to repeat the cycle of being disheartened if I was unable to find solutions yet again. While Western medicine had failed me, if TCM proved to also be a wasted effort, where else could I go?

CHAPTER 7
COMING CLEAN

I continued to navigate the trenches of living with a condition that would sentence me to a state of paralysis at a moment's notice. While it was always terrifying, I forced myself to set my sights on looking up and away from the fear that was stalking me in the shadows every day. In 2014, I was working in the Workplace Health area, overseeing the organization's Occupational Health and Safety training program. It was a place I never thought I would ever want to work in. In school, when studying human resources topics, health and safety was always a subject I never got to be interested in. While I knew it was important and a much-needed component in what makes any organization thrive, it simply wasn't an area I was passionate about. So, throughout my school and work career, when it came to occupational health and safety, I only ever expended energy and effort over this topic, just enough to get by. I took a completely different attitude when the topics of recruitment, organizational effectiveness and learning and development were discussed. Running programs or uncovering theories of what made people learn and apply new skills at work or in their daily lives proved fascinating for me. This would probably explain why, in my entire career with government, areas that had close ties with learning and development was where I stayed the longest. When an opportunity for a training manager came up with the Workplace Health team in my department, I decided to explore it. Despite it being with health and safety, the training part of the role intrigued me.

I went through the normal process of applying for the position and interviewing for the role, and when I was actually offered the position, I found myself unexpectedly hesitant. On the cusp of accepting the new job offer, I stopped myself, not knowing exactly what I wanted to do.

I knew I wanted the job. It was a good experience for me to learn a new subject area while still being able to contribute to the role by utilizing my skillsets related to designing and delivering learning and development programs. The Director of the position was a previous client of mine when I was an HR Consultant, and we got along exceptionally well. I think in the end, it was knowing that we had a positive working relationship to begin with, that I summoned all courage within to have an uncomfortable conversation with him about my health issue that I was afraid would impact my productivity in case something was to happen in the future.

"Tom, I am so very thankful for the offer you've given. But I don't think it would be fair to you if I didn't raise this one thing holding me back from accepting the offer."

Knowing I had his undivided attention, I took a deep breath before going on. "I don't normally share this widely with people, but you should know that a few years ago, I was diagnosed with this thing called hemiplegic migraine."

"I am sorry to hear Natasha. That sounds serious. What is this condition about?"

"Well… it is a type of migraine. Most people, when they get migraines, get the typical one-sided head pain for a few hours or a day. With the head pain, some may get additional auras like nausea and sensitivity to light and sound. But once the pain passes, they pretty much can go back to normal or, at least, wouldn't ever need to go to the hospital. With hemiplegic migraine, the typical auras people get are manifested into stroke-like symptoms. Sometimes, it comes with head pain, but other times just one-sided paralysis with the migraine auras. If you didn't know any better and if I was with you when an attack came on, you would see me losing feeling on one side of my body, which possibly could include one-sided facial drooping, or I could lose my ability to speak, or both could happen where I lose the ability to move and speak."

"My goodness – that is serious. How have you been coping?"

"The good news is that it doesn't happen all the time, but when it does, it comes on rather suddenly and usually without warning. I've had this for a few years now. We've learned that stroke symptoms typically go away on their own. It's gotten to the point where we've been told that unless I am completely unresponsiveness, or if the paralysis isn't going away, I don't need to go to the hospital and should just wait out the episode. I am on medication that is supposed to help prevent the attacks from happening, but to be honest, not sure how well they are working since I still get the attacks. It takes me a few days to revert to normal after an episode since my brain needs to reset itself. I guess the reason why I'm sharing this with you is that if you still decide to take me on, it'll have to be with the understanding that there may be times I'll be away from work when my hemiplegia sets in since I won't be able to function when an attack comes. I just don't want you taking on a lame duck without knowing."

"Thank you for sharing, Natasha. But I won't ever see you as a lame duck. You are one of the most competent and responsible individuals I know. In fact, sharing what you shared with me just now proves again that you are reliable. Any team would be lucky to have you. And you need to know that what you just told me is not a factor and does not affect my decision. I know I found the right person for the job in you, and I hope you'll accept our offer."

I don't think Tom will ever know just how much his words and acceptance meant and still means to me today. In many ways, like Dr. W, his empathy and understanding of what I was going through gave assurances that what I had wasn't an obstacle. That I was someone others still considered trustworthy and capable. That what I had wasn't something I needed to hide like some dirty little scandal. While it still wasn't something I would openly share with just anyone, my exchange with Tom that day helped ease future fears of sharing this 'thing,' I had whenever I was considering a new job or got a new boss. I would only hope that in working through the discomfort of disclosing, there would be another Tom on the receiving end of my confession.

***

There proved to be a lot to learn when I entered the occupational health and safety space. But I was keen to explore and was fortunate to have knowledgeable colleagues who were as much invested in their work as in their own personal health and well-being. Before long, everyone on my immediate team knew of my condition and the limitations it would have on me during and after an attack. I was well into my second year of being a hemiplegic migraineur – and the fact that not one attack had happened in the office or in public yet was nothing short of a miracle.

I remember the first winter working with my new OH&S team was an especially long and cold season. Neither acupuncture nor medication was strong enough to keep the hemiplegia from making a quick visit in the early parts of the year. But luckily, the episodes seemed not as intense as before and spared me from being disabled in bed. It was mostly numbness experienced on my left arm or leg, where the feeling of pins and needles would return in a few hours, and then I would again be given back control of my limbs. Still, the attacks always appeared on weekends or in the late evenings when I was not at work or out with friends and family. For that, I was thankful.

But the migraine was not the only thing I was battling. It was after all winter, and once Isaac survived his share of flu bugs and germs (no doubt gifted by the abundance of his daycare friends); it was also subsequently gifted to me.

I had already been with a cold for over week and while exhausted and run down, thought I was still strong enough to be at work, so long as I paced myself for the day. After another week of still not being fully recovered but in the office, I found myself simply drained and headed back home early. Once home, I went up to the bedroom and sandwiched myself in between the covers and must have fallen right to sleep, as I didn't even hear Luc and Isaac come home.

That same night, it seemed as though all the windows and doors had flung open, and the brisk winter air blown right into my very core. The cold air was so severe it jolted me awake. Pulling myself up in bed, I looked towards the bedroom window and found it tightly sealed against the frigid outdoors. I became ever more confused. If the windows were shut, why was I still shivering?

While my body was chilled to the bone, my neck and face felt like they were burning with an intensity never felt before. Still groggy, I reached for the thermometer and placed it under my tongue. The moment it beeped, I pulled it out and registered a reading of nearly thirty-eight degrees Celsius. Suddenly, everything made sense. I officially had a fever.

As though on cue, Luc came into the room to check on me, and I reported my newly registered temperature. For the remainder of the night, I was left in my peace, focused on resting so that my energy would return and chase the fever away. Sadly, the opposite happened, and for the better part of the night and into the early morning, I saw my temperature keep rising despite being fed Tylenol to keep the fever down. At its peak, I remember seeing 39.9 degrees Celsius before slipping away into sleep again, only to wake with a violent cough that didn't stop until a thick green ball of dense phlegm was finally lodged out from within. With my lungs released from the sticky mucus, it seemed that my body was finally able to rest and get some real sleep. I woke again the next day, finding the whole bed drenched with sweat, but the heavy weight of illness was no longer there, and I finally felt better.

Little did I know, the fever was only but a teaser for what was really coming my way. After a few more days of rest, I returned to the office. Leaving home and driving to work started out as a normal routine, but the moment I sat myself down , ready to review some documents, the chills and uncontrollable shaking began and only got more violent. I became powerless again against whatever poison was infecting me and could not do anything except sit where I was and let it take over.

Both my limbs began to feel numb. As I looked down at my shaking hands, I saw my nails had turned to a bluish-purple hue. In between the violent shivers and frigid chills, I wondered if this was my hemiplegia finally making its debut in the office.

I mustered all energy then to walk next door where Tom was, and upon one look, he knew I wasn't well. Immediately, I was guided back to my office so that I could sit and catch my breath and was given a shawl to help trap the heat in while Tom called Luc to fetch me. With each passing second, it was like large chunks of heat were being drained from my inner core. I heard my co-workers comment that I was getting paler by the minute, and my lips were turning a crisp purple-blue. My husband finally arrived, and before long, we were back in the ER again.

At the triage station, I was still trembling uncontrollably. Seeing these convulsions, the nurse swiftly took my temperature. The thermometer showed a near forty degrees Celsius, just like it had been a few days ago, and I was immediately bundled away to wait for subsequent tests. I was thankful that I was at least provided a bed in a private room this time. It is from here that my memory only takes me as far as lying in the hospital bed with Luc by my side as we waited for doctors to see me. A drill we both knew all too well.

***

"We're just waiting for doctors now." Snippets of lopsided, blurred images. *"Excuse me, do you know when someone will be here to see my wife?"* People running in and out. *"Should be soon..."* Voices, voices and more voices fading in and out. Blank blackness. High-pitched ringing. A scurry of noises and sounds, more echoes and then – nothing.

My eyelids raised to show me a room that housed a sink and all kinds of sterile-looking medical equipment. Luc, who must have stepped out of the room and was returning, saw that I was awake and rushed to my side.

"Hey, you..." He said with the utmost tenderness, stroking my head. "How are you doing?"

Barely able to lift my head, I forced out a coarse tremble of a whisper, "I'm so cold."

"Yeah... the nurse just came in not too long ago to take your temperature and to give you Tylenol. You remember that?" I shook my head. I had absolutely no recollection.

"They gave you Tylenol twice already since we came, but your temperature still isn't going down. I asked a few times already, and they said the doctor should be coming soon. I'll go and ask them again if there still isn't anyone to see you in a few minutes."

Comforted that Luc was once again my advocate at a time when I didn't even have the energy to speak, my eyes lowered, and I surrendered to the power of sleep. I was gently coaxed back to reality by two people that I deduced were the doctor and her nurse.

"Hi Natasha," the doctor began. "It must be a really rough day for you today, huh?" I mustered a weak nod before having her continue.

"Well, your temperature isn't really coming down, even though we have given you the Tylenol, so I think the next step is to bring you for a chest X-ray. We should know more after the imaging. Unfortunately, we are working with a longer queue than normal today and don't think we will be able to get you in until later today. In the meantime, I would like to get you out of the ER and into an actual room until it's your turn to get the X-ray done. Would that be alright with you?"

Again, I offered another weak nod and found myself wheeled into different corridors, all the while hoping that Luc was able to keep up with the multitude of twists and turns. From where I was lying, we were going so fast through the hallways that it made me want to hurl. We arrived at the destination where I was to stay, at least for the night. The trip from the ER to the room seemed to have taken such a toll that once settled, and the nurses had left, I couldn't help but fall back into a deep slumber. It felt like I hadn't slept in years.

By the time people were ready for me to take the long-coveted X-ray, it was past midnight. More than one person was needed to hoist me up from one bed to another as I was too weak to stand and walk on my own two feet. Through all the toggling and hoisting of supporting me to get to the X-ray room, I wondered if my hemiplegia was also acting up, as I could barely lift my limbs for nearly the entire day. I remembered being told once that fevers could also be another aura that the disorder might show, and I was sure the stress of everything would not have helped in staving off a migraine attack. I recall mentioning something in a sluggish speech to a nurse at one point that I had a 'migraine,' but I don't think I was very explicit in explaining its significance. The term 'hemiplegic' had too many syllables for my feverish head to conjure in that very moment.

With the X-ray taken, I was returned to Luc, who was waiting for me in the room. While Isaac was with my parents for the night, I managed to use my last drop of energy to convince Luc to go back home to get some rest. There was nothing more he could do, and we all needed a break before seeing the doctors again the next day with hopefully a diagnosis of what was going on with me.

The weight of whatever illness I had that was enabling my fever did not relent throughout the night. By morning, my temperature had held steady at just under the forty-degree Celsius mark, and I still felt haggard and battered, lying desperately in bed for any doctor to come and save me from distress.

My silent pleas for help were answered, as not one – but three doctors entered my room. Luc hadn't yet returned from the night before, and their somber expressions instantly triggered worry about what I was going to hear next.

After exchanging formalities of who was who, one of the doctors began, "Natasha, we took a look at the images you took yesterday, and it looks like you have pneumococcal pneumonia, which is a type of bacterial pneumonia."

"Well, that isn't so bad," I thought. But the doctor was just getting started.

"Normally, we would have treated the pneumonia with antibiotics right away, but through the X-ray, we saw something else that gave us some concern."

"What was it?" For all the times I thought the hemiplegia or even this fever was going to be the end of me, I was wrong. The suspense of this conversation was what was actually going to do me in.

It was now the second doctor's turn. "Well, we suspect you may have a pulmonary embolism, or in other words, a blood clot in your lungs."

This was certainly not something I expected to hear, but I let the doctor continue.

"Sometimes, this happens when a blood clot from your leg travels into your lungs, and from what we think we saw in the image yesterday, the clot is getting rather close to your heart. We had to keep a close eye on you last night in case of a cardiac arrest if the clot really did get too close."

It was as though the doctors had rehearsed this conversation before seeing me. As I was still processing the reference to 'cardiac arrest,' the third doctor took his cue and began to explain the next steps. "To make sure, we're going to have you go in right away for a CT scan and a pulmonary angiogram. A thin catheter tube will be inserted into a vein, and a special dye will be injected into it. We'll then take X-ray shots as the dye travels through the tube and along the arteries in your lungs. The X-rays from these images should be able to show the blood flow in the arteries of your lungs and tell us the position of the clot."

"What about the pneumonia?"

"Because the antibiotics used to treat pneumonia and the medications used for pulmonary embolism may counteract each other's effects, we unfortunately can't give you anything until we confirm the blood clot. If the angiogram confirms what we suspect, we'll need to manage the blood clot first, since it's so close to your heart, before treating the pneumonia."

It was at this moment that Luc arrived and was retold the plan and of what was to be done with me next. As always, he remained stoic and calm while I lied on my bed, segregated between the doctors and my husband, processing all that was just relayed. At least these two things were tactile, tangible issues with very clear approaches for treatment, unlike the hemiplegic migraine that had remained obscure and abstract in the most destructible way. So long as doctors were confident with this approach, I would be too.

I was once again wheeled off and taken to get the CT scan and angiogram, and the rest of the day was spent waiting on the results. As evening came, the doctor confirmed that the scans, in fact, showed that the blood clot seemed to have dissipated and had since traveled away from my heart and was no longer considered to be a pulmonary embolism anymore. To be safe, I was put on Warfarin (a blood thinner) for a few days and sent for another scan before being cleared of any clots. It was only then that antibiotics were given to cleanse me from the pneumonia that had wreaked havoc on my lungs for nearly a week. I was able to breathe again and live another day.

No more than a few days after the antibiotics, I was finally discharged – just in time for Honolulu. We had planned this trip with a large group of our family friends – all spouses and children in tow. For us, this winter getaway was the first of its kind, and the timing couldn't be better. While I was still in the process of gaining back lost energy, I was desperate for a holiday. Nothing was stopping me from getting onto that plane. But like a child deprived of attention, the hemiplegia couldn't resist temptation and came to me and launched a stealth attack from within the shadows just days before our departure.

In Isaac's room and standing in front of his closet to decide how best to pack his belongings, I was alone when my world began to spin. I had been unusually irritable, and my mind was unsettled as it took more energy than usual to focus on tasks throughout the day. It started with vertigo before the spinning got exponentially intense until my whole left half dissipated from feeling, crushing me to the ground. I fell against the wall with a bang and made a silent prayer of thanks that Luc and Isaac were out. My family didn't need another medical emergency when the last crisis had barely just passed. It was only after promising Isaac that mommy wasn't going to get sick again for a "really long time" did he start to become a little calmer and less anxious. I couldn't let this migraine make a liar out of me in front of my child.

But what was there left to do when the paralysis was already charging through my brain cells and innards? I stared into the distance and focused on breathing – first in, then out. As the heart rate calmed and the air was gathered back into my lungs, the hemiplegia slowly retreated and quietly slipped away. Relieved of such an anti-climactic episode, by the time Luc and Isaac came home, I had already reverted back to the same functional person I was, if not plagued by ailment. Not a word about the earlier attack was mentioned, and everyone was none the wiser.

Honolulu ended up being a joyful trip, filled with everything vacations was supposed to bring – good food, laughs, tourist activities and attractions. We even celebrated Isaac's fourth birthday there, surrounded by his friends. It may have been the warm weather or that the earlier episode was enough for an interim fix, but the hemiplegia never reared its ugly head on me the entire time we were abroad. In fact, that week in Hawaii was likely one of the few times that my head felt the lightest and my mind the clearest. Standing over the balcony one night and looking over the Hawaiian sky, the part of me that was still naïve in its ways was hopeful that the worst was over. My hemiplegia was seemingly declining in frequency and intensity. I had just taken on pneumonia and a scare of a pulmonary embolism – and survived it all. Surely, I had done my share of whatever I had to do and endured. I was cleaned out and purified to start anew.

***

Working with people who were passionate about health and safety affected me more than expected, as I found myself being more mindful of all aspects of life. It wasn't about taking a hyperfocus on the migraine or being obsessed with the ways of preventing it, but through working with my colleagues, I came to realize the importance of being holistic in approaching individual well-being. This included being more aware of the things I ingested as part of my diet and making a concerted effort to build an active, healthy lifestyle where both body and mind were in sync. It wasn't that I was adopting unhealthy rituals in my daily life before, but I don't think I ever paid that much attention to the environment around me or the things that triggered my temperament to be one way or another. There had always been so many distractions, and the diagnosis of hemiplegia was another heavy load piled onto something that was already overwhelmingly big. Between regular acupuncture visits (I was going now every month) and frequent conversations with colleagues about the importance of health and wellness, I began to feel less panicked all the time and more in control of life.

As if to show myself just how much control I had in life now, I decided to take up something I never thought I would ever want to do – running. It started with an innocent conversation with my colleague Niki in the office. She told me she was a runner and had been in several marathons before. Like an automatic reflex, I immediately commented that I wasn't born a runner and couldn't run, even if my life depended on it. I think a part of me was still trapped in the world when I was the kid who couldn't even walk a flight of stairs without wheezing or gasping for air. That part of me had yet to realize that that same child was now an adult.

Never backing down from a challenge, Niki responded with, "Give me three months, and we can train you up. Everyone can run; you just have to practice."

From there, Niki became not only my colleague but unofficial running coach. This then grew into a small team made up of a handful of colleagues from our OH&S group with some of their family members to form 'Soul-mates' who ended up speed walking a half-marathon distance of twenty-one kilometers at the annual Edmonton Marathon in the summer of 2014.

I trained more seriously with Niki after that summer, fixed on the goal that I would be running the half-marathon the following year. For the better part of 2015, I absorbed every bit of instruction, direction and advice Niki offered-from what I was to eat for every meal to the specific techniques that would make my running most effective. When we returned from our Hawaii trip, I trained indoors by running at the gym or downstairs in the basement. When the weather turned more forgiving later in the year, I would run with Niki almost every day over the lunch hour at work. I would run some more later at home after dinner, always adding a little bit more distance with every session. Under Niki's guidance and coaching, I was probably at my peak health during this time, and I will forever be grateful for her kindness and patience. In exchange for her free services, I demonstrated my gratitude by first joining in a couple of five-kilometer runs, then advanced to a few ten-kilometer events. Luc and Isaac would also be by my side. If they weren't running or walking the short distances with me, they were on the sidelines cheering me on. They were my cheerleaders, and most importantly, I wanted to show Isaac the benefits and importance of a healthy, active lifestyle.

On a more selfish note, I think I also wanted my family to witness my fitness journey so that any past remnants of a sickly wife or incapacitated mother lying helplessly in bed would be definitively replaced by a vibrant and vivacious being who had a zest for life – because that was the real me. While the trauma of the hemiplegia never left, I stayed hopeful that I was freed from the paralysis for good and prayed that the fear that so violently barged into me and my family's lives would diminish with every passing day. The time finally came when I returned to the Edmonton Marathon in 2015 with our 'Soul-mates' team and ran the half-marathon, clocking in at just under two and a half hours. Life was good again, or so I thought.

CHAPTER 8
PAPER CANNOT WRAP A FIRE

Running continued to be something I did. Through all the training that was done, I realized that it was a very effective way of numbing any kind of pain and hurt - if only for a moment of relief. In running, I was able to plug a pair of earbuds of comforting tunes and shield myself from unwanted stimuli or simply focus on my breathing as I concentrated on the motions of pumping my arms up and down to fuel my legs with motion. It was a natural remedy that I could have kept on using to heal myself. But I suppose life had other plans, despite the best of intentions.

The Chinese have a saying that translates to "the paper cannot wrap a fire." Its meaning is that no matter how careful one is, the truth can never be denied or covered up. Like paper, the hope I cultivated of no longer being plagued by paralytic ailment was too thin and fragile. I should have known better that all things true and real, like a raging fire, are always too great a force to hide or denied its existence.

As much as I planned on continuing the façade of maintaining the healthiest of outlooks to keep everything bad at bay, things were interrupted when I accepted a new job at work. As much as I enjoyed Tom and the team, health and safety was never an area I had a passion for. And after a couple of years overseeing the corporate training of the organization's health and training program, I decided that I had done all that I could and returned to the place I always felt more at home with - in organizational development. While the subject area I was overseeing wasn't foreign to me, I now, for the first time, had formal supervisory responsibilities that I never had before. In this new role, I was no longer just a program manager but was also leading a small team of consultants, and I was excited to learn and apply new skillsets of leading people. I fantasized about being the leader that helped my staff learn and grow in their work and was looking forward to being the lead of a team that achieved great things for the organization. It didn't take long for this renewed enthusiasm to be quickly squashed as a rotation of new executives was introduced as the result of another exercise to restructure the enterprise yet again.

It began with requests to change the way certain briefings were to be presented or placing restrictions that only managers at certain levels would be allowed to contact other managers within the organization. These rules riled staff in the most disengaged way but were still tolerable. But it wasn't long before those rules turned into something else that attacked people most disrespectfully, trampling their self-worth and causing them to exit the organization in droves.

By now, I had been with the organization for about a dozen years, and this was the first time I had ever witnessed it in the state that it was in. A place that once had a flourishing vibe was now dragged to the lowest of lows. Leaders were making the most unreasonable demands on their people without a care for their opinion or well-being. Staff at all levels were expected to be good workers and follow their boss's every whim and command - discouraged and even punished for voicing their opinions. As much as I tried to shield the negative energy and impacts away from my own staff, my team was not spared.

Troubled by being an ineffective leader at work, the paranoia that I could be the next one fired or demoted set a grim shadow at home. Bit by bit, I no longer found pleasure in doing things I used to enjoy, like running or reading. Despite keeping with the preventative treatment of pills, regular migraines grew to be a daily occurrence, so much so that it was odd if I was spared a day of one-sided head pain. So long as the hemiplegia part of the migraine did not show, I resolved to avoid the ER and doctors. But most distressing of all was that I grew to be ever so impatient with everyone in my family and forfeited spending quality time with my husband and son – all in the name of work. I was losing control again and didn't have the power to stop this downward spiral.

My place of work was a means to pay the bills and to survive, but the joy I used to find in doing what I did, was sucked into a bottomless black hole. I convinced myself that the sacrifice was necessary to keep food on the table and give my son the best quality of life. And I carried this mindset into the latter end of the year with the Christmas season upon us.

Amongst our circle of friends, each family would take turns hosting a Christmas party for the group every year. It was a tradition that we started in university before any of us had spouses or children, and it was something the group had managed to keep with after all these years. Exhausted from the turmoil of the work life, I was relieved that Luc and I had already hosted a few years back that we didn't have to host again for at least another couple more holiday seasons.

At our friends' place, the night was nearly ending as the adults gathered together in joyful conversation while the kids entertained each other in the next room, playing with their toys and watching shows being streamed on the television.

Even though it was a Saturday night, it had been a long week at the office, and I could feel the sleep in me threatening to take over. I looked around in search of Luc so that we could gather our child and call it a night. But he was nowhere in my vicinity. I stood up from my seat and took a step forward, and the next thing I remembered was hearing a loud "Bang" and a sudden harsh force slamming against the side of my head and then darkness.

My friends later told me that everything seemed like a blur for them, too. But the consensus was that I had stood up from the chair, and the next thing people saw was an unruly form launching forward, head-first into the wall that was across from where I had sat. Being robbed of my left side, the hemiplegia must have caused me to lose all balance and crash into the wall like a quarterback would against their opponent before sliding down to the ground, defeated and unconscious.

In the moments after the surprise attack, I heard echoes of people asking Luc whether they needed to call emergency and if I was breathing properly. But it was Isaac's cries that brought me back to reality. Right after his fearful sobs of "Mommy, mommy," I saw distorted images of my friends gently distracting him away from the chaos and back into the room where the rest of the children were. Though grateful for my friends' kindness, I knew the damage had already been done. *The paper can never wrap the fire.* The day had come when I was finally unable to protect my child of the horror that had been terrorizing his mother all this time, and for that, I was a failure.

Knowing that I was awake and conscious, Luc knew calling the emergency for such an episode would be futile. Instead, he asked our friends to clear the way so that I could lie on the couch to wait out the paralysis. The group collectively abided as they all watched intently, ready to help at a moment's notice. Though lethargic, my speech was still intact, and I was able to answer questions of concern coming my way in an effort to comfort them that everything was going to be fine. This was despite feeling the inside of me getting more unhinged as I could barely keep my composure. Not only did I fail to protect my child from the hideous reality of the hemiplegia, but the hemiplegia, in one swoop, had also shown the people closest to me just how weak of a being their friend was. That year's Christmas party ended with me hobbling home against Luc's arms with a traumatized four-year-old who thought his mother was going to die. The hemiplegia once again proved its supremacy as it came that night, knowing it would have a captive audience to make a point - that I was the paper that could never wrap its fire.

After that incident, it took days for me to explain to my son that his mother, while not with a clean bill of health, was not going to die. It was only after talking to Isaac did I realize he had walked in at the exact moment when I slammed head-first into the wall, only to see me sink lifelessly into the ground. A pattern started to emerge where, during the day, he and I would repeatedly talk about what he had witnessed at the Christmas party, and then at night, I would find him alone, hidden under the covers, crying, with only a stuffed toy to comfort him. And every time, I would assure him that all was well, with comforting words of, "Mommy may not always be healthy, and it might look really scary when I get sick. But, after the bad stuff leaves my body, mommy will be fine again." This would then be followed by a myriad of assurances that his mother would not be taken away and would be by his side for a very long time.

I knew full well that all that was promised would not necessarily be true, but there was no other way to ease the child's fears. For Isaac, that night was likely the very first time he came to realize just how uncertain the world was, in that everything could be taken from you in just an instance. But being four -years old was still too young to come to such a realization; and I've been repenting ever since that night for not being able to shield my child from such malice for just a little while longer.

While the hemiplegia left a somber note on Christmas that year, I forced my way through the exhaustion and languor. After a few physical therapy sessions, I worked through the motions of learning to walk again without a limp. At first, I mentally retraced the connection points between my brain and the nerves attached to my limbs and then got them re-acquainted with how the brain and body parts should work together. It was a slow process, but the exercises that helped regain the strength in my fingers were also introduced, and I worked tirelessly throughout the winter break to get my body back to normality. Through all the work, there would always be the hovering fear that all the progress made and gained could be lost again the next day. By the time the new year came and people were back at work, nobody would have ever known that I had just gotten through a bout of hemiplegia. It was a secret I intended to keep.

Returning to the office after a turbulent and rough year, engagement and morale continued to stay low. Then, a new opportunity was gifted to me in the form of an escape from the job I felt I could no longer be in. By the spring of 2016, I found myself with a new boss setting up a brand-new department and learning the intricacies of developing legislation and regulations in the complex government system. It was an experience of a lifetime that I never thought was something I would or could ever do. While the hours continued to be long, where I often worked twelve to fifteen-hour days, the engagement and sense of purpose in the work I was doing returned, but it wasn't without sacrifice. At one point, one of Isaac's kindergarten teachers shared that he had somehow corralled his classmates to form a line at recess for them to kiss him on the cheek. For one kiss, each kid would have to pay him a dollar. Amused by this venture, I asked Isaac why he decided to offer up such a service (for which he ended up never getting paid for). He replied, "If I got enough dollars, then you won't have to work anymore, mommy... and you won't get sick anymore." As adorable and admirable the idea was, it also broke my heart.

Through the new job, I also garnered a promotion and found myself with greater responsibilities – but the work was still interesting, and I finally felt that I was where I was supposed to be. To say I never worried that the hemiplegia would snake its way back out to taunt me again would be a lie. In fact, I lost count of the times I had asked myself if the added work stress would be an invitation for the paralysis to come inflict devastation again. But anger would take over just as quickly to defy all doubt, shaming me for letting something as trivial as a migraine dictate my life. It seemed like a never-ending argument I was having with myself, and in the end, I ignored all voices so that I could break away from the deadlock I had constructed for myself and moved on.

The summer before Isaac entered grade one, our group of friends took a trip together again – this time to Mexico. It was a joyous occasion to celebrate the union of two of our friends who had waited a long time for the world to recognize same-sex marriages. To finally witness the happy ending of a love that endured through all sorts of challenges was something made of fairytales. The weeklong vacation was filled with laughter and carefree moments of old friends being reacquainted and new friends made. Days were filled with sunny beach days and excursions, while the nights gifted us with backdrops of calming ocean waves as friends gathered for drinks and friendly banter.

For the first time in a long while, I found myself living without the weight on my shoulders and laughing freely without reserve. Snippets of joy timidly crept its way back in as I secretly swept them into my box of forbidden treasures. I must have been too brazen in the collection of such happiness and was punished for it in the end.

We were into the final stretch of our Mexico trip and took to the pool with the kids to take up whatever time was left for play and the sun. Luc was in the water with Isaac and a few of our friends while I and a few others took to our usual positions on the lounge chairs, readying ourselves for the next round of drinks. Relaxed with shades protecting me from the sun's rays, I felt my face begin to grow hefty before being pulled to one side. On impulse, I summoned my left arm for a gentle brush of the cheek or scratch to the nose, but the connection it had with my brain was no longer there. Before long, the familiar sensation of a burly weight descended through every inch of my left side, and this time, it seemed to have also taken my voice.

On the surface, I was still seemingly relaxed, lying on the lounge chair with sunglasses on. Nobody knew the mayhem that was stirring within. My brain synapses were in crisis mode, trying everything it could to direct any type of signal to all parts of my body that still had feelings. As always, my right side answered the call with clumsy thrashes in the air while my left remained deadlocked. My body was once more split and pitted against each other. The place where my inventory of words was normally stored for use was nowhere to be found, leaving no other choice but to release a primal caveman-like call for help to anyone within earshot of my useless shell of a body.

It seemed to take all of eternity before people realized my screams were not out of fun mischief but were of serious desperation. By now, nothing on my left was functional, and

I was sure my face was also in disarray and unrecognizable if someone took off my sunglasses. Luc was the first to leap out of the water and immediately fed me the medication I still carried everywhere I went. I assume that once it became common knowledge that I was suffering through another attack, people had rallied around offering help and tended to Isaac while Luc was preoccupied with me. I can only base these on assumptions because I don't remember. The combination of blurred images of people coming and going, with the humidity of the heat, kept me just under the threshold of alertness as I stayed lying on the chair that only moments ago was the seat to a blissful oasis.

Later, when I returned to full reality, I was told that while I wasn't fully mobile, I was eventually able to get up from my chair and limp slowly along the cobblestone sidewalk to our hotel room, with the help of Luc and others. When people asked if we needed to call for help, I apparently was very adamant that I didn't need emergency services and that I was "getting better." I do not recall any of this. What I do know is that what started out as a lazy pool day ended with me in bed, drugged by both medication and paralysis. It wasn't until the next morning that I was fully released from the numbness that had kept me captive for most of the night. Grasping any scraps of energy I had left, I limped my way down to the hotel restaurant, sporting a brave face for all to witness. Perhaps it was my pride or the innate defiance that was beginning to grow within, that no matter how humiliating it was in the moment, once the storm passed, I had to show up strong and unwavering. If the hemiplegia was the fire I was unable to wrap, then at least the paper of a will that I had could be reconstructed again and again.

CHAPTER 9
BACK TO SQUARE ONE

I may have been adamant about not being taken to the hospital while in Mexico. But back at home and knowing the intensity of the episode just survived, I knew I had to tell my doctors. Upon Dr. W's advice, I contacted Dr. S and found myself sitting in the waiting room of his clinic. I was back on familiar territory.

Tagged with the outpatient bracelet, I was led into the same examination room where I had done my lumbar puncture. I was interviewed by a nurse who took my vitals, followed by a practicum student who asked about my medical history and to solicit the specific reason for the day's visit. Then, Dr. S himself made his entrance, file in hand, to examine his patient.

"Ms. Chai," he began with his usual greetings. "It's good to see you again, though I wish it would have been under different circumstances."

I nodded in agreement as the doctor continued. "So, it looks like your attacks came back?"

"Yes, about a little over a week ago. We were in Mexico, and everything was great until the latter end of the trip. We were at the pool, and I was just lying on a lounge chair, and all of a sudden, the paralysis set in, and I couldn't move or talk properly again. It was all without warning, and it took me longer than usual for me to recover this time."

"How much longer did it take for you to get your mobility back?"

Pausing to recount this latest event the best I could, I answered, "Well, it used to take me a few hours and, at most, up to a couple of days to get back to normal. This time, it took me almost a week before I felt like myself again."

"Hmm…that is interesting. You were in Mexico for how long?"

"Almost a week."

"You didn't do or eat anything that was completely out of the ordinary?"

"No, nothing that I could think of. I was pretty careful with what I ate the entire time. I didn't even drink that much there either."

"Apart from the paralysis, did you suffer from migraine head pain afterward?"

"No. None. I rarely get head pain from migraines after the paralysis."

Still in thought and as if thinking out loud, he offered, "It may have been the heat and humidity there that triggered an attack. There are different things that cause migraines for different people, so we don't always know for sure. But from what you've shared, if nothing much changed other than the physical environment that you were in, it may have been just that, since we know climate and weather changes could be triggering for some people."

I suppose what he said made sense, and I continued to wait on what to do for the next steps.

"But to be sure, let's do some further checks. It's been some time since we had you going in for an MRI, and I think we should schedule one again. We'll also order some blood tests and line you up for another lumbar puncture."

Though not thrilled to be going through another round of test experiments filled with needles and scans, these were at least concrete steps to take in response to the hemiplegia that had once again decided to rear its ugly head. At the very least, I left the doctor's office with a plan.

Once the MRIs and blood test results came back, I received a call from Dr. S's office to review their findings of my delinquent body. Back in the examination room that was getting to be all too familiar, my mind ran through so many different scenarios. I was nervous to hear what was going to be shared. I was also hopeful that something *was* found to finally prove that the hemiplegia had been the symptom of something else all along and what had been haunting me all this time was something treatable with a cure.

"Well, Ms. Chai, your test results are in, and the blood work came back mostly normal. You do have low iron levels, so I suggest that you go back to your G.P. and discuss what kinds of iron supplements you could be taking to get your levels up. We know that for some people, low iron can be triggers for migraines."

I nodded, making a mental note to call Dr. W's office later while Dr. S reached for a file of what I assumed was an image of my latest brain scan.

"While your MRI was normal, we did find a trace of some white matter lesions."

He held up the scan and pointed to an area on the picture. On the top right corner of the black-and-white image of the brain scan, there was the faintest white patch highlighted against a black backdrop that MRIs and X-rays typically have.

"What are these lesions?"

"White matter lesions are abnormalities of white matter that are normally in the interior of your brain. We see it a lot with seniors since white matter usually declines as people get older. But it's also been found to be common for people who are chronic migraineurs – especially those with transient aura – like yourself – where you may get stroke-like symptoms, but your scans always come back normal."

I would hardly call myself normal, and a little shocked at how nonchalant the explanation provided was. Intuitively, I had always assumed that anything abnormal found in the brain should be a cause for concern and a call to immediate action. I ventured to ask the obvious.

"Is this something I should be concerned with?"

"For now, I suggest we simply monitor this. Short of when an aura attack happens, you seem to still be functioning normally, so there shouldn't be anything to be concerned with. In my experience, these types of lesions generally don't cause any noticeable symptoms, so there isn't anything for us to do. That said, white matter lesions could also reflect someone with MS, but you still have a lumbar puncture coming up so that procedure should help rule out that disorder."

I left his office with an added dosage of preventative medications with a scheduled date for another spinal tap. While given more information and more drugs, I was once again without a true plan for treatment because I was once again told that what I carried did not have a cure. I had been punted back to the early days of when the hemiplegia first invaded my life. Only now, I was in an older shell, worn out and beaten into exhaustion.

***

Luc seemed more frustrated than I was when I told him of my latest doctor's visit. Shaking his head in disbelief, he exclaimed, "That makes no sense! I still think they are missing something and not diagnosing you properly. How can finding something in your brain still be *normal*?"

It was a compelling point, and Luc looked to me then as though expecting a satisfactory response. But I didn't have anything more to give other than a reminder that I still had a spinal tap to do and that I was told Dr. S was the best neurologist there was in town, so surely, there was nothing more that could be done. That night, we both left the conversation unresolved and unsettled.

But we pushed on and continued with our family life routine. Isaac, now in grade school, was going through a rebellious phase where every ask that was made of him was countered with a snarky response or met with a reaction made only by a spoiled brat. There was one particular day when the kids did not have school, and I also took the day off, thinking Isaac and I would spend some quality time together. Our "Mommy and Isaac" times were getting rarer by the day as my job still kept me busy as ever, and Isaac's homework load was also getting increasingly heavy. We had planned that mother and son would each do their respective chores at home, where I was to clean the bathrooms and vacuum while Isaac would clean his room and do some reading. After work would then come the play, where we would go out for a treat and come home to binge-watch whatever movies Isaac chose. If nothing else, it was an afternoon meant for us to be lazy and unproductive through the enjoyment of each other's company. But as with many things, the day did not go as planned.

After doing my bit with the cleaning and vacuuming, I peered into Isaac's room, expecting to see the child either picking up toys or reading a book on his bed. Instead, he did neither and opted to play with his mixture of Lego pieces and action figures, making an even bigger mess on the floor.

"Isaac, why haven't you cleaned up your room yet?"

"I will."

"Have you read your book like your teacher told you to do for homework?"

"No, I don't want to."

"You should really read your book. It's your homework that you have to do, and I know you haven't read at home this whole week. If you want to go out and play later or watch a movie, you have to do your work first."

I left his room to finish up my chores before he had a chance to respond and returned a few minutes later to still find the child lazing about doing anything except what he was supposed to do.

"Isaac, did you not hear me? I asked you to either clean up your room or read. You haven't done anything."

"I will later."

"Not later – *now*."

I left again and returned a second time, only to find him in the same position as when I left him moments ago. Seeing this blatant insolence, I snapped.

Without a word, I entered his room and went over to his shelf, where his collection of childhood storybooks was stored. Then, in one fell swoop, I collected a bundle of his picture books and comics in my arms and, before any protests were made, flung them down the stairs. I went back again and repeated the dramatic gesture, pushing away Isaac's desperate pleas of begging me to stop. He didn't know that I couldn't be stopped because I was no longer in control.

Now running between his room and staircase with loads of books in hand at every stop, I yelled, "If you don't want to read, then you don't need these books. We'll give them all away to people who actually want them so we don't waste them on someone like you who don't deserve these or anything good!"

I was being taken over by a manic rush that didn't care for anyone or anything. Reality seemed to have snapped into different fragmented pieces. The books were being abused by my very hands, but at the same time, I was also just a bystander watching helplessly on the sidelines as the chaos poured through. In the background, Isaac's screams and cries were likely no longer about his fallen books but of the fact that his mother had transformed into a monster he no longer knew.

With nothing more to throw, I breathed heavily with labored breath as I surveyed the damage that was done to the paperbacks and hardcovers now scattered in a sea of mixed colors and tattered pages. I looked down and saw a pair of tremoring hands as though they also knew of the sin just committed. I felt the last trickle of uncontrollable fury drain from my toes and now looked behind me to find my child with his tear-stained cheeks barely dried, sitting on the floor in shock, destitute, and afraid.

At that moment, I so wanted to run over and wrap my arms around my baby boy. I wanted to pour every ounce of love to nourish him back to the innocent, naïve child that he was supposed to be. But I couldn't go near him. I was too ashamed.

I figured we all needed some time to ourselves and be comforted in the silence that now shrouded our home. Retreating back to my room, I realized I was still shaking, likely recuperating from the adrenaline that had coursed through my veins a short moment ago. In the calm, I realized the rage that had ravaged all my senses was not because of a defiant child but because of something else.

I had gone through another mild bout of hemiplegia the day before that had taken to taunting me the entire night. Without sleep, my mind had traced through all the doctors' visits, debilitating attacks, pain, and public humiliation the paralysis had already put me through. And while I still had the spinal tap left to do, I knew that, like the MRI, it likely wouldn't give any more useful information we didn't already know. Would I be trapped in this never-ending cycle of mobility and disability for the rest of my life? How many more attacks could my body endure before the white matter lesions would usurp my brain, rendering me paralyzed or trapped in a coma for good? If a maximum number of episodes could be handled, it would mean I only had a limited amount of time to be a mother to my child – and he still had so much life ahead of him. The thought of not being able to witness or be fully present in Isaac's life when he was still so very young made my psyche seize with fear.

It must have been that a night's worth of self-induced distress, coupled with Isaac's insolence of not following directions, triggered an unusual reaction. The anger that ensued was a backlash to a curse that would not let me go. It was of a fear that my days may be numbered and my time to teach and guide my son to reach his potential would be severely cut short. It was an unexpected retaliation against an injustice that had continuously gone unanswered, and my poor boy had just happened to be in the wrong place at the wrong time. While it wasn't an excuse, it was at least the reason.

Now that the fury had passed and I was back to my normal self, I had to take responsibility, own up to my actions, and ask forgiveness. Stepping over the heap of books still lying on the floor, I entered Isaac's room. I found the child sitting against his bed on the floor – quiet and subdued, no doubt still recovering from what he just witnessed. Ever so delicately, I sat down beside him and apologized with all that my weary heart could offer. I explained that while there was no excuse that justified the unruly behavior that had unfolded in front of him moments ago, there was a reason for the insanity. I described what I was going through the best way I could a child his age could understand. We talked about feelings and of things that we had control over and the things that we didn't have a say in but had to live with anyway. Our conversation ended with hugs and kisses, and all was forgiven. While picking up the mess of books to be salvaged and put back on the shelf, I realized just how big a heart my child had. And for that, I was so very guilty for being the luckiest mother on earth.

CHAPTER 10
GOING PUBLIC

Subsequent visits to Dr. S showed results from my last lumbar puncture as normal as any healthy human could be. Once again, there was nothing more a doctor could offer other than to increase my preventative medication of Verapamil from 30 mg to 80 mg and a discussion of my willingness to try a new abortive drug.

"Apart from the Verapamil you take for prevention, there is a new brand of medication called Cambia. This drug was originally made to treat arthritis pain, but there have been studies showing that it could be effective in relieving migraines. It is a powder mixed with water, so it enters your system a lot quicker and should provide relief a lot faster."

"Will it help get rid of the stroke symptoms I get?"

"If you take the powder the minute you feel something coming on, it should help abort the symptoms quicker. So, while it doesn't prevent or decrease the number of migraine attacks you have necessarily, it hopefully will limit the amount of time that you experience with the aura. Typically, with hemiplegic migraines, we tend to find that its symptoms ease off the older you get. So hopefully, by the time you're in your late thirties, you won't experience this type of migraine any longer."

Such a glimmer of hope was offered on a silver platter in my mid-thirties; and yet, I was hesitant to take it in fear of being disappointed in the end. But I decided it was worth a shot at trying this new drug and agreed to have yet another prescription filled. I was warned that because this was a relatively new medication to the market, it would likely not be covered by a regular insurance plan. The doctor was right. When I went to fill the prescription, I was instructed to fill out a multitude of forms to submit the expense. I had originally thought to just pay out of pocket to save time on the paperwork, but upon realizing that one box of six packets would set me back $110 each, I quickly concluded that the paperwork was well worth the time. It was also a moment of gratitude as I silently paid thanks to the insurance plans that work provided. My thoughts then went to the people who weren't as fortunate - battling something so obscure as a hemiplegic migraine and not having insurance to cover expenses for treatment. It was a reminder that no matter how dire things were, there was always something worse.

And as though on cue, my body showed there were other things to worry about other than migraines in the world. A few months after the public showing of my hemiplegia in Mexico, I discovered a cluster of unique red bumps surfacing on the upper left side of my back. At first, it was itchy and irritable to the touch, but I left it thinking it would go away on its own. But the rash grew stronger as the day went on, and I could no longer ignore it. A quick search on the Internet suggested that it was the shingles, but I was still skeptical. With the discomfort on my back increasing by the minute, we took a family trip to a walk-in clinic. The doctor looked at the infected area and immediately confirmed it to be the shingles.

Science says shingles is caused by the varicella-zoster virus, which is the same culprit that causes chickenpox. After having chickenpox, the virus stays in the body and is reactivated later in life, causing shingles. Once I was diagnosed, I was prescribed an antiviral cream and was left to my own defense in hopes that the rash and blisters would not cause too much pain. While it was the virus that set the shingles forth to invade, I wonder if it was, in fact, the stress of going through the multiple bouts of paralysis that was the true offender of yet another health issue. What were the chances that the shingles were on the left side of my body which was the same side as where the paralysis would normally lay siege? Being warned that the shingles would likely become increasingly painful, I almost wished for the hemiplegia to make another visit so as to spare me from feeling the hurt. But I was lucky in that no pain or hemiplegia came to haunt me this time. After about a couple of weeks, while the blisters eventually formed and crusted over to heal, it did not bring much pain. For once, I felt victorious and breathed a sigh of relief for surviving another health debacle. Sadly, it didn't take long for me to be reminded that every small victory exacts some sort of payment in exchange.

***

Going onto five years of my diagnosis, life forged on with work and minding a young school-aged child while I quietly gave thanks to each day that rendered itself uneventful. I think subconsciously, I was hoping that if I kept to keeping my head down and only focused on daily life routines, the hemiplegia would become restless of such a monotonous lifestyle and abandon me for good. This was naïve thinking as I had no such luck.

The morning began like any other day, as I was about to leave for work. It was the middle of February, so the sun had not yet risen, but I was already running behind schedule, knowing that leaving any later would mean dealing with heavy downtown traffic. My husband and son were still asleep when I realized I had forgotten my watch. Before leaving the house, I ran up the staircase and grabbed what I needed to grab before making my way down the stairs. And down I must have gone with an added deafening crash and a bang because the next thing I remembered was being on the bottom of the staircase where, moments ago, I was at the very top readying my first steps.

The elongated echoes of panicked cries and screams pulsated in and out of my consciousness. It felt real and artificial all at once. One minute, I was lying on the cold, hard ceramic tile at the bottom of the steps, and the next, I was on the couch, and more people were gathered around me. I want to say that I remember the EMTs and firefighters who came into my home and poked and prodded me to check my vitals and to make sure I wasn't dying. I also want to lay claim that I recall Luc talking to them and letting them know of my health history while trying to keep our son on the sidelines so that he was protected from seeing his mother hooked up with machines and wires yet again.

I want to say I remember it all, but I don't. Those were only scenes retold to me by Luc and my son, who were there with me when I couldn't respond as much to the simplest of questions. For myself, I *think* I only remember feeling the heaviness and how lifeless one side of my body was, and no matter how hard I fought, a force exponentially larger than I ever was kept me stuffed away in a black hole so that I couldn't rejoin the world where I belonged. While submerged, I was tossed and hoisted onto another platform and into another place that I now know was inside an ambulance. Like another episode of déjà vu, I was sent to the ER yet again with sirens blazing in the aftermath of another chaotic paralytic episode.

When the hemiplegia let me back into the world, I found myself lying on my back on a stretcher, my arm attached to an IV drip in the ER ward. Luc was by my side, and I assumed my parents were asked to take Isaac again for the day.

Seeing that my eyes were open and more alert than they were hours before, Luc leaned in and whispered gently," Hey… we're waiting for a doctor to come. Shouldn't be too long."

Fully conscious of how heavy my body was and how my head was also increasingly feeling strained and bruised, I managed a nod and looked around, curious of all the hustle and noise about us. The entire room was filled with patients and their loved ones. Some looked to be in pain, hooked on IVs like me, talking to nurses, while others seemed to be asleep, likely waiting for a doctor to tell them of their fate. As for what my future held, a doctor now approached and introduced himself as Dr. Mark.

Dr. Mark was an older man, mild-mannered and had a kindness in his eyes that immediately put you at ease -

without judgment or prejudice. One look at me and the state that I was in, and I was whisked off for an MRI. When I was wheeled back to where I left Luc, he was nowhere to be seen. I figured he must have stepped out to take a work call or for a coffee. Exhausted from all the commotion, I drifted into sleep when Dr. Mark returned to check on his new patient.

"How are you doing, dear?" he asked, ever so gently and with care.

His question was met with a meek, "I'm ok."

He patted my shoulder and reviewed the chart before saying, "Your MRI should be coming out soon. In the meantime, rest some more. Your body and brain have gone through a lot of traumas in a very short amount of time."

I nearly cried to hear the empathy and genuine concern that came from him, and wondered why he wasn't my neurologist. I had always appreciated Dr. S of his professionalism and thoughtful responses to questions, but I never realized that what was lacking in his medical expertise was the absence of sincere care expressed to the patient. Call it bedside manner or just the overall ability to be empathetic – but shouldn't all health care professionals have this sort of competency?

In the midst of the pleasant shock of having such an understanding doctor tend to me, I nodded and gave him my thanks. He let me know that I had a bump on the side of my head, and my pupils were dilated, which suggested a concussion – a side-effect of tumbling down an entire staircase. I was given anti-nausea medication through the IV, and if I was still feeling nauseous, the amount could be increased. I just needed to let him or one of the nurses know. With that, he gave me another comforting pat on the shoulder and left me to sleep – but not before reassuring me that he would come back again once the MRI results were out so that he could go over them with me.

A few minutes after Dr. Mark's departure, an elderly man was wheeled across from my station. Unable to succumb to sleep, I naturally let my ears absorb the conversation that began between this new patient who had just arrived and the ER doctors tending to him. I learned the man was named Raymond, a seventy-six-year-old who lived alone. He was admitted because of chest pains but was very adamant to everyone fussing over him that he was "just fine and healthy."

The doctors and nurses were patient as ever and kept coaxing him to keep his IV in and oxygen mask on until at least all tests were done. I shifted my eyes for a second to the nurse who came to check on my IV when I heard a long-sustained sound of a *BEEEPPPP*. In a flash, and before I could process what was happening all at once, my nurse dropped what she was doing and sprinted over to Raymond's bed alongside other doctors and nurses who were all scrambling and calling out his name in search of a response. They tried to resuscitate the man by giving him CPR and used what looked like a defibrillator to shock his heart back to life. But it was all to be done in vain.

In a matter of seconds, Raymond went from being a headstrong, stubborn man to someone lying lifeless and dead. In the blink of an eye, the life that had existed was taken away. It was done without warning and permission. As his death was declared and the doctors and nurses who had tried so desperately to save the man walked away to their next case, I overheard someone say, "Hope we'll have better luck next time."

My energy levels were still too depleted to show or do anything on the outside, but on the inside, I was reeling. A life-and-death situation was just attributed to luck. I suppose such a comment would be considered heartless, almost crude, to someone who didn't work in the healthcare world. But maybe that was how people working in hospitals and high-stress environments coped. The nonchalant comments and dark humor were perhaps the only way to survive an occupation that saw death daily. I realized then that I couldn't judge. Just like people had no right to judge and make comments about the struggles of my condition, I had no right to be their critic when it wasn't me on the front lines, literally fighting to save lives every day. While I had no right to judge them, I did have a right to lend an opinion of what I thought life was – and that it was a very fickle, unpredictable, fragile thing.

***

It wasn't until later in the afternoon that Luc and Dr. Mark eventually both returned to my bedside, ready to discuss the latest findings of my brain that the MRI showed. And like me, I could tell Luc took an immediate liking to Dr. Mark, who was just as caring and genuine as when I first met him in the early morning hours.

"So, the MRI came out normal, which is to be expected for someone with hemiplegic migraine and is also good since it means no brain swelling or bleeding from your head bump."

"So, is there still nothing that can be done?" asked Luc, his frustrations beginning to surface again. I hoped for Dr. Mark's sake there was more to this debrief than what had been provided so far.

As though sensing my husband's exasperation, Dr. Mark carefully voiced his next words. "Well, while you know there isn't a cure for this, there are a number of ways to help prevent it." He then turned directly to me and asked, "I assume you're on some preventative medications?"

Instinctively, I nodded while motioning for Luc to pass me my phone for the list of medication names before answering, "Yes…right now, what's working best seems to be the Verapamil, then there's the Cambia that I recently started as an abortive drug."

The doctor nodded knowingly and asked further, "And… are you often nauseous when the auras come?"

I bobbed my head up and down and looked at my phone notes again. "Yeah… I take the Metoclopramide for the nausea."

"Good… because the IV we gave you is also for the nausea. It looks like you've been keeping track of your medications. Have you taken any others to help cope with the migraine?"

I got Luc to help scroll through my list and began regurgitating the list of drugs that have been assigned to me in these last few years. "I've tried Acetazolamide,

Amitriptyline, Nortriptyline and Zofran too, I think for nausea as well."

"And I assume you only take the Verapamil now?"

"Yes…those other drugs made me even more sick or gave me lots of brain fog that I couldn't function very well during the day. The Verapamil also gives me brain fog and makes me tired, but it seems to be the medication that gives me the least side effects."

He checked my chart again before finding another option for me to consider. "Have you heard of Topiramate or Topamax?"

Both Luc and I shook our heads.

"Ahh…well, Topiramate can also be called Topamax and is usually used for seizures or epilepsy. But there have been instances where patients have said it's effective on migraines, too. Usually, during migraine attacks, there is an electrical activity that causes the nerve cells in your brain to get overly excited, which causes a chain reaction that moves across your brain – like a wave – resulting in swelling and sometimes pain in your head. The Topamax calms that process down so that your nerve cells don't get too excited and, in turn, could decrease the number of migraines you experience."

Through all the times I had been incapacitated by this thing, I never truly made an effort to uncover exactly what went on in my head during an attack. I always assumed that it was because of inflamed blood vessels pulsing through my brain that brought me the grief of paralysis or head pain or both. But after hearing what Dr. Mark described, I came to realize that during a migraine, my brain was turned into the epicenter of an electrical storm. Just how many electrical storms had my brain survived? I had lost count.

I decided to give this Topiramate a try, and Dr. Mark was kind enough to give me a few samples alongside another box of Cambia for good measure. Since I was still quite weak and attached to the IV, he had me stay until later that night for observation before signing off on my release, but not before noting on my file that I was to see Dr. S again for a follow-up.

When I was allowed to leave, Luc helped me off my bed, and as I was getting myself coordinated to replace the hospital wear with my own clothes, I noticed how weighted one side of my body still felt. Trying to move, I coaxed my brain to attach its signal to my left arm and leg to thread through the openings of my shirt and pants. While my limbs technically followed directions, the amount of effort to complete the task was nothing I had experienced before. I made a mindful effort to make sure I *felt* my left arm and leg - and I did - but it didn't feel that they were completely my body parts. It was as though they were on loan from somewhere else, and while I was able to direct their motions, they weren't my own. It was the most surreal sensation I had ever felt and became even more unsettling as I nearly stumbled over my feet, thinking I was able to walk when I couldn't, which also surprised Luc.

A nurse who saw me struggle came to help and commented that it would take some time for the hemiplegia to completely go away. When I mentioned this was the first time I had experienced such lingering mobility issues after an attack, she reasoned that all episodes and their 'post-domes' manifested differently. It seemed that instead of leaving me because of my boring lifestyle, my migraine had decided instead to gift me with another added challenge to make my life anything but monotonous.

The one-sided weakness lingered for over a week. It got to the point where I had to borrow my mother's cane from when she had to use it for her walking issues, and I never had the chance to return it to her. That episode was the first-time other family members, like my parents and sisters, saw how the hemiplegia could cripple me without mercy. While my internal pride never allowed it to show, every step I took with the cane in public took a slice of my dignity. People in their mid-thirties were still considered young and were not supposed to be dependent on walking aids. But here I was, learning how to stay coordinated and graceful with the aid of a cane meant for seniors. That was also the first time I had to take an extended leave away from work, as I couldn't see myself functioning properly in the office and didn't want to draw attention to myself when I continued to fear the paralysis was preying on me around the corner.

Thankfully, another attack did not come, but I was due for another visit to Dr. S. This session involved him encouraging me to stop working, as he theorized it had been the work stress that was the trigger for my latest attack. I immediately protested, adamant that I wasn't anymore stressed than I normally was, so it didn't make sense for the hemiplegia to have made its visit when it did. Dr. S wasn't convinced and added that the extended time it took for me to get back to my full mobility this time around was another sign that these frequent attacks were taking their toll on my body.

I asked how it was possible for my MRIs and other tests to come out normal when there wasn't anything normal with my mobility. Surely, that was a sign that either there was something wrong with the tests or that my mind was somehow playing tricks on me that was preventing me from being functional because I certainly wasn't faking all this. The doctor wasn't the least bit phased and defended that MRIs and CT scans detected the mechanics of what was wrong with the body parts. When intricate nerve cells or muscular weakness were the issues, these were things that X-rays or MRIs couldn't always detect, but it didn't mean the problems weren't there. He further reasoned it was the same logic as if we placed two people going through a migraine attack and put them under an MRI at the same time. There would be a possibility that one scan would show evidence of an attack happening while the other person would still give a normal scan – even though it was clear that both people were suffering the same thing. It was just another indication of how elusive the human brain was and just how little we all knew about it.

He then went on to mention that given the frequency of my attacks and visits to the hospital, my file was flagged to caution doctors when providing me with MRIs and CT scans if I ever returned to the ER. Given my diagnosis, the scans and imaging likely wouldn't return significant results, and it wouldn't be a good idea to undergo such regular testing at any rate, given the radiation and other potential effects from CT scans and MRIs.

"So… should I even go to the hospital when I get the hemiplegia now? What should I tell my family or people I work with to do if they see me during an attack?"

"I think that on the onset of an attack if you are conscious and feel that it is a regular episode where the numbness lasts for a few minutes and you feel the sensation coming back to your arms and legs, it's probably just as good if you take the Cambia as the abortive drug and rest at home. Of course, if you are unresponsive or if the paralysis is getting worse or not going away after an extended time, you should still take the abortive medication and have someone call emergency for you. I think the longer you are with this condition, the more familiar it will be, and you will know when an episode isn't your typical attack and to head to the ER at that time."

When I left the doctor's office that day, he was still insistent that I take an extended break from work if I wasn't ready to quit altogether. He suggested that I talk to Dr. W if I wanted a second opinion. In the meantime, he wrote me a prescription for Topamax and instructed that I take it with Verapamil for added potency that could help strengthen the hold against the hemiplegia from coming back in the short term. I took the prescription without having anymore fight in me and looked to calling Dr. W for a second opinion.

Dr. W also agreed that I should take the time away from work – three weeks of extended leave, to be exact. She reiterated that the severity of the migraine attacks wasn't so much in the moment of the attack but that once the episodes were over, my brain needed the time to recover and reset. While my work wasn't physically demanding, it did require me to be a slave to the computer and its screen for long hours every day. The repetitive process of going through the paralysis and hurrying up the recovery period so that I could get back to work or whatever life routine that was required of me wasn't helping my brain rest and recuperate – especially when my latest recovery time took so long to get back to normal baseline.

With it being two for two, I relented and approached my boss to let her know what the consensus was from both the doctor and specialist. While supportive of having me take the leave, conversations quickly migrated to who would replace me and what would happen if the three weeks were to be extended for an even longer time. It was an intense period for our unit as a piece of legislation and its regulations were being passed for the first time in provincial history. All hands had to be on deck to implement, and here I was asking for time off.

Reason hollered I had every right to take the time. From the original order of having me quit the job to be at home indefinitely, I knew asking for three weeks instead was nothing. Work would always be around, and everyone was replaceable. There was no obligation to sacrifice anything in the name of work – especially when it was for my health. If there were any obligations to be had, it was to my family. My head knew all of this. But even so, no matter how much I recoiled away from it, every part of me screamed shame. I found an innate shame that stemmed from within, scolding me for being incompetent and incapable. I was dishonoring all that was given to me in the past and was relinquishing any future opportunities I could have reaped – just because I was too feeble a person to fight a migraine headache. The shame tore me apart from the inside while I feigned dignity and self-respect on the outside. I knew it wasn't right, but it was what lingered.

In the end, as much as it made me cringe, I handed off the files to my teammates and followed doctors' orders to take the three weeks off. Admittedly, the extra sleep I gained in exchange for surrendering the work helped. It gave me time to see a physiotherapist and learn exercises that would bring back some of the strength in my hands, arms and legs. For the first time since my maternity leave, I was able to take leisurely walks in the middle of the day around the neighborhood without needing to rush to be anywhere. I was able to reconnect with friends that I hadn't seen for so long because work and life had always monopolized my time. It dawned on me that I had neglected so many beautiful things in life and made me wonder if I had let the wrong things dominate the definition of what made me. But before any conclusion was made, my three weeks were up, and I went back to the grind, hoping that I would never have to take an extended health leave again.

The three weeks off was nothing in the whole grand scheme of things. It took only a morning of the first day for me to feel like I had never left. The hint of calm and serenity that had graced my life was but a distant memory and I soon found myself submerged back into the frantic sea of deadlines and rigid, tight schedules.

Time itself kept moving forward, and soon spring was in the air with my birthday around the corner. One of the greatest gifts my mom gave me in my youth was getting me to apply to be a retailer at an optometrist shop when I was in high school. It was a local business that had a few locations situated on the south side of the city and also in Chinatown. It was part-time work that helped hone my Chinese dialects of both Cantonese and Mandarin; and also sharpened my business acumen and customer service skills that would forever serve me well in the workforce. But the true gift was the friendships I made with the group of girls I met while working there all those years ago. What started out as casual colleagues working together flourished into something breathtakingly beautiful and became a permanent staple of my life. Through the years, our group grew from a handful of girls into a core ensemble of nine, with our partners and children added to the mix to make us whole. These girls were like my second family, and while life had evolved for all of us, a tradition that stayed was getting together on our birthdays to celebrate. Gifts were not needed and no longer a thing for this group, but good food and laughter at these dinners was always expected.

The year I turned thirty-eight, my group of girlfriends brought me out alongside our families for a gathering of Korean food, and it was a joyful evening where we relished in each other's company. Sitting at the end of the table, I reached out to grab my teacup for a sip of tea when a sensation came over and caught me off guard. I fought to set the teacup back down before being engulfed by the paralytic wave. My first instinct was to survey my surroundings to find Isaac playing with the other children. Then I looked across the table in hopes of sending a telepathic message to Luc, letting him know I was not well again. At the same time, my friend who was sitting beside me saw my slouched figure in the process of being incapacitated.

In a flurry of activity, Luc bolted over to my side, medication at the ready for me to ingest. All my friends, like others who had witnessed this before, hovered on the sidelines, not knowing what to do or how to help. If only someone was able to tell them that I was helpless.

By now, Luc was able to tell a mild attack from a serious one that needed professional help. Luckily, this was a minor incident that just needed some unsettling patience to wait out the episode for the weakness to pass. When it did, we reassured everyone that I was well enough to walk, and we all left the restaurant in a somber mood. I don't think the restaurant owners even knew that a medical situation had just imploded at their facility. This attack left as quickly as it came before I was released from its paralytic grip - but it was not without its consequences.

The attack at the restaurant was my hemiplegia's debut to a group of friends that I held most close. While I always talked about the condition I had, none of them had ever witnessed what an attack was like in the moment until now. It must have shocked them to their core because the very next day and all throughout that week, I received calls and texts from each of them— sometimes even a few messages a day to check in to make sure I was alright. Though touched, I was also so very sorry of the scare I inflicted.

The guilt continued as I had to do damage control with Isaac. No doubt, seeing his mom take a tumble from the top of the stairs only months before and now another instance where she was again rendered disabled had given him an insecurity he wasn't able to shake off. Not only was he clingier to me than normal, but his teachers had also reported bursts of inappropriate language being used on the playground and being a little too rough and too angry with his friends when we all knew him to be a gentle, playful character in nature. And if the days for him were filled with feisty angst, I found his nights filled with the silent weeps of a frightened child. For more nights than I could bear to count, I laid with my child in bed, reassuring him that all was well. While I could no longer promise that I would not be sick anymore, I vowed to do all that I could to keep healthy. Through it all, I tried to have him see just how healthy I was now and that while horrific in the moment, once the attacks made their pass at me, I would always return. I told him that because his mom was strong, he, in turn, could also be strong. To this day, I still don't know if my words provided him with any comfort – but I do know with certainty that the hugs he gave me were all the strength I needed to carry on.

At a family BBQ, the hemiplegia made another public appearance a few months later. This time, it was a gathering at my parents' place, where my sisters and some family friends were invited over for the night. Once again, without warning, the paralysis invaded and forced me to relinquish all control. Like a bad movie scene on repeat, a flurry of people with shock, horror and panic floated in and out as I fought to stay present and alert amidst the concerned faces. Somehow, I was helped into my parents' room for some privacy, where I gave up the fight and slumped onto the bed out of spark. I remember my mom and Luc at my side, rubbing and massaging the side of my body that had fallen limp. Had I the energy to speak, I would have told them to stop wasting their efforts as it was all for naught. I wasn't able to feel anything. But then, it probably was best to have them continue what they were doing if it made them feel useful that they were doing something to help.

Though not fully alert, I was still conscious and knew that the hospital could not help any more than the back rubs my mom was giving me. I was thankful Luc saw through my strained eye signals, and weak head shakes as he declined people's advice of going to the emergency. I don't know how long I laid on my parents' bed for - only that when I was dragged into their room, there was still light in the sky, and when the pins and needles returned to prick my sensation back to feeling, it was dark. That public show cost me another couple week's worth of mobility. I didn't go to Dr. W or Dr. S to report the latest episode, as I knew by now, I was my own doctor and physiotherapist.

Later that year, on the morning of New Year's Eve, my nemesis made another pass at me. Normally the first to wake in the household, Luc found it strange that I was still lying peacefully in bed when he was already getting up from his slumber. Thinking that I had slept in, he made his way over to my side of the bed and shook me back and forth, but I wouldn't stir. Giving my body a more aggressive shake, I still did not budge a muscle, even though Luc was now calling my name out in panic mode. But as lifeless as I was, he caught a glimpse of my face that had grown lopsided sometime during the night and immediately knew what was wrong.

CHAPTER 11
KEEPING TOGETHER

It was a horrific end of a year and a rocky start to a new one. When my world came back into focus again, I saw a man and child frantic and scared. I didn't know what had happened, but judging by their looks, I made an educated guess.

After taking the medication and being left in bed to rest for the better part of the morning, the sense of feeling returned in the form of pricks and needling sensations all through my limbs and face. Depleted and drained, I pulled myself out of bed and reached for the trusted cane. Most awkwardly, I jutted out one foot ahead of the other, approaching closer and closer to where my family was binge-watching a movie. Alerted by my clumsy shuffles, Isaac rushed over and helped me to a place on the couch, ready to be cuddled. Seeing that I was still having issues moving about, even after taking the drugs, Luc asked if we needed to go to the hospital. I shook my head - enough to convince both of us that the disability would soon pass like it always did. It was New Year's Eve, after all, and I didn't want to subject my family to spending the last day of the year in an ER ward.

The paralysis eventually loosened its grip but left me once again with a set of limbs that were shaken and fragile, too frightened to do what they were meant to do. After five days, I was still limping like a newborn calf that had yet to find its footing and continued to depend on a cane if the walking meant taking more than a few steps. Any effort made to break free from the walking stick, would be punished with quivering legs that sent all of me falling in defeat to the ground. While I never said a word, my head began to whisper fears that this latest attack would be *the one* rendering me permanently damaged.

Still, when such murmurs echoed through, I did my utmost to forge ahead. I kept up with doing everything I was told to do by everyone who knew best. For my doctors, I stayed with the daily intake of Verapamil and ingested the Cambia and Metoclopramide at the earliest onset of a migraine aura of all sorts. The pills still gave me the greatest of all brain fogs – sometimes leaving me mentally destitute, on the verge of a catatonic slumber. But such a split from the world's reality was worth it if it meant preventing another attack. For my parents, I continued going to an acupuncturist, having my body needled and cupped in hopes of stimulating a flow of energy that was to miraculously free me from the hemiplegic curse. While I couldn't say for sure if these traditional treatments were making a difference, I knew that it made Mom and Dad feel better. So, if it wasn't causing any harm, I kept with those appointments. It was the least I could do for my parents to make them feel they were helping their daughter. I boasted to my friends of how diligent I had become in getting back on a regular exercise routine that included free weight training and group gym classes, all the while showing Luc that I was managing the stress of everything in the most constructive way. I was leaving nothing to chance in letting the hemiplegia get to me and loudly showed the world that I was still in control. But in fact, I was breaking apart from the inside out, bit by bit.

The concept of control was all but an illusion. The hemiplegia would attack whenever it wanted. If it felt generous enough, it sometimes would send a brief warning, signaling my body to prepare itself to go under siege. But often, attacks would overtake the body without advance notice. There wasn't the ability to negotiate, no matter the effort taken to prepare myself for the unexpected.

One winter, I was driving home with Isaac in the back seat after a day's worth of work and school. Stopping at a traffic light, we were about ten minutes away when a familiar wave of sensation began creeping through my left toes and slid its way up my thighs. I knew I only had minutes before the paralysis would invade, leaving the whole left half of me useless inside a moving vehicle that I was supposed to be driving.

Still waiting for the light to turn green, I took a deep breath and tightened my grip on the steering wheel with my right hand before stealing a glance at Isaac through the rearview mirror. He was in the backseat, looking out the window - no doubt daydreaming about things eight-year-old boys usually fantasized about, like dinosaurs and cars.

This had to be handled in the most delicate but swiftest way. Ignoring the beads of sweat forming around my temples, despite being thirty-below outside, I steadied my voice before calling out to my boy.

"Sweetie, do you remember when we talked about how sometimes mommy's hemiplegic migraine might come for a visit again by surprise?"

"Yeah."

"And do you remember what we said you should do if you see mommy going through a migraine?"

"Yeah. I'm supposed to see if you are awake and if you can talk. If you can talk, you are supposed to tell me what to do to help you move. If you can't talk, I'm supposed to call 9-1-1 and then Daddy."

"That's right, buddy! So, I think my hemiplegia is coming for a visit to my arms and legs really soon. I can get us home, but once we're in the garage, you'll have to help me into the house. Can you help me do that?"

"Okay. You can still talk when we're at home, right?"

"Of course, I will be."

As if on cue, the light turned green and I shifted my weight the best I could to my right side as I stepped on the gas pedal, praying for a safe passage home. I once heard that the brain could only concentrate on one thing and that there was no such thing as multitasking. This was then my time to test the theory in an experiment where I put whatever brainpower I had left in me to focus on driving while ignoring the numbness that was spilling over my left side without mercy.

I don't remember what was said and what stories were exchanged, other than I knew that I had to keep up the casual banter with my child to mask the terror that was consuming me. While we were now only minutes away from home, it seemed that every block that my car advanced forward was done in exchange for an inch of leg muscle to be seized and made disabled. In my hidden angst, I silently begged whatever force was willing to listen that the paralysis would not plague my face or take away the ability to speak.

With one hand and a leg maneuvering the car, I could finally pull onto the driveway and press the button to open the garage door. Once I shifted the vehicle to 'park' and turned off the ignition, I let myself exhale a sigh of relief. We at least made it home in one piece – together.

My sweet, sweet boy, at this time, got out of the car and opened the door on the driver's side. The crisp winter air pierced through one side of me like a knife slicing through tender flesh, reminding me that I wasn't entirely without feeling. Undeterred by the cold or his mother's disability, Isaac, with all the authority, announced, "Don't worry, Mommy. I'm going to problem-solve this and get into the house with you."

Before I could respond, he wrapped both arms around me and with all his boyish might, tried to hoist me out of the seat that I was now confined to. If we weren't already in such tragic circumstances, it likely would have been an amusing sight to watch. A child not even half the size of the grown-up trying to lift her out of the car was like an ant thinking it could roll a boulder up a hill on its own. The nature of physics simply wouldn't allow it.

By now, the cold air was seeping through our winter coats, and I could see my boy was beginning to succumb to the blistery wind pelting through the garage – his cheeks and hands turning bright pink. I asked Isaac to stop momentarily and had him put on his mitts and scarf. Glancing over at my work bag to where my cell phone was, I thought of calling Luc. But he was still at work, and it would have taken him over an hour to get back home with rush hour in full swing. Rather than instilling more worry and panic, I resolved to focus on what Isaac and I could do together now.

A quick mental check was done to validate that I was still paralyzed on the one-half. I was fighting so very hard to keep a clear mind and sucked in another breath of frosted air before asking Isaac to dig out my keys from my bag and had him open the door to the house. If we ever made it to the top of the steps, at least the door would be unlocked for us to enter our home.

Like a solider, Isaac followed through and made good on my instructions to unlock the door with the key. By the time he returned, I had managed to lift myself out with the help of my one good leg and arm and leaned against the outside of the car, panting and out of breath. To buy more time, I had Isaac take our work and school bags inside the house first so that the only thing we needed to focus on afterward was getting me indoors. I now prepared myself for man's longest trek from garage to house door. Holding onto Isaac for balance while still leaving most of my weight against the side of the car, I moved forward inch by inch with lopsided one-legged bunny hops. They were the most ungraceful jumps and not the least bit coordinated, but at least I was moving and making progress. Now drenched in sweat, I finally reached the bottom of the stairs. We only needed to make our way through five more steps, and we would be home free. But how could I travel up the steps with just one leg?

Gently turning down Isaac's offer to piggyback me up the stairs, I lowered myself onto the concrete ground, heaved through with my good right arm and leg, and did a self-hoist that lifted me just high enough to land my bottom onto the next wooden step. My boy, ever the coach, talked me through the whole way, giving a status report of how many more steps I had before finally making it inside the house. Once in, I immediately slumped onto the ceramic tile that comprised most of our main floor. Still ever determined to help, Isaac pulled my arms upwards so that he could drag me across the floor and into our living room. From there, I drew in everything I had to make one final crooked heave onto the couch before the darkness swallowed me whole.

Luc was sitting on the couch, waiting for me to wake up, when I came to. By that time, Isaac had already given him a recount of the full story of what had happened, and I was given a gentle but stern scolding by my husband of how dangerous the situation could have been. While I knew what he was saying, I couldn't help but feel the anger churn inside as he continued his lecture on safety.

"Well, what was I supposed to do, then?" I snapped back, daring him to answer.

Not the least bit phased, Luc responded, "If you knew something was coming on, you should have just pulled over."

"Pull over and wait for how long for it to pass? It was freezing cold outside, and if I pulled over to call you or anyone else to wait for help, it would have caused a scene and scared Isaac."

"I think Isaac was already scared."

"Of course, he was scared, but he was also able to help me through things when we got home."

"He's only a child."

I knew he was a child. He was a boy with the biggest heart, who could light up the darkest room with simply a smile and deserved the best. But by some sort of twisted fate or bad luck, he ended up being *my* child. My child, whose mother was not always fully ready or capable. I was his mother who didn't deserve her son's love. Even so, the cards were already dealt with no choice but to move forward. If I was fated to be cursed with paralysis, then my boy was fated to be subjected to an imperfect childhood that would haunt him his entire life. My job as his mother was to condition him so that he could weather whatever storm life threw at him, even if I were gone. If there was a silver lining to all of this, it would be that in watching my struggle, Isaac would learn of resilience and grit, and this deficient mother would have taught her son the skills to survive almost anything, no matter the cost.

***

As feisty as I was with Luc, the hemiplegia that struck while driving left me sleepless for countless nights. No sooner would I have fallen asleep in bed the nightmares would come of me being handcuffed or blindfolded in a moving car and smashing head-first into a wall, or worse, directly into Isaac, who happened to have been crossing a crosswalk at the moment a paralytic attack came. Whatever version these night terrors came in, the one common theme was that I had absolutely no control and no way of taking back the control I so needed to run my life.

Nearly a month after the car incident, I found myself back in Dr. S's office. After recounting the latest episode, Dr. S reasoned that while he wouldn't subject me to an official driver's medical exam that could legally revoke my license, I was to voluntarily restrict my driving to only operating the vehicle for going to work. Highway driving was never permitted so long as I had a hemiplegic condition, and I was to also limit my driving over the weekends and when going out at night. In short, if there were other people or other options for transport, I was to use them first and driving on my own was the last resort – and only if I was certain that I was feeling well. Any hint of exhaustion or fatigue, no matter the time of day, would render me unfit to operate a vehicle. Given that I was still silently getting over the shock of the latest incident, I didn't challenge the doctor and conceded.

The sense of déjà vu returned again as he gave me a prescription that topped up my medications of Verapamil, Topiramate and Metoclopramide while stressing that I really should think of not working so that I could let my body "rest up." I responded with my usual defense that I was financially incapable of doing so. Besides, my job was probably one of the few things that had enough power to distract my mind from the cruel taunts of the hemiplegia. However stressful my work was, too much toil and effort had already gone into it, and I couldn't let it go. I had never gone without a paid job since I was nine- years old. Quitting the work-life now would be the official declaration that the hemiplegia had won over my existence. As tiring as it was, I wasn't defeated yet.

***

Months later, we were over at my parents' place, mapping a summer trip to visit family in Asia. The original plan was that it would only be Isaac and I going with Mom and Dad. This trip was a pricey endeavor, and with the purpose of the travel mainly to visit family from my side, it was only logical that Luc would stay behind. However, while going there with my parents, Isaac and I were to return home to Canada first so that he wouldn't miss any classes when the school year started in the fall.

Mom and Dad, who had been stressing over my latest hemiplegic episode, went into parental mode and declared that I could not travel alone with Isaac. God forbid that if the hemiplegia attacked while enroute back home without family members, it would be the most disastrous thing for their one and only grandson to be left stranded alone in a foreign place with his mother, who could not speak or move. My husband, who rarely went against his in-laws, shuffled his schedule to accommodate this unexpected voyage. Plans were reconstructed to be set in motion, and a few months later, we all found ourselves traveling overseas to visit my extended family.

Looking back, it was well worth the trip in the company of family and friends whom I had not seen in years, while both Luc and Isaac got acquainted with my aunts, uncles, and cousins for the first time. I was reminded of the importance of family and found myself sad knowing that once we left, we would be once again so far removed from kin. As much as Canada was home for us, I had forgotten the strength and warmth the family bond brought when together.

Perhaps it was because of the renewed sense of vigor forged through family ties that kept the hemiplegia at bay. Though always in the shadows, the paralysis did not manifest itself for the entire duration of the trip - going there or coming back. And while relieved, what should have been taken as a victory became more of a sense of dread that my life's autonomy was at stake. From needing a walking cane to not being able to drive freely or be trusted to travel alone with my son – little by little, paralysis was gnawing away and shredding apart the pieces that made me whole. And slowly, slowly, I was being reduced to nothing.

CHAPTER 12
PERSPECTIVE

For as long as I can remember, I always admired my mother. Her childhood in 1950s Hong Kong was tainted with family neglect and extreme poverty to the point it nearly killed her. But she survived a malnourished start to life and created an existence for herself against all odds that relied on nothing but steel determination and cold-hard grit. Out of nothing, she made something of herself and must have thought that happiness was finally within reach when she married my dad. She couldn't have been more wrong.

Being married proved harder than a single life, and it got even more brutal after moving to Canada from Australia when the University of Alberta accepted my dad for his post-doctorate. I was about two years old at the time, and we lived in a basic one-bedroom apartment. In some ways, we were your typical story of the Asian immigrant family in pursuit of a better life in Western society, only to discover that the grass wasn't always greener on the other side. In fact, where we were in Edmonton, Alberta, the grass was covered in heavy white snow for much of the year. I learned from a very young age that money was scarce in our household. My parents struggled to make ends meet while their relationship suffered even more. In the early years, the home was a place where anger dwelled and laughter a rare commodity. Yelling, screaming and sometimes hitting happened frequently between the adults as they dueled out their regret and resentment with each other realizing too late that they should never have built a life together, while I was often caught in-between their crossfire.

Whatever glorious vision my dad had of uprooting his wife and child across the world for a better life soon disintegrated into ashes as he could never secure a stable job after completing his work at the University. It was a different place and time back then, and being a socially awkward but hardworking, knowledgeable academic was not enough for a Chinese living on foreign soil dominated by white men. My dad never stood a chance. Unable to find suitable work during his prime years, this let-down turned him into an unreliable husband and father.

But in between the grays that colored my childhood, there were moments when I was given love, though it wasn't shown in the most obvious ways (we were Asian, after all). While he never was the parent who gave comfort in providing the most stable home, my dad was responsible enough. He drove me to school and activities, showed up for parent-teacher interviews and prepared meals for me when needed. Since the man was incapable of providing for his family, my mom stepped up in every way to fill in the gaps that the father of her children lacked.

Deprived of a formal education herself, my mom was convinced that the only way to a decent life was through school. She always ensured I had the resources to concentrate on my schoolwork. And when she couldn't be there, she would find the help I needed at all costs. Tutors, Kumon sessions, music lessons, dance lessons and many other extra-curriculars – were all expenses my mom took upon herself to fund and support me in. It didn't matter how many jobs and side gigs she had to take on. She was adamant that I had the proper education so that doors would be open for me when I was ready to take on the world. This intense focus on ensuring I was always in good health with the required schooling was made just as fierce for my sisters when they came into the world. Our mother's only purpose was to ensure all her daughters would lead a better life than she had. If this was my mother's dream, then looking at what her girls have become today, I would say she succeeded in making her dreams a reality. I owe everything I have today to my mother, but I also know it was at the greatest of all costs for her. And for that, I am sorry.

The years of hardship where one challenge was met with another and yet another obstacle in a never-ending iterative cycle drove my mom into a deep depressive state. But with her children still young and not yet on their own, she used up all her energy in our youth to suppress the darkness until it manifested into something so unruly it devoured her from within and was only given an official label of severe depressive disorder in her senior years when her daughters were at long last grown and independent. At a time when our mom was supposed to finally begin to enjoy life's pleasures, happiness once again kicked her onto the curbside to be treated like bait for the depression to consume her. As if the depression was insufficient, breast cancer also came to torment her two times over. But no matter how much the depression and cancer have tried to rip her apart, my mother continued to stand her ground – though ragged and broken.

For my mom, the cancer was like a walk in the park compared to her depression. I have come to realize that like the hemiplegic migraine, depression is real. It is not something that is formulated in the mind at random to solicit attention, nor is it something that can be controlled. While manageable with lots of help, it is not an inconvenience that someone can just get over and move on. With its destructive ability, it has the power to destroy the most formidable. For me, I have seen it break down my mother's spirit. From a person who was once vibrantly optimistic and strong, she has turned into someone so very bitter and somber that there are days I do not recognize the woman who raised me. This disease has devoured her mind, feeding her venomous lies that she is uncared for and alone – no matter how much effort her children, husband and friends try to help. It has raped her soul and left it quivering in the darkness, not letting anything or anyone in or out. Like hemiplegia, depression leaves victims trapped within their own shells without escape until it decides when it is finished with them. Sometimes, I think it is a fate worse than death itself. Seeing the one who gave me life suffer at the hands of her internal demons has been one of the most excruciating things I have been forced to helplessly witness.

***

When my hemiplegic migraine struck again for the third consecutive Christmas, my clouded thoughts led me to my mother and all the misfortunes that had plagued her life. In bed, paralyzed and in a catatonic state for nearly three days, I thought of the numerous times that my mom had tried to end the pain in exchange for her own life. And how, with every failed attempt, she was instead subjected to more hurt without reprieve. I began to wonder how successful I would be if I tried what my mom hadn't yet achieved so that I could grant myself release from the agony that had been holding me captive for so long.

For over half a decade, it was becoming apparent that I had no control. The hemiplegia had made it clear through the years that it was my master and that my livelihood was subject to it granting me mercy. All the medicines, tests, therapy and miracle treatments were simply illusions of hope, rendering me the fool to think I could ever escape. When the hemiplegia came, my will meant nothing. It was time for me to wake up. I was imprisoned in a battered body with a broken spirit, so what was the point?

Then Isaac walked into my room. To him, my eyes were closed as though sleeping, and he stepped closer to my bedside. I saw him silently survey the blankets to ensure I was still warmly wrapped under the embrace of the bedsheet covers. After stroking my head as though to soothe my pain, he left the room and returned just as quickly with a glass of water to place on my nightstand. Instead of just leaving, Isaac climbed into bed and cozied up to me as he placed one hand on my chest – ensuring he could still detect his mother's heartbeat. We lay there and drifted off to sleep in blissful peace.

Waking alone in bed, I glanced over to my nightstand and saw that the glass of water was still there, validating that what I saw earlier was not a hallucination and that my son had, in fact, paid me a visit. Pulling myself up the best I could, I leaned against the headboard and conducted a self-examination of my left leg, arms, and face. Though unsteady and weak, the pressure of the paralysis was gone for now. My hemiplegic captor had freed me until the next time.

It was now Luc's turn to check on me, and as he saw my sad efforts of trying to get out of bed, he rushed over to my side, grabbing the cane. It was time for me to get back to work.

Gulping down the Cambia, I leaned on the cane with my good right side while Luc continued to steady me on my left. Knowing that my sense of feeling on my left was not fully intact, I was helped to the bathroom and then was carefully guided out to be helped into some clothes that were not pajamas. By this time, Isaac knew I was awake, and he ran to help me shuffle slowly into the family room. It was the first time in a long while I felt sunlight on my skin through our windows.

The trek from bedroom to family room had taken the wind out of me and I needed to lay back on the couch to catch my breath and steady my trembling body. With hands too weak to maneuver anything, Luc fed me soup by the spoonful. I only needed to open and close my mouth as I willed the liquid to slide down my throat as though doing so would bring back the energy. If only it were that easy. Satisfied that I was settled and more alert than I had been in days, Luc gave me a hug and headed downstairs to prepare dinner for the night. Isaac stayed close and returned to his toys.

Left alone once more, I recounted the dark, hazy thoughts that had swirled in my mind not so long ago when I was submerged in bed. I thought of Mom again and remembered her telling me once that when her depression came, it was like a burning hot flame engulfing her heart. It was a sinister force so evil she wouldn't wish it on her worst enemies. My sentiment for the hemiplegia was very similar to my mom's struggles with her depressive burden. But in the same instance, I also knew we weren't the same.

As impossible as it was to push through, something else more important depended on my survival. Out of the corner of my eye, I caught Isaac's stealth glances of stealing quick checks while seemingly preoccupied with his play in case the hemiplegia came back for another surprise attack. I remembered the vow I gave my child the day he came into our world. I had promised to protect and nurture him so that he would be the best version of himself. I was the one who had brought my son into this world, and for that, he deserved more than a mother who spent her days wallowing in self-pity and bitter resentment.

I thought of my husband and the vow we gave each other of 'for better or for worse'. If it were the other way around, I would have expected Luc to fulfill the promise we gave each other and to forge through and endure. I once told Luc that marriage to me was one of the most sacred things two people pledged to each other. It was a commitment that couldn't be broken on a whim. I married this man because I knew he felt the same way I did. From the day I was diagnosed with hemiplegic migraine and through all the hospital visits, test procedures and medications, no matter how terrifying it was, this man had always been by my side. Without so much of a whimper or complaint, he had endured my frequent outbursts of irrational rage when a migraine attack was coming on and was my personal nurse aid when I had to relearn basic life routines. No words can describe how humiliating it is to not being able to pull down your own pants to go to the toilet or how mortifying it is when robbed of the ability to walk, dress or feed yourself. But my husband had always been my rock to steady whatever storm came my way and always did what had to be done without fuss or commotion in getting me rehabilitated back to my normal – every single time. In every instance when the paralysis left me crushed and depleted, he had been my de-facto drill sergeant, urging me to get back on my feet no matter how many times I was beaten down to a pulp. Luc never strayed from the vows he gave me on our wedding day, and for that, he also deserved more than a wife who thought of only her own perils.

I was not my mother, after all. I was much more fortunate than her. At the very least, my home was erected on a foundation of endurance and perseverance. My obligations to the home that I had built with Luc were not nearly fulfilled, and until they were, I had no right to step down. The hemiplegia could cheat me of my limbs and cloud my mind whenever it wanted, but it could not take away my spirit the way depression raided my mother's. I had my husband and son by my side, and as long as they were here, I would be able to fight. It was what I owed them.

With renewed determination and perspective, I spent the next three weeks relearning the motor functions of basic life skills. I had to build up my stamina to stand while showering and brushing my teeth in the bathroom. I had to learn again the art of going to the bathroom and dressing myself, controlling my trembling hands and legs when sliding them through my sweaters and jogger pants. Communication between my brain and limbs had to be reestablished so that I would be able to use my chopsticks, spoon or fork to feed myself. My cane was my everyday walking aid until I built up enough confidence to regain the balance I had lost and was able to move on my own without help. Brain fog was still an issue, impacting my concentration and focus. The ability to tolerate electronic screens, whether with the laptop, phone or television, had to be carefully paced in fear that being exposed too much too soon would trigger another attack.

By now, while the frequency of the hemiplegic episodes was a lot less as compared to when I was first diagnosed, each attack left me with a longer recovery period.

Where it used to take a maximum of three days to get back to normal, it now took at least three to four weeks – and even then, I was unable to fully recuperate my strength.

Where I was once able to lift twelve-pound weights, with every paralytic invasion, I would be knocked down to only being able to maneuver three pounds with the greatest physical exertion and it would take weeks before I would be able to lift heavier weights again.

Where I once ran half-marathons, my lung capacity would also be reduced to letting me go just a few kilometers before finding myself gasping for air, barely able to breathe. I didn't know if it was because the attacks were becoming more intense or if it was because my body was beginning to succumb to the repeated trauma and stress of the hemiplegia. I only knew that I was getting weaker with each episode.

***

"It absolutely is because of the numerous attacks you've been having, and your body is getting older, so it naturally takes more time to heal." Those were Dr. W's words when I returned to her clinic in hopes of getting a doctor's note to excuse me from the weeks of work I had to miss from the last round. While still working for the government, I was in the middle of transferring to another division in the department to lead a unit accountable for the organization's corporate learning and development programming. This latest attack had set me back almost a full month, and while I had been upfront with my new boss about the condition I had from the very beginning, it was a miracle that I was not yet fired with the amount of sick leave I had needed to take with each episode.

Seeing me still very weak and dependent on my cane to walk, the doctor conducted the regular exams of checking my reflexes and confirming all limbs had at least regained feeling. Knowing that her next step was likely to refill my prescriptions, I told Dr. W that she only needed to top up my Verapamil and Cambia, as the Topamax had proven to make me more brain-fogged during the day instead of preventing migraines. Dr. W surveyed me once again and sighed, "I really wish that Dr. S was able to see the condition you are in right after you have an episode and not weeks or months later. Seeing the patient and how they are right after an incident compared to later gives a different perspective and might help better inform treatment."

I nodded my head in agreement.

I assume he's never seen you limping like the way you are now, even though it's been weeks after your hemiplegia?"

I shook my head responding, "No… I don't think so. Other than the first time we met at the hospital; all my other visits have been through appointments. I think the quickest he's seen me after an episode was probably about four to six weeks, and that was when my recovery period was quicker."

"Unfortunately, that's how our system works here. But for someone with your condition, you need to see someone more immediately."

I couldn't agree more. While forever grateful for a public healthcare system where people had equal access to medical services, it was also an imperfect approach. A public system meant longer patient queues where demand for doctors and nurses would always surpass the supply of health care workers. There seemed to never be enough funding to fill the gap between supply and demand; and whatever money the government provided to fix the issues were only used as band-aid solutions, without ever getting to the root cause of a seemingly broken system. Still, even in my most dire of states, I would always choose public over private. Given the number of ambulance calls and hospital visits I have had to make in these recent years, we would never have been able to afford the hefty bills that would have been charged, let alone the countless times I have had to see doctors and specialists. At least with a public system, there would at least always be a chance to gain access to help, so long as we endured the long wait times.

After a few more moments of pondering, Dr. W announced, "I am going to write you a referral to a medical clinic in the city that specializes in neurology. It may be a longer wait, but hopefully, once they take you in, you'll at least be able to access their neurologist quicker than with Dr. S in the hospital. Your file will still be with Dr. S, and you'll also have a file with this clinic. Between the two specialists, there should be someone who can provide quicker treatment and follow-ups."

I was thankful for Dr. W's help and curious if a new neurologist would be able to offer some further insight on how to rid me of my nemesis, though I secretly wasn't all that optimistic. Online searches of the latest on hemiplegic migraines continued to report on research findings of newly discovered genomes tied to the disease or of additional medications that have been found to 'potentially' help some people in preventing its recurrence, but there was still no mention of anything on a possibility of a cure. Despite Dr. W's good intentions of finding me another approach to deal with what I had, I knew that unless it was an antidote, I would continue to be trapped and always be kept a prisoner.

Despite my cynical doubts, I patiently waited over six months before receiving a call from the neurology clinic for my initial consultation with a Dr. Nelly. The initial visit covered the routine motions of a nurse, first going over the paperwork of confirming my particulars and getting me to summarize my issue and why I was referred to their practice. Then, Dr. Nelly appeared and introduced himself to Luc and me. He was a younger specialist - or at least younger than Dr. S, and I suppose friendly enough. But there was just something about him that was missing. Throughout the sharing of my story of the hemiplegic migraine, he didn't ask any questions to validate or confirm facts and reacted rather indifferently to what I was going through. Without so much as carrying my file with him, he tore open a blank sheet of paper to make hurried notes of the steps I should take if a migraine attack were to come. It was information I already knew, but not wanting to make it awkward on the first visit, I didn't let him know that what he was lecturing us about wasn't providing any added value. Perhaps the most important piece of information he shared was telling us that if a migraine did come on again, I would be able to contact the clinic as their patient to get an IV to soothe the pain or nausea that typically accompanied the attacks. This was probably the only useful news during the whole visit, knowing that I now had another option other than the ER to get some relief when it was needed. He closed off the appointment by asking what types of medications I was on – something he should have known if he had taken the time to read my file – and decided to increase my Verapamil dosage by about five milligrams, as though doing so would cure me of the hemiplegia. It was done so arbitrarily. He then declared that I was to see him every three months for follow-up before writing up a requisition for blood work and sending Luc and me on our way.

"Hmm... I don't know about this doctor. He doesn't seem like a very good one," was Luc's assessment of him after our first visit. I couldn't agree with him more.

CHAPTER 13
WHEN THE WORLD CHANGED

Ask anyone on the planet about the year 2020, and it's guaranteed everyone who was not an infant at the time would have the COVID pandemic on their mind. When the World Health Organization announced that the world was in a global pandemic with the COVID-19 virus, it officially marked this era as one of the most impressionable time periods of the twenty-first century and of our lifetime. There, of course, had been other modern-day pandemics that garnered global attention that preceded COVID, like SARS, the swine flu, Ebola, Zika virus and others, but none of them were as easily transmittable as the Coronavirus. With COVID, the spread of the virus was achieved by both those with symptoms and those without them. If contracted, some would simply get over it, like the common cold, whereas for others, it caused severe respiratory illness or other complications that threatened or became the cause for the end of life. Often, it was the elderly or those who already had underlying health issues at the most risk. The ease of transmitting this disease from person to person forced the world into a competition to develop vaccines for the human race while social distancing measures were mandated across the globe to combat the spread. This disease drove healthcare systems across the world, with its hospitals, doctors and nurses to the brink of collapse. It was an international mayhem that would loom over the world for at least the next three years.

While the world continued to reel over the devastation done by the pandemic, I was trying to calibrate the virus' residual effects at home and work. Schools had transitioned their classrooms all online and Isaac had to learn in an entirely new environment at home in front of a laptop computer. Thankfully, at age nine, he was able to mostly manage on his own in maneuvering a virtual classroom with his teachers and classmates, so there was not much I needed to help him with while working at home myself.

At the office, work-from-home measures were implemented literally overnight, and support was needed to help staff transition their jobs from office to home. Our unit's business model of primarily delivering training and programs in-person had to pivot on its head, where all our learning products had to now be adaptable to various online platforms like MS Teams, Zoom and Webex. In between this chaos, the department underwent another re-organization with the goal of doing more with fewer resources. It witnessed the elimination of various senior and executive leaders, demotions, and reassignment of duties for those who were spared of the layoffs and cuts.

For me, while I was neither demoted or let go, I was given a larger unit to oversee with a new boss. From being accountable for a team of six, I was now managing a unit of nearly thirty staff. In addition to being responsible for corporate learning supports, I was now also in charge of the delivery of corporate performance management and succession processes, as well as executive development. As the director of this newly established unit, I had to not only learn about my new subject areas; but had to simultaneously assert a renewed vision for the unit.

With a pandemic still in full force around us, it was a time of great uncertainty and flux. Night after night, I lost sleep over my staff's well-being and morale while growing increasingly worried about how I was to support my team in continuing to deliver on our priorities to the rest of the organization. With an expanded unit and larger mandate, I was constantly battling the imposter syndrome lurking within, waiting for someone, anyone, to call me out and expose me a fake.

But it was quite the opposite. No sooner did the restructuring complete its course that I found myself in a meeting with my new boss, Sue. We were discussing our next steps in stabilizing a newly established team that was still quite shaken by yet another restructuring exercise, when out of the blue, Sue asked, "Can I offer you an observation?"

Surely, this was the moment I had been dreading the entire time. I was going to be reprimanded for being in a role that was way above my capability. But whether it was because of pride or defiance, I didn't let my fear show and forced a bold response of, "Yes, of course."

"I have been watching you work like crazy these last few weeks. You have such great energy about you and are obviously very competent. But I haven't seen you stop to even catch your breath all this time. I wonder if you needed to slow down a bit so that you can take care of your own well-being, too."

Such relief washed over me when I heard her words. Before being my supervisor, I always heard that Sue was a formidable executive - always knowledgeable and capable of leading the most complex work. What I didn't know was just how personable and warm a person she was. I knew then how very lucky I was to have her as my superior. As leaders go, she had both skill and compassion. She was the full package. And just like what Tom did all those years ago, it was at that moment Sue offered a safe place for me to disclose both my most inner secret and burden. I confided in her about my health condition and all the hardships and damage it had already done to me and my family.

But most importantly, I let her know what could be expected if an attack were to pounce on me unexpectedly and the amount of time that would be required to recover from the hemiplegia. Despite feeling initially safe to disclose, I was still partially guarded and looked for any signs of suspicion and doubt about the story I shared. I only saw empathy and the interest to understand more of my situation throughout the conversation and felt ever the more grateful. Little did I know while Sue may have eased some of my worries, my hemiplegia was not yet fully convinced that it was still being taken seriously.

***

Having worked with my new team for over six months, COVID-19 and all the stresses that a global pandemic offered were still going full tilt, leaving the world in survival mode. There were a few months when some governments (including ours) tried to bring people back into schools and workplaces despite repeated caution from healthcare providers and experts. But no sooner was that done, orders were reversed, and people were sent back home again in light of rising COVID cases.

Even so, there were instances where management and workers alike were permitted and chose to be in the office for at least a few days a week. I was one of them. While being at home alleviated many stresses often tied to the work commute – like gas prices and traffic – I didn't realize how much I enjoyed being in the company of people until I was told to be at home every day. For me, the synergy and momentum garnered through in-person connections would always surpass virtual platforms. And so, given the choice, I chose to be with other colleagues in the office for a few days and worked from home the remainder of the week, still mindful that we were in the midst of a pandemic that could claim anyone's life in an instant.

Still on Verapamil and going to an acupuncturist on a monthly basis, my hemiplegia had not surfaced since the end of the previous year. In another couple of months, I would have been free from paralysis for a year. It was a hope I carried with me, and I silently counted down the days.

In the meantime, life carried on, and it was an on-site workday when I was in a virtual meeting with Sue and a few of my other colleagues from different areas of the department. As the discussion began and when it was my turn to talk, I began expressing my viewpoint. I remember uttering a few sentences when the all-too-familiar sensation made a comeback to both my head and limbs on my left side. In an instant, the numbness pounced not only on my arms and legs but also on the left side of my face, taking away my words. All motion slowed, and surrounding noise morphed into a distinct ringing in my ears as I witnessed the drooping of my left eyelid, cheek and mouth on camera. In all of the seven years that the hemiplegia had been haunting me, this was the first time I was able to see with my very own eyes the metamorphosis that took place during an attack. I was mortified by what I saw on screen and could only imagine the horror I caused my colleagues, who were also forced to watch the transformation. Instinct had me fight through the brute force that was seizing my limbs and distorting my face, but it was of no use. Like the world was against COVID, I was powerless against the paralysis.

In a flurry of activity, a colleague of mine, Shelley, who was working a few cubicles down, rushed down the hall and helped maneuver me to the floor - my entire left side was now useless and completely out of commission. I later found out that once Sue realized what was happening, she had messaged Shelley to tend to me. Luckily, both of them knew of my health condition, though it likely didn't ease their fear of what was happening to me. I don't remember much afterward beyond being helped to the ground, though Shelley told me later that while I was still unable to speak, I had managed to guide her through messy scribbles in a notebook to call Luc to come get me. I had no recollection of doing such a thing. While waiting for my husband, 911 was also contacted as nobody felt it right to simply watch me work through the paralysis that was coursing through my body.

By the time paramedics came, the prickled sensation of pins and needles was poking all the corners of my face, lips, and tongue. It was a discomfort that brought great relief as it was the first telltale sign that the paralysis was subsiding. Even greater comfort was that I was finally able to talk again. Propped against my desk drawer and with labored breath, I responded to the paramedic's questions while explaining to her that I was going through a type of migraine attack and not a stroke. It was the first time she had encountered such a case like mine where, for a minute, there were obvious signs of a stroke, and in the next, all symptoms of a drooped face, aphasia and hemiplegia would recede, and the person reverted back to normal. She was perplexed and fascinated all at once. If I didn't already feel that I had just been mowed down by a ten-ton truck and needed to attune back into the world, I would have also shared her awe in this most baffling phenomenon.

Other paramedics soon joined the commotion, and just like the first paramedic, none of them had heard or was even aware of what a hemiplegic migraine was. Just the same, my explanation was still not enough to convince them that I wasn't having a stroke. My sweater was raised over my head, leaving me exposed with only my bra, but I was way too exhausted to care. A number of electrode probes were then placed on my chest. I noticed the probes were connected to a rectangular box that resembled a laptop. I learned that this apparatus was set up to take my ECG and provided an immediate result. A few more readings were taken, and as my results were examined, Luc finally arrived on scene. He took one look at me and said, "Oh, it's not so bad this time."

All heads turned to him in disbelief. People must have thought him to be the most insensitive and senseless husband on earth. But he was right. At the very least, I was conscious and able to communicate. And though still extremely drowsy and brain fogged, I was alert enough to know what was going on. It really wasn't so bad this time, all things considered.

Clearing the way for Luc to reach me, now sitting meekly on a chair, one of the paramedics explained what had happened and verified with him that what I had was a hemiplegic migraine. He validated everything I had already told the first paramedic. It was then announced that while my ECG reading looked good, it was still advisable for me to go to the ER, as my left side was still numb and without feeling. Both Luc and I reiterated that that was how the hemiplegic migraine manifested itself and that it usually took a couple of days before my limbs reverted completely back to normal. In the midst of a pandemic and where there were already shortages of hospital beds and help, the ER was the last place for me. I knew with all conviction that I was better off at home in my own bed to wait for the storm inside me to pass. But despite both me and Luc's push back, none of the paramedics were convinced.

Finally, the team ended up contacting the on-call doctor who was assigned to their unit for consultation and to get a second opinion. I only hoped this doctor had some familiarity with hemiplegic migraines. I was given the phone and confirmed with the doctor that I was certain this was a typical migraine attack for me and that while my limbs were still quite heavy and not entirely back with the rest of my body, I could feel some progress. I really, really didn't need the hospital today. Relenting to my insistence, the doctor made me promise that if my condition didn't improve or got worse within the hour, then I had to be rushed to emergency services. I gave her my word. To seal the deal, the paramedics gave me some documentation to sign, officially declaring that I had refused to go to the ER, and I was set free. Still weak and unable to walk, I was hoisted onto a stretcher and brought down to the bottom of the building where Luc's car was waiting. The rest of the day became a hazy merging of blurry activities that had me bedridden, drifting in and out of a sea of consciousness.

Like another bout of déjà vu, the days that followed were filled with doctor visits and exercises with long periods of sleep and rest in between – all in an anxious rush to get back to functional so that I could return to my daily routine. My colleagues who had witnessed my fall from grace were so very kind and sympathetic, sending me messages of concern and encouragement. Sue was just as supportive, assuring me I had all the time in the world to recover and recuperate. She even arranged for the entire branch to pitch in and gift me and my family a gift card from Skip the Dishes, so that we didn't have to worry about cooking a meal or two at home.

As comforted and touched as I was by everyone's kindness, I couldn't help but feel sheepish and embarrassed. While many people at work now knew of my condition, it was one thing describing to people what I had, but it was something else entirely to publicly showcase what the paralysis was capable of in distorting my face and rendering my speech and the rest of the body disabled. To this day, I still can't get rid of the terrifying image of the deformed face that had stared back at me that morning in the office – a reflection of me but wasn't me. And I fear it will forever taunt me to no end.

The latest office attack brought me back to Dr. Nelly. As I described to him the event that led to the latest paralysis, he ripped out another blank page in his notebook and began listing out the medications I was to take for when the attacks came again.

"I need you to keep taking Verapamil, then when an attack comes or when you're recovering from it, take Metoclopramide for your nausea and Benadryl together. I'm also going to prescribe you Ritzatriptan. It's also a medication that has been shown to help people with their migraines, but what's good about this drug is that it's a pill that dissolves in your mouth. If you happen to be unconscious or have difficulty swallowing because your tongue is numb, you can take this for relief from your head pain."

I reminded him that my hemiplegia these days no longer gave me the residual migraine head pain, but he didn't seem all that interested in what I had to say. I also wasn't so sure about the advice on Benadryl. In all the years I had been with Dr. S or Dr. W, neither had ever hinted of this over-the-counter concoction as a remedy, nor did I ever come across this in the research I had done myself online with migraine treatments. Feeling skeptical of the advice, I pushed for more information.

"The Metoclopramide is to help with your nausea, and the Benadryl will help you sleep. But, if you're finding the Metoclopramide not doing anything for the nausea, you can take Zofran as an alternative to help with the queasiness." Adding another drug to the list, both Luc and I were starting to get confused with the old and new medicinal fixes being cited. I wondered whether the list of drugs was meant to help with the migraine or to get me so drowsy and high that I wouldn't know the difference if I was getting better or not.

Looking back now, I wish I had been more adamant with Dr. Nelly to at least clarify that I didn't go to him hoping for more drugs. In fact, it was quite the opposite. I had learned that many of the side effects of the chemicals in these drugs just made you more brain fogged and drained you of energy. The Verapamil was probably the most I was able to tolerate as a preventative – and even then, I couldn't remember the last time I was truly alert or present. The Cambia and Metoclopramide I resolved to take only as a last resort and avoided anything else beyond those three pills when it came to migraine. In the early days of the disorder, I had been told that the drugs I was given would prevent the migraine and was also told that the hemiplegia was temporary and that once I was in my late thirties, hemiplegic migraines would be a thing of my past. Both predictions had yet to come to fruition and yet, I was being loaded up with more drugs with every doctor's visit; and given empty promises that all the pills I ingested would be the right fix.

These thoughts were all in my head, all leading to a voice telling me that medication was not the answer. And yet, as Dr. Nelly wrote the Cambia, Rizatriptan, Metoclopramide, Topiramate, Zofran and Verapamil and another reminder to get the Benadryl on my prescription, I said not a word. I didn't know how to express my frustration, nor did I think he would care to understand. He was the doctor, and I was the patient. A good patient did what the doctor said, or at least would appear to follow orders, and that is what I did. I was too tired, too slow, too exasperated to argue.

When Luc brought home all the drugs that were prescribed to me later that day, I put all the medications that weren't the Verapamil, Metoclopramide and Cambia to the very back of the shelf, knowing that I would dispose of them one day without using them. As if just to prove to myself that I still had some sense, I contacted my pharmacist sister and asked her about the Benadryl.

"No, I wouldn't take it like that. Especially combined with the medications that you've been given, it'll make you so drowsy, you won't be able to wake up!" That was all I needed to hear to prove my point and enough to forget about the Benadryl. People often preach that while doctors can be helpful, you need to listen to your own body first. I was beginning to appreciate for the first time what that meant. My body had been telling me for a long time it didn't need or want the drugs.

So, instead of taking everything that Dr. Nelly had prescribed, I ramped up my visits to the acupuncturist to help with my sleep and energy levels. Like a vitamin, I was still taking Verapamil every day but avoided all other drugs – even the Metoclopramide, and resolved to apply natural oils like peppermint to ease the urge to vomit.

With a week left before I was expected to be back in the office, I was still using the cane to walk but felt I was nearing ready to let it go and move on my own again. It was the end of the day, and everyone in the household was preparing for bed. I don't remember what it was I thought I needed that night, but I recall taking the cane from my upstairs bedroom to help get me down the stairs to the main floor. I made no more than two steps before the bottom of my cane strayed away from its grip on the carpeted step, causing me to lose balance and plunge headfirst into the side wall before tumbling downwards in a rough, tangled mess. The loud boom brought Luc and Isaac out from wherever they were in the house as they both rushed to me on the middle of the staircase while I was still processing what had just happened.

"Why didn't you look after Mom, Isaac?" Luc scolded our son as they both lifted me up from the staircase and headed toward the bedroom.

Isaac, not one to take the blame for just anything, especially when it wasn't his fault, snapped back at his father with just as much vigor. "What?! It wasn't me. I didn't do anything wrong!" He was right. The burden that was mine to carry was to always be with me and no one else – let alone a child. Not wanting the sudden chaos to escalate further, I quickly defended my boy and tried to talk reason to the husband, who was still working through his adrenaline. "It's fine. Isaac was doing what he was supposed to be doing in his room. I just wanted to go downstairs to get something and must have lost my balance with the cane. It wasn't his fault."

Letting a stressed-out sigh, Luc now turned his frustration on me. "You should be more careful – especially when you're going down the steps! Make sure you hold onto the banister with your right side and carry the cane down with you *before* using it on level flooring."

Thankful that Luc was no longer taking his anger out on Isaac, I relented to his lecture on stairway safety and let myself be helped onto the bed. Though a little shaken and bruised with some rug burns on the side of my thighs and arms, I was relieved to be able to still feel both of my limbs. There was also no facial sagging or sensation of waves of numbness. My speech was still intact, which gave all the positive signs that I didn't have another attack but rather was the victim of my own clumsiness in losing my footing. Though I should have been relieved, guilt consumed me that night, knowing I had caused another scare to my loved ones, except this time, I couldn't push the blame on the hemiplegia.

Despite the fall, I was determined to get back on my feet and back to normal. I didn't want to be a burden any longer than I needed to be. As weary as my body was, I ignored the exhaustion and fatigue and worked tirelessly to wean myself off of the cane so that I would be able to walk with as little a limp as possible. I walked everywhere in my house and then outside around the neighborhood until moving with my legs felt like second nature again. The same went with my hands and arms. While my left hand was still shaky, I nurtured its strength back by lifting the smaller pound weights every day, preaching to myself that if I was able to get the strength back before, I could do it again. I had to, there was no other choice.

The day finally came when I was ready to head back to the office. Even though COVID was still running rampant in the world, and staff continued to work from home for the most part, there were days when management was called in to hold down the fort in the office. I had already been sheltered at home for over a week and looked forward to the change in scenery, even if it meant risking to be infected by the virus that was still winning the war against mankind.

It was good to direct my attention to something other than my health problems, and my team members who were at the office seemed both pleased and impressed that I had returned, looking as though nothing had happened to me. What they didn't know was that it was just a façade. I didn't even realize it myself until I was at my desk trying to read an email. I remember seeing the words and even reading them. But I didn't *understand* what the message was saying. It took me nearly half an hour for me to read and re-read one email before finally grasping what the content was about. It was as though the part of my brain responsible for comprehension couldn't latch onto the hook that gave me cognitive ability, leaving my mind doomed to wander into the aimless ether. This was the same for when people were talking to me. In meetings, I soon noticed that I wasn't able to focus on the words and sentences that people were saying. Like the emails, I was able to hear them just fine, but I couldn't conjure up a quick response, even for the easiest of issues that were being discussed or asked.

I simply couldn't focus. I found myself trembling with anxiety whenever being called into virtual meetings. The fear consumed so much of me that I wasn't ever able to concentrate on the actual content of the call. When I did have a thought to share, my mind and words lost their ability to sync together in unison, which resulted in endless stuttering of speech that made it difficult for people to follow what I wanted to say. Adding to this, I worried that in an instant, whatever I was saying would turn into a glob of mumbo jumbo where my face would once again be distorted into an unrecognizable melted heap. People were either too kind or I must have hidden my incompetence very well. Nobody said anything to me.

Things were no better on the home front. Bouts of angry outbursts would explode in reaction to the most minor things. From Isaac leaving his cookie crumbs on the floor to Luc forgetting to pick up something from the grocery store, were all met with the wrath of my rage. It was unreasonable anger that I couldn't control. Usually, when I was this irritable, an attack was bound to happen, so I waited and prepared for the paralysis to invade, but it never came. Instead, while the bad temper stayed, my appetite left, and so did my ability to get a full night's worth of sleep. I would be jolted awake every few hours by heart palpitations that beat so fast it felt as though my chest was imploding. The angst that woke me would also be accompanied by sweat trickling down my temples in fear that I was once again immobilized within my body shell. This lasted all of four days, but it felt like four years. Finally, on an afternoon while working from home, I caught myself just staring into the space of nowhere. I remember feeling nothing. There was no emotion, no passion, no intensity. I was just a shell of something that was just tired. I was so very, very exhausted, drained out of everything that ever made me who I was. Every breath I drew in and every sigh I let out cost me so much energy that I could no longer afford to move forward.

The light within was all gone, and I had been shepherded over to a world of a place that had nothing, and I was locked inside it.

CHAPTER 14
SELF-CALIBRATION

As empty as I was during that time, there must have been a flicker of light left somewhere that prompted me to reach for the phone and call for help. The pandemic changed even the way doctors cared for their patients, where phone consultations were the default to comply with social distancing policies. However, once I spoke to Dr. W, she immediately told me to come in person to her clinic so that she could see me herself.

"Your pupils are still dilated. How long ago did you say you had your fall on the staircase?"

"It was less than a week ago. But other than soreness and some minor rug burns, I don't think I broke anything. I haven't been getting any paralysis, so I don't think it was the hemiplegia. I haven't even been getting any headaches or head pain."

While divulging my story of restlessness and lack of focus, Dr. W continued her examination. She felt for lumps and bumps all over my head. *There weren't any.* She tested my motor skills by knocking my knees with the reflex hammer. *They jerked up as expected.* Coordination skills were also put to the test as I touched my nose with my eyes closed. *I found my nose with no issue.* The bottom of my feet was scraped by an apparatus. *My toes moved as they should have.* Lastly, I was asked to stand on one leg – first with the right and then the left. While still a little wobbly, I managed to complete the exercise to Dr. W's satisfaction. I was asked about other symptoms like repetitive vomiting and neck pain – and answered no to both.

"Given your fall, I think you have a mild concussion and also think that what you've been going through may be a form of PTSD. Have you thought of going to a therapist to talk things through?" While I was able to rationalize the mild concussion, PTSD was something I hadn't ever considered. I wasn't in the military, had never fought in a war, nor was I ever in a life-threatening incident where I was a survivor of bombs or car crashes. But then, maybe I heard wrong. Maybe Dr. W had said something else that only sounded like PTSD.

"PTSD – as in posttraumatic stress order? The kind that soldiers and first responders can sometimes get?"

Almost amused, Dr. W responded, "There are many in those professions who suffer from PTSD – yes. But PTSD can happen to people who have experienced or seen traumatic events that may not necessarily have been life-threatening in the typical sense."

"So, you think the hemiplegic migraine is giving me PTSD? How is that possible? I've been living with this thing for seven, almost eight years now. It's also not the first time that I've fallen or had concussions. So how could I all of a sudden have PTSD now?"

"It may have been that you've always had a little of it with mood changes, trouble with your sleep and fatigue."

"I thought those were all because of the hemiplegia causing those symptoms."

"Yes – that could have been possible. You could have very well been dealing with both since they have very similar symptoms." Still processing my thoughts and unsure how to respond, Dr. W offered more of her opinion. "Listen, what you've been going through is a lot. A regular migraine on a normal day is debilitating for anyone, but the kind that you have fires up lots of things in your brain and, given that you've had repeats of these occurrences, is a lot to handle. Every time you experience a hemiplegic migraine, your brain has to reset itself. Think about all the motor skills and cognitive ability that is temporarily lost when you get your attacks. It's a lot of work for your brain to reorganize itself for you to function again. Now, you pair that with the occasional fall that gives you concussions and the recovery period that you have to go through every time; it *is* a traumatic experience. We know that PTSD can surface years after a distressing event. In your case, you've been experiencing and reliving your trauma over and over again, spanning multiple years. So, I think it is absolutely reasonable that you would be showing signs of this delayed onset of PTSD."

All of what Dr. W said was logical and within reason. However, I still could not identify myself as someone with PTSD. As taxing and draining the hemiplegia was when it came, it was *still* just a migraine. A notch up from a headache that could set you back a day or two, and in my case, a few weeks at most. But it wasn't enough of a life stressor that warranted something as serious as this mental health condition. I wasn't worthy of this diagnosis.

While I continued to be hung up on whether I was truly suffering from PTSD, Dr. W was more concerned about what I was going to do next and already had orders for me to follow. "I know work is busy." *She knew me so very well.* "But I need you to take at least six weeks off. You need to be away from sitting in front of a screen all day – whether that be a phone, laptop or desktop. The stimulus from constant use of electronics and everyday work stress isn't doing you any favors when your body is still trying to recover from hemiplegia and concussion. So, while you're off from work, the only screen time you can have is streaming Netflix on the TV and sometimes on your phone to message and text your social contacts - if needed. But that's it. You are to disconnect and stay away from work for these six weeks. I'll also write you some sleeping pills to help with your sleep." Knowing how hesitant I was with taking drugs, she continued on, "Sleep is where the bulk of your healing happens. If you can't sleep or don't sleep well, you don't heal properly. So, these sleeping pills are meant as a last resort if you truly can't get a solid few hours in. Take frequent naps, do some light activities like walking on a regular basis and sleep early. Once you've recovered some more, you won't need to take them anymore."

I left her office with some concrete actions to follow through, including handing off what I needed to do in the office for the next six weeks. Sue's unwavering support and admittance that she wasn't surprised, as I didn't look ready to be back to work, made me feel that I had once again let her and the rest of my team down. But with Dr. W's note in hand, I knew I couldn't ignore her orders and forged on. My next course of action was to look for a psychologist who could help me process all that I had been going through so far. I reasoned that PTSD or no PTSD, therapy could help to resolve some of the anxiety issues that I had been going through. It was another moment where I gave silent thanks to an insurance plan that covered drug and therapy expenses. It was hard enough to find good people to help with medical issues, and I couldn't imagine someone going through what I was going through without having at least one understanding doctor (like I had) or the financial help to access the support needed (like my work gave). Of all the pain and hardships, I was reminded of how lucky I was. There were always worse things.

***

As skeptical as I was with Dr. Nelly's advice many a time, there was one thing he had suggested that stuck with me. At one of my visits, he mentioned the importance of not thinking that once an attack came, I had to stay in bed for long lengths of time. It was one thing if I was paralyzed and couldn't move. Still, when the hemiplegia had subsided, and the shock passed, my recovery could be expedited if I started to do some activity that stimulated the neurons in my brain.

"I don't mean for you to get up and run a marathon or start working ten-hour days. You still have to pace yourself. But get back to taking short walks the minute you are able to maneuver yourself better or try something new. Doing an entirely new activity or learning a new skill is always good for your neurons, even if you don't have brain trauma. If you're not feeling up for physical activity yet, painting is another great activity to do and helps with your motor skills."

For whatever reason, this advice stayed with me, and I was reminded of it again during the first week of my leave. Scrolling through my social media feeds one day, a string of videos and reels popped up promoting the benefits of 'paint-by-numbers'. Never an artist, let alone a painter, I was intrigued to see how easy this activity was to do, where the painter would simply paint the image by using the paint corresponding to the numbers already labeled on the drawing. It reminded me of coloring books I used to doodle in when I was a child, but the finished product proved to be way more sophisticated, even worthy of being framed as a professionally painted portrait in many instances. With nothing to lose (or work to do), I took a chance and bought my first paint-by-numbers kit.

My first experience with the painting kit was a positive one. Not expecting much to come out of the activity, I was surprised to find how the motions of matching the paint color to the number on the canvas gave such calming serenity to my entire psyche. Through painting, I was able to shut out all distractions and white noise surrounding me every day and simply focus on the task at hand. It was a kind of peace I don't think I had ever encountered before but had always unknowingly craved. I was finally relieved of all tension, if only for the few hours that I was with my painting. Not only was I able to de-stress, but I was also able to achieve something I never thought I ever could: creating images on a canvas.

My newfound hobby with painting triggered an extended interest in creative art design. If I was able to paint, then would I also be able to learn how to make other artistic creations without any guidance other than my own vision? I began searching for resources, apps and other software that offered tips and tricks on how to design and stumbled upon Redbubble. I discovered that Redbubble was an online market that sold products on-demand based on user-submitted artwork. By creating an account and setting up a virtual kiosk, I was able to upload my digital creations onto various products like T-shirts, stickers and water bottles and sell them. An improbable phenomenon became another reality as I created my own brand called 'Chai Concepts' and posted my designs and all other creative works, like my paint-by-number creations, for the world to see through Facebook and Instagram. It was one of the boldest and likely most shameless things I had ever done, but I did it anyway.

And while I was far from being able to quit my day job, I managed to pick up a few projects under my Chai Concept's brand through Facebook, IG and simple word of mouth that has since generated a little side income for me through my paintings and online designs. But financial gains aside, I was gifted joy and contentment, knowing that I was still capable of creating things without being a burden to anyone else. I had found something I could call my own, where I was safe and secure.

Artwork wasn't the only new thing I tried during my extended leave from work. My last visit with Dr. W and her diagnosis of PTSD lingered in the back of my mind for a long time. I suppose I had thought from time to time through the years that as much as I needed to help my physical self, I also needed to maintain good mental health. After all, body and mind together were what defined health and well-being. But like many things, while I had thought of it, I never felt the urgency to act on it. At least not until now.

As with all things new, I did some research on the best types of therapies to treat PTSD and came across an approach called Eye Movement Desensitization and Reprocessing or EMDR. I read that it was a type of therapy where a trained therapist would have the patient focus briefly on the traumatic memory while getting the individual to experience another sort of stimulation (like eye movements) at the same time. Such an exercise was proven to help reduce the intensity of the emotion normally associated with the traumatic memory. It was a helpful treatment for disorders like anxiety, depression and other distressing life experiences. The psychologist I eventually ended up seeing to undergo EMDR would later explain that this sort of therapy helped the brain process whatever stressful memories there were impeding our everyday life and allowed it to heal on its own. The ultimate goal of EMDR was that it would strip away the overwhelming emotions associated with the traumatic memory so that the person would still be able to remember the event but without the stressful emotion.

Frankly, the EMDR exercises that I was guided through weren't all that effective for me. There was a mixture of visualization activities coupled with various bilateral stimuli through a hand-held device or self-tapping techniques. The point was to change my perception of the traumatic event by activating both halves of the brain to create new neuron connections through the pairing of memories with the bilateral stimulation, allowing for my memories to transition from an emotional form to more logical thoughts, all without the stressors that were once there. Numerous sessions later, I was disappointed to find that my fight, flight and freeze instincts were still intact– still always in anticipation of when the next hemiplegic attack would come. And when it didn't come, it made me more anxious, convinced that the longer the attacks lagged in between, the more serious a blow I would suffer when it really did set in to invade again later on.

But while the anxiety never truly left, I did feel a sense of relief to share my worries and stresses with someone who didn't have a vested interest in the person that I was so that I wasn't judged (at least not openly) and was able to speak freely without reservation. It was a kind of healing that let me recalibrate myself so that I was able to rekindle the spark that gave me back the will to move on.

CHAPTER 15
IRON SHOTS

The paralysis attack of November 2020 was an especially impressionable one as it not only forced me to be out of commission from work for six weeks (the longest time I've ever taken from work, other than maternity leave), but it also left me with a body and mind so badly weakened I would never be the same again. Weeks after the hemiplegia passed, my left hand would continue to tremble when using utensils or lifting the lightest things. It found the greatest comfort in being held closely against my chest, curled and bent, letting my right hand do all the work. While doable, it took the greatest of energy to have it outstretched and mobile. Holding a regular frying pan to cook was a challenge as it felt like the pan had gained over fifty pounds overnight. Returning to work, I was still having difficulty concentrating, and my stuttering had grown worse. I would often be in mid-sentence with a colleague or client and would either forget midway what I was trying to say or simply couldn't force the words out, even though I wasn't having a hemiplegic attack.

Both Dr. W and Dr. Nelly validated that these symptoms in the post-dome of migraine were 'normal'. It was just my body getting older and taking a longer time to recover. If they thought the explanation would make me feel better – it didn't. While I wasn't dying, my body certainly was deteriorating. Where I used to be able to pull off over ten-hour workdays and be up and ready to go back to the office the next morning, I found myself near the point of collapse at the end of a regular eight-hour shift. It didn't matter if I was working from home or in the office. In fact, it didn't matter if it was even a workday or weekend. By the end of the day, after doing any sort of activity – be it work, grocery shopping, or running errands, sheer exhaustion would sweep over me like a tsunami and I was done for. The fatigue was so overwhelming that I didn't even have the energy to sleep.

***

Entering a year since the world announced it was in a pandemic, vaccines were finally developed, and governments were urging people to get their shots. Though never one to be scared of needles or against vaccinations and immunizations, I hesitated to take the COVID-19 vaccine. While doctors were adamant in claiming there was absolutely no correlation, previous years of getting the seasonal flu shot would leave me dragged through bouts of hemiplegia. The attacks post-flu shot were typically shorter than normal, but waves of the paralysis would leave me bedridden for at least a day or two. It became so much of a pattern I stopped getting the flu shot in recent years and instead resorted to acupuncture to boost my immunity and energy levels as an alternative way to avoid illness. Getting needles and being cupped on a regular basis by TCM practitioners in exchange for getting one shot a year to avoid paralysis seemed to work well. While I was constantly battling migraines and hemiplegia, I couldn't remember the last time I fell sick with the flu or any sort of cold. So, when vaccines were mandated by work, I felt I had to discuss with my doctors to talk out the risks for someone with my condition.

When I raised it with Dr. Nelly at one of my regular visits, he, like many others before him, didn't think the vaccine had a direct relation to hemiplegia. "The vaccine may give some people flu-like symptoms where you feel sore and tired for a few days - maybe even a fever, and that's normal as with many vaccines and immunizations. But there should be no causation effect between getting the vaccine and your hemiplegic migraine. If anything, it may be your body experiencing flu-like symptoms that could trigger headaches or migraines, but that would result from the flu symptoms, not the vaccine."

But I had a different perspective. Whether direct or indirect, it didn't make a difference if the end result was that I was going to get paralysis after being vaccinated. Regardless, this vaccine was for the goodness (and longevity) of mankind. I knew from the beginning that I was going to get vaccinated, but I wanted to be prepared for what could come.

Dr. Nelly actually carried a flip chart with him that day of what I assumed carried my information. Skimming through the papers in front of him that likely contained my latest blood test results, he commented, "I see that you're really low on your iron levels – almost near zero. Have you always been this low with iron?"

I nodded my head.

"Have you done an iron transfusion before?"

The nodding turned to a shake of the head. I had heard of blood transfusions before but didn't know that iron transfusions were a thing.

"It may be worth looking into increasing your iron levels since low iron can also be a trigger for migraines." *Why wasn't I told this before?* "This might be why you've been getting migraines all this time too."

"I've been taking iron supplements for years, but for some reason, my body never absorbs the nutrients, and I've never been able to get my iron levels up. What is the normal iron level for women?"

"It's a pretty wide range, anywhere from ten to thirty, but it looks like you're currently at a three based on your last blood test. The one before that, you were at a six, which was also low, but your levels are continuously dropping. Iron transfusions aren't my specialty, so you need to go back to your G.P. and look into getting a transfusion. If you increase your iron levels, you may not react as badly as you did before with your shots."

I took Dr. Nelly's advice and contacted Dr. W to discuss the possibility of an iron transfusion. "I'm looking at your file now, and your iron level is low, but it isn't *that* low. Puzzled by her comment, I pushed to know more. Dr. Nelly had said my level was at a three. Three points away from zero, which I assumed would indicate my body to be completely out of ferritin. How much lower did I have to be for it to be truly low?

"Dr. Nelly said that my last test showed a three."

"Well, that's interesting because what I see on your file is a twelve. So, while it's not high, it isn't as bad. Threshold levels to get into the program for iron transfusions have since gone up, and I'm not sure if having iron levels of twelve would be enough now to get it. A level three reading definitely would get you in. But given that I don't have anything here that says you're at a three, I'll write you a job requisition for a test to confirm, and then we can go from there."

Despite getting a blood test recently, my results obviously weren't showing for all my doctors, so I went back to draw another blood sample. Results for this round of tests showed that I was indeed at a level three for iron and also showed a significant drop in hemoglobin levels that officially tagged me to be anemic. Upon receiving my results, Dr. W immediately got me accepted into the program.

While waiting for the transfusion, I explored more of the implications of what having iron deficiency anemia could mean. I learned that hemoglobin is a protein in red cells that carries oxygen from my lungs to all other organs in my body. Having anemia meant that I did not have enough healthy red blood cells (or hemoglobin) to carry the oxygen where it needed to go throughout my body, causing me to constantly be tired, weak, and even short of breath. I had been exhausted for so long and had always attributed my fatigue and lack of alertness to the hemiplegia and the drugs I took to prevent the migraine. But now, with this newfound information, was the source of my brain fog because of something else entirely?

Through my preliminary research, I came across a number of articles that also supported Dr. Nelly's claim that low iron had been linked to migraines, causing a variety of symptoms, including dizziness, anxiety, and depression. There were also studies that showed people with iron deficiency anemia have a higher rate of migraines. Further studies also indicated that low Vitamin D levels could also prevent the absorption of iron, while a deficiency in Vitamin B12 could prevent the production of the red blood cells needed to be healthy. I recalled that in my early days of being diagnosed, Dr. S had also suggested I take up a daily regimen of Vitamin B and D to help with migraine prevention. How interesting that both Vitamins B and D were once again named. The more I read, the more evidence I saw that showed just how strong a linkage migraine had with iron levels. I made a note to ramp up efforts to ingest more of my vitamins. I once again felt a glimmer of hope that maybe, just maybe, getting more iron was the answer to relieving me from the hemiplegia.

Two weeks later, I was admitted as an out-patient for my very first iron transfusion. Because of Covid restrictions still firmly in place, the hospital was a deserted place when I got into its lobby to register. There were strict protocols of being masked and sanitizing my hands before I was directed to the back of the lobby to take a seat for a nurse to hook me up to the IV, where the iron was to be transmitted into my bloodstream. The process took a little over two and a half hours, with minimal side effects.

With the iron transfusion now complete, I was ready for my first COVID-19 vaccination. Getting the needle itself was rather uneventful, but it was the waiting afterward to see if my body would rebel and strike me with a hemiplegic blow that rattled my nerves. I remembered that the hemiplegic migraine would come for an attack about three to seven days after getting a flu shot and used that as a gauge to see if I would be hit with something similar post-Covid vaccine. A week after getting the vaccination, I was still paralysis-free and cautiously breathed a sigh of relief as I scheduled myself for my second COVID shot to complete the vaccination series.

A little over a month later, after getting the second shot, I held my breath once again in hopes that I would be spared from the hemiplegia. During this second round of shots, if the increased iron levels were meant to be my defense, its barrier was strong enough to fend off a full-on attack but was unable to fight off the waves of numbness and tingles that seized my left side in short bouts. It was as though the hemiplegia was warning me of my naivety by reminding me that I would never have the strength to completely stave off its grip. That I would always be its captive, forever and for always.

CHAPTER 16

PSYCH

About a year after my attack at the office where Sue and my other colleagues got to see a demonstration of how debilitating the hemiplegia was, my branch welcomed a new executive director. I think the international crisis of COVID caused many to re-evaluate life priorities, and Sue was one who decided life was way too short to put off retirement when she already had her numbers. She had put in her fair share of the work over an impressive span of over thirty years, and it was time to put her family first. I didn't blame her.

With my new boss, Layla, on board, I found myself cautiously optimistic that she would be just as empathetic and understanding as Sue was when it came time to disclosing my medical issue. The organization I was still a part of didn't always have leaders who were kind and compassionate. Remnants of the guilt I felt back then for taking a lunch or coffee break were still very real to me in the present, as was with many others who also had suffered through the tyranny of a leadership team that focused only on results and not its people.

My first impression of Layla was a positive one. Though not Sue, she seemed just as understanding and had a genuine concern for people. I took a chance and disclosed my medical secret to yet another person, hoping that I wouldn't be penalized for what I was about to share. Just like I did with Sue when we were first acquainted, I explained to Layla that my medical condition was labeled a migraine but inflicted stroke-like symptoms. I went on to assure her that my attacks were not frequent but were something I had no control over (though I was on preventative medication), and when the attacks came, I would typically be out of commission for a few weeks. After hearing my story, Layla was as understanding as I had hoped, and I silently gave my thanks for being once again so fortunate to have such a boss. However, in the backdrop of my mind, I also knew that there would be a day when my luck would run out.

***

Towards the end of 2021, I was fully functional and was on a good path in regaining most of my physical strength. The iron transfusion had helped raise my iron levels and my hemoglobin range. While iron and hemoglobin ratings were still low, I was no longer considered anemic. My sister suggested I try a different iron supplement to maintain my iron levels. I was pleased to find that the Proferrin did not cause the constipation and cramping that all other iron supplements had previously given. This brand of supplement was made from animal proteins (like cows), and while each pill did not provide as much iron as the other conventional brands like FeraMax, its selling feature was that it was very easily absorbed into the system while always gentle on the stomach. It went for about a dollar a tablet (as opposed to other brands that charged no more than seventy cents a capsule), but not feeling any negative or painful side effects on a daily basis was well worth the price. Having completely given up on the Topiramate by now, I was still feeling brain-fogged from the Verapamil use on most days and was relieved that I at least no longer had to deal with the constant stomach pains.

When COVID hit, the annual MRIs, CT scans, and periodic lumbar punctures were put on hold as healthcare resourcing was redirected to more immediate priorities (and understandably so). Now approaching year two of the pandemic, the brain scans that were missed were rescheduled, and the latest results came back normal, short for a few white lesions that had previously been shown and dismissed as something typical for chronic migraineurs. Once again, it was confirmed that I didn't have any other ailments, and there was nothing more that could be done to rid the paralysis plaguing me.

Even though I had just passed the one-year mark of being paralysis-free, the fear that another attack was on the horizon haunted me every day. It was this same fear that drove me to see a naturopath to explore if there were other more natural vitamins that could potentially replace the Verapamil as a preventative supplement against migraines. I had been taking Verapamil for years because it had the least side effects, but I was never entirely convinced that it was doing its job of preventing the debilitating attacks. I started taking magnesium glycinate, which worked to relieve anxiety and to help with sleep. As sleep and anxiety were connected to migraine frequency, the logic was that taking this supplement would help keep the hemiplegia at bay. After the naturopath, I continued to see my psychologist on a monthly basis. By now, we had moved away from the EMDR and simply spent my visits voicing all the unease and distress that was caged inside to calm the angst and avoid the self-fulfilling prophecy I knew could happen any minute if I let down my guard. And maybe that was why, while I hadn't had an attack for some time, I was still so very exhausted, always depleted, and never fully alert in the moment, no matter how much I tried to sleep. It was likely because I was always on guard all the time.

By December 2021, Covid had evolved into the Omicron variant. Different countries across the world imposed different policies with various degrees of restrictions to limit the spread. In Alberta, where I was, people were strongly urged to scale back their gatherings during the Christmas season. It became another quiet holiday spent with immediate family members with no friend gatherings in our household. Though sad that after almost two years, the world was still not yet free from this pandemic, I was also relieved to use COVID-19 as the reason to stay low-key at home. If the hemiplegia decided to show itself again, I at least would be steps away from my bed, out of sight and away from people. Christmas Eve then Christmas Day came, but the migraine never showed. I found myself feeling once again a sensation of hope and optimism that maybe – just maybe, this was *the* year when I would be able to go through Christmas and New Year's without fuss and drama.

I made it through New Year's Eve but started the first day of 2022 in a blur. I don't remember much of what happened and was told that I was found in bed in the late morning when I should have already been awake. Like before, Luc and Isaac had to shake me back to life while shouting out my name to solicit any sort of reaction, and when my eyes finally opened, they were empty – soulless and confused. This apparently lasted a few minutes before my senses returned, and I was brought back to reality - back to my husband and son. At home, one-half of me was no longer mobile as the paralysis coursed through my nerves, seizing not only limbs but the better part of my consciousness. While in bed and able to respond to questions, it was all done through a fog of muffled stupor. I was there, but not there.

In the early days when I was first diagnosed, doctors mentioned that while uncommon, hemiplegic migraines could be serious enough to drive people into comas. Apart from the obvious, this was another reason why prevention of hemiplegic attacks was critical, as the more frequent the attack, the more the brain needed to reset back in place. Without prevention, there would be a risk that the brain would one day be so overtaxed that it would simply relent in exhaustion and let the body succumb to coma.

There had already been a handful of times in previous years when I was found unable to wake from sleep. And while I was always shaken back into consciousness, the drowsiness and brain fog would still have me lagging and barely responsive. I wonder through all those times, including what happened in 2022, if I wasn't showing signs of sliding on the edge of being comatose.

With the streak of being migraine-free now broken, we went through the regular motions of going to my doctors for sick notes and reloading up my prescriptions in preparation for another attack. All hope was once again shattered, and my body was left to relearn (yet again) the basic skills of walking, eating, and getting dressed, all while putting on a brave front for the sake of everyone around me who were also suffering.

Where months before, there were once remnants of color that triggered faith, my world had crashed once more into a dark chasm, reminding me that I wasn't worthy of a good life. I found myself stewing over this mental slump on the couch one night as the family watched a movie. While on the outside it looked as though I was focused on the show, something sinister was brewing on the inside within the intricate fabric of my brain cells. A couple of weeks had passed from the last attack that came to me during sleep, and while I was still using my cane, I was confident that I would be able to limp again on my own without help within the week. But while the paralysis had retreated from my limbs for the time being, it was my head that was now becoming unhinged.

Images on the television started to morph and jump out of the screen like demented gargoyles, dragging me into its center of lurid colors that stabbed every neuron fiber of my brain. Alongside the stabbing, every blood vessel in my head was being wrung and squeezed. Once twisted into tangled knots, both ends of my neurons and blood vessels were pulled and tugged in a continuous torturous pattern, making even the motion of inhaling and exhaling air most painful. People who claimed that the brain didn't have pain receptors were liars.

I closed my eyes as a means to escape, to shield myself away from the raw colors and images surrounding the senses. While I could no longer see, the sounds that were emitted were just as excruciating. I felt the inside of my head swell and pulsate so much it made my right eyeball bulge out of its socket. This sudden bomb of stimulation made me want to convulse with what little food was in my stomach, right on the center of my lap.

Isaac, who now saw me reduced to a fetal position with hands on my head, whimpering in pain, called out to his dad, who was downstairs. Rushing back upstairs, Luc found me crippled and tremoring all over.

"Sweetie, are you alright?" Luc asked; concern and worry evident in his every word and touch. The scare from the latest attack was still very fresh for both him and Isaac, and to witness something like this so soon afterward was likely nothing short of terrifying.

"My head… it hurts so much," was all that I could manage to mumble before returning to wordless sobs.

"You just had your medicine. Do you need to take something else? Should we go to the hospital?"

No response as he was met with more painful cries.

Despite battling the onslaught of piercing pain, I must have given some sort of signal that I didn't want to go to the ER, perhaps knowing intuitively there was nothing that could be done even if we made the hospital visit. Not given permission to dial 911, Luc did the next best thing and simply put his arms around me and applied pressure against my temples and upper back in an effort to ease my pain while my body continued to hunch over, coiled into a tangled, tremoring ball.

I must have blacked out in Luc's arms for some time as I succumbed to the torture. When I came to, I heard faint echoes of my name being called for me to take a sip of some ginger tea that had been made to help with the nausea. Apparently, I had done some dry heaving earlier on and had murmured something of wanting to vomit but couldn't.

The night bled into the next day, with the pain finally retreating a little at the crack of dawn, leaving still yet a throbbing pressure pulsating on my right temple. Though not completely in the clear, at least the stimulation that had brutalized me the whole night before had calmed somewhat. With the intensity of the pain lowered, I was finally able to rest.

The next morning was a school and workday. While knowing that both my husband and son would have much rather stayed at home to monitor my condition, I assured Luc that I was fine and that the episode the night before was likely a fluke incident. Actual migraine head pain after a hemiplegia attack was something I almost never got anymore. What I experienced the night before, was probably an anomaly, with the chance of it recurring again low. At least I wasn't paralyzed. All I needed was a good day's worth of sleep and some proper meals for sustenance to continue with my recovery.

Barely an hour after kissing my family goodbye, the pain returned with just as much vengeance as it had the previous night. Being curled up in a ball for the better part of the morning, once again nauseous and frazzled, I reached for the phone to call Dr. Nelly's office. I could endure no more and needed help.

"Dr. Nelly's office."

"Hi…I'm hoping to get into Dr. Nelly's office for an IV treatment. I've been going through some pretty severe migraines all last night and today and need some help."

"Could I get your name?"

"Natasha Chai."

After listening to the clickety-clack of keyboard typing, the receptionist returned to the line.

"I'm afraid I won't be able to get you in. It looks as though you are no longer a patient here." Assuming I heard wrong, I asked the message to be relayed to me again.

"It seems that your migraine attacks haven't been occurring as frequently anymore, so, as a result, you have been removed from the patient list."

What nonsense was this? "But I just saw him not long ago. Why was I not told of this?"

"You'll have to check with your G.P. But for today, I won't be able to get you in." As though sensing my desperation, the receptionist suggested calling Dr. W's office instead, or if the pain was too much, I should go to the ER. The whole point of having Dr. Nelly as a doctor was to receive immediate care and to avoid going to the hospital. But here I was back at square one again – with no doctor nor reinforcements to help.

Barely able to open my eyes, much less talk, I somehow managed to phone Dr. W and explained the new information that I had serendipitously uncovered. Dr. W was equally surprised and also unaware that I had been removed from Dr. Nelly's patient list. She assured me that another referral would be written immediately, asking him to place me back on his patient list in hopes that I wouldn't have to wait another six months.

In the meantime, there was still the harrowing pain still raging inside my brain to deal with. "I completely understand why you wouldn't want to go to the ER when we're still dealing with Covid." *Another example of why I was grateful to at least have Dr. W on my side.* "But we need to target the migraine so that you can actually get some real rest. Sleep is needed for your body to recuperate, and if the pain isn't letting your body rest, it'll continue to be a trigger to experience more headaches and migraines, and you'll just find yourself in a vicious cycle of continuous pain and exhaustion. Did I hear right that you're not experiencing any hemiplegia this time round?"

"No…I had the hemiplegia recently, but it hasn't come back. Just the really bad migraine this time," I whispered through the phone, feeling myself being consumed by the torture with each passing minute.

"On a scale of one to ten, how would you rate your pain now?"

"A ten, if not an eleven."

"Okay, then. I'm going to prescribe you Ketorolac Tromethamine – ten milligrams and take it up to three days a week as needed. It's a stronger painkiller medication. See how this helps with the pain, and if it doesn't, get in touch with me again."

Grateful that relief was around the corner, I called Luc, asking for his help to pick up the medicine that was to grant me the escape from the pain so that I could finally sleep. Upon taking the Ketorolac, I found that while it lessened the intensity, the pain in my head did not relent. Everything around me, from the car sounds outside the house to people chewing their food at the dinner table, was still just as raw and amplified. The new pills did a good job creating a cloud of dense mist all around my consciousness that I couldn't tell the difference between day and night, but I was still able to feel the *pain*. I was still unable to sleep or eat.

Within a week, I called Dr. W's office again wanting to ask for another doctor's note to extend my sick leave from work and to ask for something stronger. At this rate, I just wanted to be knocked out of my misery – at all costs.

When I called, Dr. W was on vacation, and I instead got her backfill – Dr. Toy, who, after hearing a summary of my woes and reviewing my file, decided to put me on Tramadol in place of Ketorolac for the week.

"But the Tramadol is our last resort. It's a stronger painkiller than the Ketorolac, and if it still doesn't work with relieving your pain, we'll have to take you to the ER and look at giving you something through intravenous."

It sounded like a fair enough deal, and I rushed for the Tramadol as though it were my last hope. Fifty milligrams of the pill were prescribed, and I was to take it once or twice a day as needed. It turned out that Tramadol was indeed the magic pill for pain relief. It gave me the sleep and rest I needed, but it came at a price.

This pill was the gateway that relieved me from all torment while altering all components of reality that contained time, space, and people. With Tramadol, I no longer felt burden or fear. In fact, I no longer felt anything. I was a feather that was tossed in the atmosphere and was content in following whatever direction the wind fancied to blow me into. On the outside, my family saw me finally out of pain and held their breath for the day that I got back to "normal" again. For me, the Tramadol gave my insides – head, heart, and limbs – freedom.

Before Tramadol, I had never touched a regular cigarette, much less taken up cannabis or any other type of recreational drug, nor did I ever feel the need to get high or pollute my lungs and head with foreign substances. So, when the effects of the Tramadol flooded my senses, it didn't even occur to me until afterward that what I was floating on was the release of dopamine that gifted me euphoria. *When people spoke of "out of body experiences", was this how it felt? Was this what being "high" meant?* These types of thoughts would flutter in and out of my consciousness in between woozy naps during the day and randomly as I sat with my husband and son at the dinner table or went about the day running errands. But I was now always relaxed and calm as my mind took me through the carefree journey to ponder the essence of such ecstasy.

But once the week's supply of Tramadol was all consumed and over, the burden and fear I had all too easily forgotten returned. I found myself missing, almost obsessively, the bliss I had lived in only a week before and yearned for more. I was terrified of going back to battling the weight that everyday life had in store for me, and I found myself staring up at the ceiling in the darkness every night, unable to sleep, thinking about the tiny magic pill. Missing it so very, very much.

With still another week left until I was expected back to work, the head pain and nausea returned. Anxious that this was a warning sign for another paralytic attack coming my way, I resorted to taking the Rizatripan in hopes of aborting any debilitating symptoms that another round of a hemiplegic migraine attack would bring. But the more I took the medication, the more insistent the migraine was, embedded inside my brain. I was once again held prisoner by my own head.

It was at this time that I received a call from Dr. Nelly's office. I was informed that I was once again made his patient, and I was scheduled to see him later that week for a consult. *Another moment where I gave my infinite thanks to Dr. W for her quick action.*

The timing couldn't have been more perfect as I could feel the migraine pain becoming more intense by the day. Before the week's end, Luc and I found ourselves back in an all-too-familiar examination room waiting for Dr. Nelly.

Without acknowledging the previous incident of getting removed from his patient list *(was he even aware that it had happened?),* he jumped straight into asking how I was doing and the details of my latest episode.

Both Luc and I gave an earful of all the events that had happened, from waking up dazed and confused on the first day of the new year to the most recent episodes where there had been no hemiplegia but severe migraine head pain. I told him about the exhaustion, the brain fog, and the head pain that always seemed to linger despite taking the medication.

"So, you're still taking Verapamil daily, but just how much Rizatriptan have you been taking?"

"I followed instructions and have taken only one a day whenever I feel an onset of migraine pain coming."

"How long have you been taking it for?"

"I've been taking it every day, once a day now, for about two weeks, give or take."

"That may be the issue. Rizatriptan is supposed to only be taken on a periodic basis and should really not be taken more than twelve times per month. Frequent ingestion of the drug could actually cause drowsiness and nausea and, ironically, might even trigger headaches. I suspect your brain fog and exhaustion is not only because of your body still trying to recover from your latest episodes, but it's also because you're experiencing the side effects of taking too much Rizatriptan."

As though jumping to my defense, Luc responded with, "We didn't know. The instructions said to take one a day as needed."

Unphased, the doctor replied, "Well, that's just the instructions, but in reality, twelve pills a month should be the maximum, or else you run into issues like what you've been experiencing."

We were then sent off with a doctor's note to extend my leave for another couple of weeks, and I was directed to stay off the Rizatriptan for at least two to three weeks. If I experienced any more head pain, I was to try to tolerate it, and only if the hemiplegia returned could I take Cambia or, if it wasn't severe paralysis, "wait it out." In essence, I was being placed on a self-directed detox program, getting weaned off of the Rizatriptan.

One day, in the aftermath of this particular instance, I reviewed the list of medications that I was placed on and dug deeper into the drugs I had been prescribed to help with my head pain. After several Google searches and further queries with my sister and other pharmacy friends, I soon discovered that the Ketorolac initially prescribed was usually used for inflammation and to treat acute, moderate pain. While not morphine, it was found to be just as effective and was normally provided after surgery. While the findings of Ketorolac were interesting, the information on Tramadol gave me a shock.

Like Ketorolac, Tramadol was a strong painkiller. But what brought the Tramadol to the next level (at least in my mind) was that it was a narcotic. Its use was to typically treat short-term severe pain and used when other non-opioid pain medications have been exhausted and found ineffective. Like other narcotics such as oxycontin and codeine, it had the risk of being misused, causing addiction – even under a doctor's care.

I remembered the weightless joy I had felt during the week I was on Tramadol and recalled even more clearly how I had mistaken that euphoria to be happiness. In that moment, I would have given anything to feel that thrill over and over again. Had the doctor prescribed more than a week's worth of the opioid, or if I had been a little more desperate, I fear I would have driven myself to become dependent on the drug that only gave the illusion of happiness.

Faced with this newfound information has made me wonder why I was prescribed such strong medications in the first place without even needing to see the doctor in person. Granted, it was during a time when the world was still dealing with a global pandemic, but these were medications that were normally prescribed at a hospital after a person had gone through surgery - the epitome of bodily trauma. I merely had to only make a few calls and, while completely genuine, cry about pain before getting access to some of the most addictive and potent drugs. Not only was I given the drugs, but they were also provided to me with limited information on what the medications were and their implications. I gathered the onus should have been on me to ask, but already distracted with pain, I really didn't know what to ask. And while initially being given a limited supply, had I asked for more of the medication afterward, I was fairly certain I would have been given what I wanted. I suppose it was due to assumptions that I was not from an "at-risk" lifestyle, that I had a legitimate condition that caused chronic challenges, so that stronger medications were warranted. But even so, should such strong drugs be prescribed to people even in my condition? Looking back today, had I not been thinking of the Tramadol in the aftermath, I would not have turned to overdosing on the Rizatriptan for consolation.

When I finally returned to work and back to my normal life routine in late February 2022, I was topped up my prescription for Rizatriptan again. Picking it up from the pharmacy, I flipped over the box and saw that the product label on the drug still read, *"Take 1 tablet by mouth each day as needed."*

CHAPTER 17
COMPETITIVE EXPOSURE

In the spring of 2022, cities and their countries slowly and cautiously allowed visitors to cross their borders again with minimal or no restrictions. While Covid was still around, it had become less severe and deadly compared to previous years. The world could finally breathe a sigh of relief and begin the long road back to a new sense of normalcy.

I found myself a mother of a boy who, at eleven years old, had already surpassed my height, just graduated elementary school and was on the cusp of entering junior high. With the fiasco of what happened in the first part of the year still fresh in my mind, I had ramped up efforts to continue looking for potential treatments that didn't involve drugs and pills. While I still kept with the Verapamil, my daily routine also included vitamins and supplements like Proferrin, magnesium glycinate and saffron, which was a newfound herb to help with mood and anxiety. If I had to take pills, I wanted them to at least be plant-based and organic and not be a chemically processed medicine.

Monthly appointments with my acupuncturist, Livia, now turned into biweekly visits and also incorporated additional mini sessions of cupping and 'gua-sha'. Gua sha was a TCM practice where a tool was used to scrape the skin (typically on the back or limbs) to produce small dots that looked like sand-like bruises after treatment, and cupping involved suctioning the skin with glass. Both types of therapy were meant to release unhealthy toxins to stimulate new blood flow in the body for further recovery, and done in conjunction with acupuncture, would provide the maximum benefit of unblocking my flow of energy (or qi), which in turn would prevent the hemiplegia or migraine of returning. The catch was that these were not 'one and done' treatments. I was warned from the beginning that I had to remain patient and tenacious if I wanted to claim the lifelong benefits that TCM would bring. If not for my previous experiences where acupuncture had rid me of the asthma I once had, and various other maladies (like slipped discs and endometriosis), my faith in this practice would likely not have persisted.

By now, I had been under Livia's care for over three years, and she was well aware of my invisible disability. As someone who had her share of health issues in the past, Livia had also turned to TCM in hopes of curing her ailments. This turned into a journey of actually studying the ancient practice and becoming a certified TCM practitioner herself. Though never pushy or aggressive, in her eyes, it was Chinese medicine that had saved her from being condemned to a lifetime of never-ending visits to doctors, hospitals, and drugs. She was a great believer, and her story gave me hope that TCM could once again save me from my affliction as it had done before.

***

With the stresses at work unrelenting and juggling Isaac's busy schedule of extra-curricular and tutoring sessions, the summer of 2022 proved to be busy. All of July was dedicated to Isaac's wushu training as he prepared for the 2022 Canadian National Martial Arts Championship in Thunderbay with the rest of his teammates. This Championship was his first national competition, and he was entered to compete in three events: hand-form, spear and sword.

While it was Isaac's first national competition, it was also our first time in Thunderbay, Ontario. Our team had arrived a couple of days before the start of the competition so that it could reap the benefits of additional practice time and getting used to the space where athletes would compete. We could feel the sultry air simmering in the summer heat from the moment we landed. The three-day event was held at Lakehead University in their gymnasium. Considering that it had to hold hundreds of people at a time doing strenuous physical activity, it was a small venue, and without any air conditioning, the humidity and heat that came with the late July sun made the space insufferable, especially in the afternoons. Thunderbay was two hours ahead of our time zone in Edmonton; and with athletes needing to arrive at the venue early every morning made for extremely long days. Not only did we have to get up early for practice, but we also often had to stay late into the night until all the kids from our school had competed in their events to show team spirit and support.

Though tiring, I felt lucky that we at least were traveling with a couple of our family friends whose kids were also in Isaac's wushu cohort and competing in the competition. I had gotten to know Carrie when Isaac, in grade one, declared he was Tyson's best friend for life. Tyson was Carrie's oldest son, who had a younger sister, Melanie. When we first met, it didn't take long for us to realize that between her and her husband, Jesse, we had a multitude of mutual connections and friends. It was a little surprising that it took until now, when we were already married with kids, to meet and bond with each other as more than acquaintances. Angela and Peter were another couple I had crossed paths with in my youth, but only after having their two girls attend the same school and now wushu classes with my son, did we really get to know them as friends.

While it all started with our kids attending the same elementary school, my friendship with Carrie and Angela grew and blossomed when we all somehow got enveloped into the world of wushu because of our children's involvement. We became each other's peer support group when it came to organizing ourselves in having our kids attend their martial arts classes and preparing for their performances and competitions. It isn't an everyday occurrence where both the kids and their parents get along and just 'click' with each other. Watching our kids play and grow together through the years has been one of the most fulfilling and rewarding things. I only wished to have known them sooner in life. Both Carrie and Angela knew of my condition. Like my sister, Carrie was also a pharmacist by trade, and I had, on occasion, asked for her opinion on certain medications and interactions between drugs to garner more information on potential treatment options. Angela also had her share of ailments and was just as empathetic upon learning what could happen if an attack came for me.

***

Before leaving for Thunderbay, I had already been silently nursing a headache for days. After the Wushu competition, we had plane tickets to travel with my parents to Malaysia and Singapore to visit my extended family. This trip would be the first time that I would be away from work for over a month that wasn't because of a sick leave and I had to get as much done as possible before jetting off to vacation. The dull ache had started at the base of my neck, as with all tension headaches and was left there to stew until it realized there was more space to invade if it broadened its reach upwards and outwards into the membrane of my head. A headache I could tolerate, but I was adamant that the hemiplegia would not hinder the travel plans that had taken weeks to prepare. As a precaution, I had taken both the Cambia and Tylenol on a rotational basis to chase the headache out of my system. While the medications didn't fully alleviate the head pain, it was enough to let me travel without issue.

Now that we had been in Thunderbay for a few days, not only was the headache still there, but the increasingly loud ring in my ears also made me restless and jittery, while every small thing that didn't align with my expectations annoyed me to no end. If Isaac or Luc happened to forget to do something, I would chase them down the hotel hallway in angry fervor, shaming them for being so reckless. Even with my friends, I found that if the group swayed away from something I thought we had decided together (like where to pick up lunch for the kids before their next competition), I would turn cold and quiet as though punishing them for being so selfish to not include me on the big decision. It was all so irrational and unreasonable, but it was as though my head and heart had separated along the way. While my head knew better, the rest of me did not and resorted to lashing out. But once the internal rage waned, I would revert to my regular pleasant nature, not knowing why I had overreacted in the first place. Though no one said anything of my fluctuating temperaments, I'm sure people noticed.

The explosive ups and downs of going from being even-keeled to severe irritability and wrath were all very uncharacteristic of me, but it felt most natural in the moment. Reflecting on this time, I think I was submitting to the illness set to strike. This was what experts called the "pro-dome phase". More specifically, it was when the early symptoms of the migraine appeared before the major symptoms started. The features that defined me and what I held dear – being respectful, kind, and altruistic were let to vaporize, and in their place was left with nothing but hostility and malice. It was something I couldn't control. *How could you control something when you never had control over it in the first place?*

For numerous consecutive nights leading up to Thunderbay, I could not settle and calm my mind. It may have been that on a subliminal level, I knew that it was only a matter of time before the paralysis would set in; and staying awake was the only way to fight off an imminent attack if it decided to invade in the darkness as it had done so before. No matter the reason, the sleepless nights coupled with the busy days leading up to the kids' competition must have been the last straw that pushed me over the edge.

It started with me sitting in the bleachers waiting for Isaac's turn to compete while Luc was down on the gym floor where the athletes were, scouting out a good place to take the perfect video and picture. Outside on campus grounds, there was some cloud coverage, but it was another muggy and humid day. Between the heat and the hordes of people in the cramped gym space, the collection of voices and a myriad of the athletes, coaches and spectators moving in every which way soon converged into a bleary, noxious collective. All the commotion surrounding me became painstakingly intense for my senses, and I wasn't able to focus on anything other than my agony. It felt like the entire gym had turned into a giant duvet, and I had been dragged into its center, face shoved against the covers to be throttled and deprived of air.

What was all the whirring noise? Why was everything, everywhere, so stifling? I couldn't breathe, I couldn't think, I couldn't do anything. I had to get out. Why was there no way out? Get me out!

There were people, lots of people surrounding me, breathing heavy breaths. *What was happening?*

"Should we get the onsite doctor?" I heard one voice. "I don't know what happened!" "She looks like she's having a stroke" were more words that entered my ears. "Where is her husband?" *So much whirring and ringing. Why are people yelling and shouting? Where was I? Why couldn't I move? Who were all these people, and what were they doing around me? What was happening?*

I don't know how I got to the state I was in, but in an instant, I was surrounded by people I didn't want to be around, and I couldn't move to protect myself. I tried to speak or make some noise but couldn't force anything out of my throat. I was trapped.

Somehow, through the chaos and commotion, Luc and my friends, who realized by now what was happening, came at once and protectively stood between me and the growing number of strangers, curious to know what all the fuss was about. With my eyes open and seemingly conscious, they assured the crowd that they knew what was happening and that I wasn't having a stroke, nor was it an emergency – at least, not the kind where 9-1-1 could help (for now). The words "migraine" and "condition," with phrases of "stroke symptoms" and "she'll be ok," were scattered through faint echoes around pockets of space circling above me before I drifted off again to a realm I would never remember.

When I returned to reality, I realized that people, including Luc, had thought I was conscious the entire time. I didn't have anything in me to explain that I had been in a trance, as though transported elsewhere while slouching lopsided against the seat of the bleacher chairs. My left side was completely seized and frozen without feeling. I knew Luc had thought I was alert because he was in mid-sentence scolding me that I should have stayed at the hotel if I wasn't feeling well when I was brought back to the world I belonged to. But how could I stay at the hotel and miss my son's first competition? I was already a bad parent for not keeping good health. What kind of a mother would I be if I skipped out on his key life milestone events? It was nerve-racking enough to compete in anything – even for adults; and to not be by your child's side for support when being judged by a panel of total strangers would be wrong. For over a week now, I had fought with all willpower to shield myself against this cursed disease. And now that I had finally made it this far, I wouldn't let my son down for some migraine headache.

"Well, it would have been better than you making a scene here. Everyone is focused on you. Is that what you want?"

Had we been at home and I with the ability to speak at a quicker pace and response rate, I would have demanded a divorce right then and there. How dare this man imply I was seeking out attention. Everything I did and all that I endured was for my child and nothing else. He didn't know the colossal amount of strength needed to fight this thing I had every day. He had no idea the depth of humiliation and shame that came with being forced against your will to showcase to the world a disability that shouldn't have belonged to you in the first place when you knew at your core that you were not incapable, that you *were* useful, that you *were* worthy. People like him, lucky enough to be spared such a fate, had no right to judge.

Looking back, I now know that Luc's comment, while hurtful, was because of his own fear of not being able to grasp control of something that had taken over his life. It was enough fury and frustration to account for both our woes. But half of me was still unable to move and I was resolved to stay where I was to watch my son perform, at all costs. My son needed me, and I had to be there for him. If nothing else, when he looked up, I wanted him to see me in the bleachers looking well as he competed, letting him focus on what he needed to do. I wasn't going anywhere.

One of the most unjust things about hemiplegic migraine is that it only gives you glimpses and snapshots of a memory when it takes over you. Just like when my limbs lose their sensation and get severed from my brain receptors to move, there are instances where the body and mind are sliced apart as the paralytic storm rages between the neurons in the brain. With neither part of the self whole, nothing functions as it should, including recollecting events.

My recollection of things that day includes short snippets of exchanges with several kind strangers and some from our wushu school who had witnessed my hemiplegic demise. But when trying to retrieve images of when Isaac was competing, I come up short, entirely blank.

In the moment, I must have looked the part as the doting mother (albeit drowsy) who watched her son fling his spear or thrust his sword, but what I *remember* has been based on videos and pictures that Luc and other parents took of Isaac. Even when we returned home, and I found pictures on my phone that must have been taken by me, I had not the slightest imprint of a memory that I had actually taken the image. All claims of what I remembered from that day were only borrowed and synthetically reproduced before being artificially placed back in my brain disguised as a memory. It was yet another life moment that was ruthlessly stolen from me and my family; and I was too weak to do anything but to surrender to its poison.

Word must have gotten out quickly and spread like wildfire in the University gym as I spent the rest of that day powerlessly enduring people's gawks and concerned looks. But I stayed in my seat, determined to preserve whatever dignity I had left, even if it were only an illusion for myself. Undoubtedly, Isaac was already in the know that I had another episode while he was preparing for his turn to compete. He had come to sit beside me after his first event but didn't say a word. After a few minutes, Isaac left to go to the bathroom, and when he returned, his eyes were glossed over, watery and red. Still, he didn't say anything other than to hold my hand, as though letting me know everything would be fine. It broke my heart. And in that instance, I remember thinking to myself that he deserved a better mother than the one he had.

Isaac's Wushu master also approached me, offering to have the onsite doctor examine me if I wasn't going to the ER. Not wanting to waste anyone's time, I gently declined the proposition and explained my condition to her the best I could in my broken Chinese. She was nothing short of fascinated with my story to the point of asking how "hemiplegic migraine" was spelled so that she could note it on her phone to do further research on it later herself. Normally, a martial arts Master with a strict demeanor, I was taken aback by the empathy she showed and was even more touched by the kindness from the other parents who offered to drive us back to the hotel when the day was finally over, seeing as I was still unable to walk properly. Carrie, Angela, and their families were just as considerate and thoughtful, looking for any way to lessen our burden and ease the struggle.

Though grateful to be in such good company where everyone around me was eager to keep me safe, at the same time, I wanted to crawl into a hole in the wall with every kind gesture that was offered. Contrary to Luc's earlier accusation, I *didn't* want the focus to be on me. I never did. I was an introvert by nature, and any excess attention garnered would make my insides cringe in agony. But life had conditioned me to play the part as I forced a strained smile while people kept showering me with their warmth and goodwill and met with my automatic rejection of their offer for help. By default, I was already a burden to my family and didn't want to make trouble for anyone else.

***

While forced to miss out on Isaac's first set of competitions, somewhere in the cosmos, I was gifted mercy overnight, where I got out of bed the next day, able to speak and walk with a shaky limp without help. This was a miracle in the face of the fact that it normally took at least a week's worth of work to get back to full mobility.

I also surprised Carrie and Angela later that day when I returned to the gym to witness another day's worth of competition, hoping that I could at least be present for Isaac's last event.

"Do you normally recover this quickly? You still look pretty exhausted, but you're walking pretty well, all things considered," commented Carrie, who was in awe, fully expecting that I would be resting at the hotel, given the state they had left me in the previous night.

"Yeah, I'm pretty surprised myself. I feel like I was just run over by a bus, but I'm not complaining. At least I can move and talk."

Leaving the gym impaired and returning as a mostly mobile person surprised everyone else who had seen how I was the day before. I did my best to ignore the stares and pretended not to hear the whispers behind my back as I focused on the only reason I was there – my son. While Luc was preoccupied with Isaac and when not minding their children, Carrie and Angela took turns keeping an extra eye out for me in case I had a relapse. Groggy and weak, I was still rather unstable with my steps. My friends made sure to help me get to the bathroom and checked in regularly to make sure I didn't need them to grab me a coffee or food. Someone was always by my side, and I was not left to go or do anything alone for the entire day.

Parents and students from our Wushu school also rotated through the circuit of asking after my well-being and took the chance to offer up their wisdom about what I should do with my condition. "I'm in the healthcare system, you know," one of the senior students said. "My wife also has migraines, and she has a respirator to give her more oxygen whenever she gets a headache." He then suggested that Luc and me should also get a similar machine. When Luc asked him what he did, he told him he was a dentist.

***

Despite the drama that had happened to his mother, Isaac brought home a few medals - a gold and a silver - at the end of his first competition experience. The hemiplegia may have wanted to compete against Isaac in Thunderbay, but my son persevered against the greatest odds, and I couldn't be prouder. After returning home, we hopped back on a plane with my parents to Malaysia the next morning.

We never told them of the episode that had grazed me a few days ago. Nothing was gained by telling them, and I was in a hurry to put this latest episode behind me.

Luckily, the head pain and paralysis, along with any other pro-dome auras, all seemed to dissipate while in Asia, and I was freed from its grasp for the entire duration of the three week trip. Though no longer naïve enough to think that I would ever be released from the migraine curse, I remember being thankful to at least be given this small reprieve and silently held my breath until my nemesis was ready to fight me for another round.

CHAPTER 18

NEUROBLOCKER

Coincidently, when we returned from Singapore, I was scheduled to visit Dr. Nelly again for my quarterly check-ins. Since Dr. Nelly was on vacation, I was told that some Dr. Nemes was looking after his patients in his absence.

I immediately took a liking to Dr. Nemes the minute she entered the room. For starters, she had my patient file in her hands and had reviewed its content before seeing that I was already seated in the chair waiting for her. Her smile was contagious, and you couldn't help but feel the sincerity that oozed out of her. With Dr. Nemes, you felt that you were important and not just another case study.

"So, I see here that you've been battling some pretty brutal head pain and hemiplegic migraine for quite some time," she started, flipping through the pages of my medical story. "How is the head pain now? Have you been experiencing any more episodes?"

"I had an episode about a month ago. We were in Ontario, and it came on after about a week's worth of regular headaches. It was pretty hot and humid when we were there, so not sure if that may have triggered the attack."

"Hmm…that may have been the case. Changes in weather patterns that set off air pressure changes have been known to be triggers for lots of people with migraines. Unfortunately, I'm sorry to say that if you are a chronic migraineur, Alberta may be one of the worst places on earth for you to live in, given its constant fluctuations in its air pressure." *Wonderful.*

"When I was with my family in Singapore and Malaysia this past month, I noticed that while it was super-hot and humid, I don't remember feeling the extra pressure or the ongoing ache that's always at the back of my head. My head felt a little lighter there. But the minute I returned, no more than a couple of days, my head started feeling heavier again, and the dull throbbing sensation was back."

Nodding in agreement, she validated, "I'm not surprised. On that side of the world, the climate is relatively consistent, which doesn't trigger as many changes in the barometric pressure. This is different from where we live – between the different seasons and more instances of changing weather patterns in recent years. Are you finding that you're getting more head pain now?"

"I used to get only migraine headaches but not the hemiplegia. But then the headaches stopped for a while and then came back after having a baby. When the hemiplegia came on, I used to only get paralysis but no head pain. But lately, in this last year or so, I've noticed that my head is also starting to hurt again."

She asked where the pain usually was. Using my finger as a probe, I explained that the pulsating throbs would usually start somewhere in my neck or base of my skull and then migrate to either side of my head. Sometimes, if I pressed on the middle back end of my head, there could be a sensation of pain, but most of the time, I couldn't distinctively pinpoint a location; only that it hurt. Sometimes, the pain would radiate to my ears or behind the eyes, but it would always be on one side of the head, rarely both and would be most nauseating.

After scribbling a few more notes in my file, Dr. Nemes asked, "Have you ever heard of a neuro-blocker to help with the headaches?"

I shook my head. I had heard more often nowadays of people applying botox to treat their migraine pain, but never a neuro-blocker. I was interested to learn more.

"The procedure is meant to provide some temporary relief so that you're not always distracted with the head pain when going about your daily routine. It works similar to what a dentist uses when they work on their patients." *Didn't a toddler recently suffer permanent brain damage after receiving local anesthetic from her dentist's office for a routine procedure?* "We take some anti-inflammatory medication and local anesthetic and inject it into the back of your head where the pain usually is. This injection normally numbs your entire skull to above your eyebrows, in front of your forehead, so you don't feel any pain."

"But don't you need to feel *something* in case you get hit in the head or some other trauma happens so that you know to get help?"

"The injection is meant for you to not feel pain so that you can go about your daily life." *Didn't answer my question, but alright.*

"What are the side effects of this treatment?"

"There are always the standard risks of infection or bleeding, but that's rare. Some patients experience balding in the area where we do the injection. Still, if that happens to you, we'll just administer the anti-inflammatory medication and not use the anesthetic, which seems to mitigate that side effect." *Balding in exchange for no feeling...*

"How long does this treatment last for?"

"Hmm....it varies. I've had patients who have only had to do it once, and they never returned. I've had others who come back after four months for another treatment. On average, it lasts about four to six months before the numbness completely disappears."

"And is this something I would do in a hospital?"

"No, it would be an outpatient procedure. If you were willing, I could do it for you today, now, if you wanted."

Even though I was never one to shy away from needles, I only endured them on an as-needed basis. What Dr. Nemes presented was an option, but it sounded like an extreme measure. When I probed further on whether the neuro-blocker would help with the hemiplegia, she confirmed that it was meant to only relieve the pain. The paralysis experienced as part of my migraines was an aura and would not be impacted by the injections. She further explained that if the aura were meant to occur, even if it weren't the paralysis, like nausea or seeing flashing lights or anything similar, the neuro-blocker would not be able to help with those symptoms. It was only meant to do one thing and one thing only – to relieve the feeling of pain.

Dr. Nemes asked eagerly again, "Were you interested in doing this today? We can have you prepped right away."

Instinct told me this was a bad idea. I was extremely uncomfortable knowing that I would not be able to *feel* my head and forehead for months. Yes, the migraine was debilitating at times, but I also knew that pain was Mother Nature's way of signaling when something was wrong with a part of our bodies. If the ability to feel such a sensation was lost, I feared that I would potentially be putting myself in danger. The thought of sticking a needle and injecting a foreign substance directly into brain cells that might have already been somewhat scarred from white lesions and other migraine-related damage was unnerving and made me even more uneasy. I decided then that I would rather endure the periodic excruciating pain that the migraine brought on than risk giving up feelings of any kind. If I wasn't ever interested in botox treatment for my head, surely the neuro-blocker was also not an option for me. It seemed too risky for my body, which was already internally battered.

But looking across at Dr. Nemes, who seemed keen and hopeful that I would take her up on the offer, I didn't have the heart to reject her immediately. "Umm…I think I need to discuss this with my husband. Dr. Nelly had never mentioned this treatment before, and I would like to think things through before making a decision."

I don't know if it was what I saw in actuality or if my mind was playing tricks, but there seemed to be an immediate tension in the air that wasn't there moments ago. Dr. Nemes sounding a little let down, responded with an even tone, "Sure. I'll put a note in your file and have the office follow up with you in a few days."

Logic and reason would rationalize that while doctors were the experts, the decision to go with whatever treatment they recommended always lies with the patient. That's why patients or their closest kin are often asked to sign consent forms to confirm that it was the patient who made the final decision. Doctors provide their expertise, but what they advise on how to treat an illness or ailment is just that – advice – meant to be taken or not. On the surface, that would be how the relationship between doctor and patient goes. But many a time, it is not how it is in reality.

Throughout all my years of being brought through the healthcare system, a power imbalance exists between a doctor and patient when a healthcare provider attends and treats you. Most of the time, it is silent, but there is an underlying expectation that through rendering their services, the doctor is the decision-maker on the course of action, and the patient needs only to follow. This is because the doctor or specialist went to school to garner knowledge and spent even more years soliciting experience, while the patient assumingly has limited know-how. I have learned through the years that this imbalance if tipped over too much with the doctor as a decision-maker, can be dangerous for the patient.

Doctors should never forget how vulnerable patients are, and as the adage goes, *with great power comes great responsibility*. When a person comes to them for help, it is because they need it. Even so, just because the patient had come to the physician first for help doesn't mean the doctor should dictate the patient's actions. But I had seen and experienced many instances where there would be a cooling of relations upon not following the doctor's advice – even when the relationship had always been positive – ultimately souring the communications and potentially the quality of care in the long run. When treating and healing someone's health, ego should never be part of the process. Sadly, often, patients are left to deal with their doctor's pride, and this unsaid pressure often forces patients to make decisions that may not be in their best interest.

I had felt this friction with Dr. S whenever he wanted me to try a new medication, and it was the same with Dr. Nelly. *I was not some lab rat to experiment on just because something might work. But just because I wasn't comfortable with certain medications didn't mean that I would be against everything.* Both would be beside themselves with resignation with every rejection of a drug or treatment recommendation. It always made for awkward connections, leaving me to wonder if they were truly making every effort to explore treatment options for me despite their bruised egos. As exceptional a doctor as Dr. W was for me, I even felt similar strains when I pushed back against her advice when she wanted to write me off work longer than I felt was necessary. Had I succumbed to feeling the need to stroke Dr. Nemes' ego, I would have felt obligated to agree with the neuro-blocker, but it would have been against my will despite agreeing to it in writing. Admittedly, even after all this time, rejecting a doctor's advice has been one of the most difficult things to do. But as patients, we must never forget that we owe it to ourselves to stand up for our bodies because we only have this one shell for better or for worse.

We must never forget that *we know our bodies best*. Physicians must always be mindful that the power imbalance will always be tipped to their advantage like something already pre-populated on a form for every patient – even before meeting them. It is a fact of life, and with this realization, if doctors had gone into their profession for the right reasons, they then must know to temper every advice and recommendation they give with the notion that it is the patient's right to decide the approach or treatment that they want to pursue. They had every right to solicit a second opinion if they didn't like what they heard. It isn't about ego, and it isn't about pride. It is all about getting the information needed for the patient to make the right decision for themselves in the circumstances that they are in because we only have one life.

***

A few days later, when Dr. Nelly's office called to follow up on whether I was going to go ahead with the neuro-blocker treatment, I officially declined the offer. I hung up the phone, feeling lousy, though knowing it was my right decision. It took another few days to get past the guilt as I tried to push out the image of Dr. Nemes' disappointed expression.

CHAPTER 19
A RE-RUN OF A SHOW

After the last attack in Thunderbay, while I was paralysis-free for the most part, the migraine head pain continued to come and go in waves throughout the rest of the year. Visiting Dr. W for my annual physical exam, she commented that while it was initially thought I would eventually grow out of the condition, as many people did, given that I was still getting at least one or two hemiplegic attacks a year, it was likely that I would be the lucky few who would be living with the hemiplegic migraine for the rest of my life. *Yes, lucky indeed.*

Verapamil remained a daily staple, alongside iron supplements and vitamins. With Cambia's diminishing efficacy, I relied solely on Rizatriptan for any head pain or signs of paralysis. It was the cheaper drug to finance anyway, compared with the Cambia. I would always be careful with my dosage of Rizatriptan and took extra care in noting the number of tablets I had already taken, never allowing myself more than the twelve pills per month. If further relief was needed once I hit the allowable Rizatriptan maximum, I would either revert to the Cambia or endure the pain without taking anything the best way I could. I discovered that pending the level of intensity of the head pain, acupuncture also helped ease the pulsating head throbs, so long as I was able to get to Livia in time.

I was still seeing Dr. Nelly on a quarterly basis and yearly MRIs and CT scans with blood tests and the periodic lumbar puncture were still a thing. While I went through the motions of taking these tests, I no longer held the hope I once had that the images or test samples drawn would show anything more than normal readings. I must have been the only person in the world who wished for a bad reading of some sort with these tests and scans. At least any sign of something abnormal would be something concrete and tangible than a diagnosis made through exclusion. Most importantly, if it was something more palpable, there would be the possibility of a cure. But sadly, I was never so lucky.

***

In 2023, I gave thanks to another winter holiday and new year season that was without a hemiplegia attack. By this time, being tired and depleted by the end of every day was the norm and the daily brain fog I still had was becoming something that was a part of me; and like the exhaustion, no longer worth mentioning. It was what it was.

Outside in the greater world, life was getting back to normal and it was difficult to believe that barely a year ago we were all still dealing with a global pandemic. Though still and will likely always be with us, Covid was either not mentioned at all; or if it was, would be talked about like the common flu. The entire world was keen on putting this international crisis behind itself.

With the lifting of all health restrictions, we thought it would be nice to host a Nerf gun get-together for Isaac's twelfth birthday with his school friends. We hadn't coordinated any party for the kid since second grade and Covid had ruined the original plan to host a birthday two years ago when he hit his first decade milestone year. In truth, the birthday may have been the excuse, but think people – both children and parents - were just happy to be able to go about freely, spending time with each other in person.

One of the many things Isaac has been blessed with has been his good fortune in making strong friendships with many of the kids who have been in his class since grade one. Even his teachers through his elementary school years had commented that such bonds between kids in an entire cohort class were rare. Perhaps it was due to the children all being in a bilingual program (where they were taught both Chinese Mandarin and English) – that had them placed in the same class year after year, which in turn fostered a long-lasting kinship bond. And it had been with their bond did many of us parents were also able to become more than just mere acquaintances. There were even a handful of parents whom I felt safe enough disclosing my struggles with the hemiplegic migraine. Whenever I shared such a story, I was always been met with kindness and understanding.

I have often thought that since the world always needed to find its balance, the good luck that Isaac has had in finding such great companions was the consolation for having a mother with limitations like me. Perhaps in times when I couldn't be with him, he'll have his friends to turn to for comfort and care.

***

The birthday party went off without a hitch and I soon found myself back in the office, the beginning of another work week. It was the last Monday of January and I was tired from organizing Isaac's party over the weekend; but not so exhausted that I couldn't function. It was in all, a typical winter Monday morning.

I was sitting in a virtual team meeting with my office door closed when it was my turn to provide some input on an issue. I no longer remember what we were all talking about, only that when I started to talk, an overwhelming wave of sensation, without any warning, came over me. As I looked at the faces that were watching me on the screen, everything came to a head. My colleagues' faces where a moment ago were all in their own dedicated boxes, were now meshed into one melting pot, while the familiar blanket of numbness took over the left side of my lips, tongue and cheeks, dragging my left eye downwards. Before my brain had time to even process what was happening, I was already sliding down, down and down, as though the carpeted floor was sucking me into its fabric. In retrospect, it likely was because my left side was once again overtaken by the paralysis, that caused my body to lose balance from its once sitting position.

From that point onwards, like a spectator on the sidelines, I have had to rely on witnesses to find out how everything played out. A few colleagues on the call who were in their offices on the same floor as me, came running to my rescue when they noticed something wasn't right and that I had somehow "disappeared" from the screen. Luckily, these were the same colleagues who knew about my condition that could render me immobile when suffering an attack and one of them was also a first aider. I was moved into a recovery position and apparently gave signals through forced grunts and Frankenstein-like pointing of my good arm to where I kept the Rizatriptan. Glimpses of memory have me vaguely remember being guided to lower my chin so that at least one-half of my mouth would open to receive the pill.

When asked if I needed to go to the hospital, I mumbled a whole lot of incomprehensible noises but the word "No" was heard quite clearly numerous times. As I was conscious and stubbornly unwavering in expressing what I didn't want, they resolved to call Luc instead of 9-1-1 to collect me. Joyce, a friend who was also my co-worker offered to make the actual call to my husband. From there, my two colleagues ushered Joyce out of the office and closed the door for privacy as they continued to watch over me lying on the floor, motionless and quiet. While waiting for Luc to arrive, they would periodically call out my name or gently shake me to get a small rise of a reaction to confirm that I was not all lost and still conscious. I do not remember any of this.

When I did come around to opening my eyes - weak, but more alert, Luc and Isaac were both by my side. Schools were off that day and I recall that despite the mental fog, I was still able to silently curse the paralysis for making another showing in front of my son.

To me, it had been no more than a half-hour from when the attack started until present time. In reality, two hours had already passed. But no matter how exhausted and desperate I was of wanting to leave the office, I couldn't. My left leg and arm were without feeling, forbidding me to move with my own free will. My co-worker Hazel stayed with my family and me in my office – on the one hand, waiting out the paralysis in hopes that I would be able to hobble myself out of the building and at the same time brainstorming with Luc of ways that I could be shuffled out despite the disability. Luc had tried a number of times to hoist my good right arm over his broad shoulders so that he would be able to support me as I tried to hop my way along leaning against his body while dragging a weighted left leg. But there was no way I would be able to hop the distance from my office to the elevator doors and then down to the car. Even with both Luc and Isaac each taking a side to haul me upright, it took no more than a few paces before their man-made walk-aide collapsed with my one-sided weight. I was out of breath with sweat dripping from my temples on the verge of passing out with the even more intense expenditure of energy; while my family and Hazel were left to continue to think of another viable option to get me out.

Hearing that I was now alert, Joyce also peeked her head into my office to see how I was fairing. Between her and Hazel, they concocted a brilliant idea. My office chair had wheels and they suggested that I could sit in the chair for them to wheel me into the elevator and down to the car where Luc had parked. With the help of all four people, I managed to heavily plop myself onto the chair and was wheeled out into the hallway and down the lobby before being carefully maneuvered into Luc's car. There were a few stares and I remember Hazel responding to questions. I don't recall what the exchange was like, but assumed people were satisfied with whatever Hazel said, as I was finally on my way home to rest, away from the world. That fiasco only took four hours from start to finish.

***

The following day when I was scheduled to go to the doctor's, I had another episode. It was mild and happened in bed, with the hemiplegia laying its weight only on the left leg, sparing my arm and face. Being unable to move, we did the next best thing and resorted to a telephone consult with Dr. W as Dr. Nelly was fully booked. I don't remember what the doctor said, and quite frankly, not quite sure if I remember having this medical appointment or if it was recounted to me later on. But the sick note that was eventually emailed to me, was proof enough that I was in fact seen by the doctor; and was likely given the same advice as was always given. When it came to the hemiplegia, there was no longer the element of surprise with doctors' visits.

The next seventy-two hours were spent in bed where I fazed in and out of consciousness. It was as though I was being submerged under a brain fogged cloud, while waiting for the pins and needles to prick my nerves, marking the return of feeling. Even opening my eyes while lying down required substantial energy when I was awake. While it was completely normal to be tired and worn out after a hemiplegic episode, the aftermath of this attack felt different. This time, it felt that the paralysis completely drained everything out of me. The thought of breathing where it was required to inhale and exhale air was exhausting; and envisioning the motions of opening my mouth, chewing, and then swallowing food seemed unfathomable.

It felt so taxing on my beaten brain that I wasn't able to garner the energy to take in food for two straight days, other than to ingest water and the occasional anti-nausea medication to keep me from dry heaving. I didn't even have the energy to pull myself into a sitting position in bed, needing help from either Luc or Isaac to lift me off my back to at least have me lean against the headboard so that I wouldn't choke from drinking water. Once the fluid was consumed, it didn't take long before I asked to be relieved from the sitting position to lay on the bed once again, because of all the power it took to sit. No matter how much Luc begged and coaxed, I didn't have it in me to take in any more sustenance. It was as though my body was running on fumes and needed to conserve what little fuel it had left for it to breathe. I suppose on some primal level, it knew that eventually, food and water were key ingredients to keep me breathing, but with such little energy left, it could only manage to focus on the immediate and didn't have the capacity to think for the longer term. I was in survival mode.

The moments after Luc and Isaac finished checking in on me, were my darkest hours. Lying alone in bed, I would begin to think about the meaning of life and how very futile it all was. What was the purpose of moving forward if life always had to inevitably end? Besides, it clearly didn't matter how hard I tried. In these years past, I had done all the right things – taking the medications I was supposed to, exercising, eating healthy and maintaining a positive outlook. But in the end, nobody cared and nothing mattered. The hemiplegia would never leave and I would always remain a captive in my own body of a force that nobody, not even doctors, could ever see or manage. With uncertainty of when the next attack would come, I would forever be a ticking time bomb. These thoughts drove me to make a silent prayer above that I be sent away during sleep so that at least those around me would no longer suffer alongside my misfortune.

The world seemed colorless and bleak, devoid of hope. After three days of bed rest and requiring assistance for basic needs, I hit rock bottom. I remembered a conversation I once had with a friend who believed in God where she so passionately insisted that we were all God's children. If that were true, then I most certainly was a neglected child - not entirely abandoned, but definitely not one who was treasured or deemed precious. I was a spare part, a freak of nature, only good enough to be a plaything for a vicious menace, to be tortured over and over again until there was nothing left of me - inside and out. How I longed for it all to end.

CHAPTER 20
A DIFFERENT WAY

So much crying and sobbing. The darkness around was filled with such heavy sorrow, that it was suffocating. But where was I? Had my prayers been answered, and had I been taken away? I looked up, down and around all four corners and realized I was trapped in a human-sized box, too small for me to stand upright, so that I could only crouch and hover near the floor. The crying grew louder and increasingly unbearable. It was so much that I had to cover my ears and shut my eyes while rocking myself back and forth as if doing so would prevent the pain from seeping in. But the bawling continued and its echoes were made only louder as the sorrow closed in on me. Then, salted water began to slide onto my lips gently making its way into my mouth, lapping the tastebuds of my tongue. The trickles grew into a flowing stream until my entire face was drenched and I was forced to drink in the melancholy. The sobbing continued and I realized that I couldn't drown out the crying because the wailing was coming from me.

Every drop of regret and anger; all desires, disgust, fears, and dreams that ever existed and defined me were being squeezed out into the open and turned into desperate howls and wails. The despair was so great it made every inch of me convulse. It was all so overwhelming, my senses hypersensitive. I wished for the paralysis to overtake me so that I wouldn't have to feel the exhaustion, the pain, the hurt, the fear...

"Tash, Tash…," from a distance was the faint but familiar echo of a voice that I knew. Something was stroking the top of my head while gently whispering, "You've been sleeping all morning, it's time to wake up." Like magic, I was released from the grip that had locked me beneath the surface and I was finally allowed to come up. I opened my eyes while gasping for air and looked up to see a familiar face.

"You've been in bed for too many days now. You really should try to start moving again. At least get up and eat something."

Without a word *(because talking was too tiring)*, I obeyed and tried to push through the barrier that confined me to bed. Sluggishly, I jutted out my right leg and moved it to the side of the bed, while using my hands to guide my left leg to do the same, all the while checking that every part of my left side now had its feeling returned. Luc steered me to face him with my shoulders and I was ready to take my first step in four days.

As expected, the stance and eventual walk were wobbly and unstable at best. It improved slightly with the help of the cane. Before even reaching the door of the bedroom, I already felt the fatigue overcome my limbs. But Luc was determined to get me out of the room that day and demanded that I at least hobble my way to where the bonus room was, that was some extra forty to fifty steps away. I finally made it to the couch after what seemed like an eternity. The daylight that streamed through the windows made me squint my eyes as I looked at Luc, rather annoyed that he had the audacity to make me do so much activity after the trauma I had had to endure again. All I wanted was to be back in bed, tucked away from the world and disappear into the night. If my husband knew of my resentment, he didn't show it and was oblivious as ever as he went downstairs after settling me on the couch to bring me lunch. He was equally as demanding when I protested the amount of food he wanted me to ingest. After a few failed attempts, I gave up complaining and focused on eating. Once I remembered how to carry the soup from bowl to mouth using a spoon, I surprised myself by actually finishing the entire bowl of soup. I suppose there were times when my husband knew me better than I knew myself.

With being satisfied that I finally had somewhat of a proper meal, I thought that I would be rewarded by being let back into my room, into bed. But I was so very wrong. After passing the near-empty soup bowl over, I was told to walk around the house for as long as I could. "In these situations, it's really not good to be in bed. You have to keep moving so that your muscles don't become stiff," preached the man who used to be my husband, now turned drill sergeant. He hadn't ever experienced paralysis or any disability. What did he know about my situation? *Since when did I marry such a jerk of a man?*

Still, uttering any words would over-extend what little energy reserve I had left. I did the next best thing and did what I was told, albeit reluctantly. Like Groundhog Day, the rest of the afternoon was filled with iterative motions of pitiful attempts to walk up and down the carpeted walkway between the bedroom and the bonus room. At times, it felt worse than going through the paralysis. When my body could no longer take the stress of walking, I let myself crash heavily onto the couch, huffing and puffing as though I had just run a marathon. With my body shaking and out of breath, Luc was finally content with the effort I made and while I was still not permitted to go to bed, I was allowed to lounge on the couch in front of the television until Isaac returned from school and it was time for supper.

The subsequent days mirrored this routine. After Luc returned home from driving Isaac to school, he would march straight to my bed to shake me awake for me to begin my walking routine. By now, I had been secluded inside my house for a week and the thought of walking outdoors in public still made me uneasy, almost scared. But Luc was adamant and continued to push me to keep moving. One morning after dropping Isaac off at school, I was driven to West Edmonton Mall (or WEM). This venue was considered the largest mall in North America and many seniors liked to take advantage of its indoor space to do their walking in the early morning – especially when it was too cold on a winter's day for any outdoor activity.

Luc thought it would be a good idea for us to visit the mall for me to also practice my walking. I had just weaned myself off the cane, but still rather unstable in my strides, I was only able to take baby steps at an exponentially slow, shaky pace. There were seniors that day who moved way quicker than I ever could. I watched them whisk by me and Luc as I slowly limped on, feeling as though I would topple with even the slightest wind's touch. I remember how envious I was of those people and their mobility. We arrived at WEM around eight in the morning and left a little after noon. It took me four hours to finish walking one small part of the mall; and by the time we made it back into the car to go home, I was panting heavily with sweat trickling down both sides of my temples, so winded that I couldn't even finish a full sentence. It was obvious that I was still quite weak where not only leisurely walks, but holding up simple items like chopsticks, spoons or a toothbrush would bring about the tremors and extreme exhaustion. This was abnormal – even for me, where typically after a week, I would feel at least a good portion of strength return to my core; whereas this time, everything still seemed off – uncalibrated and off kilter. But I only had a week left before my sick leave expired and I was expected back into the office. The anxiety of not being able to show up as scheduled started to creep in. I had no choice but to get better. There was no other way.

***

The last time I was wheeled out of the office was on January 30, and I returned on February 20, feeling nervous and unlike myself. I remember sitting in front of my multiple computer screens with work files clenched between quivering hands in fear that the paralysis was going to pounce all over me again; though logic reasoned the chances of such a thing to happen so soon after multiple episodes was unlikely. Apart from the muffled fear that I tried to suppress; I don't recall much else of my first day back in the office. I don't even remember driving myself to and from work that day, only that I was beyond depleted once I managed to return home later that night. Luckily, because I had to cancel the last in-person appointment with Dr. W a month ago, her office had rescheduled me to go in to see her and it happened to be the following day.

Dr. W was on vacation, and another doctor was covering for her that week. Dr. Toule seemed young but looked to be a responsible and studious type who read all his patient's files. Or at the very least, he had read up on my background and history by the time I got to the examination room.

"So, it seems that you've been dealing with this hemiplegic migraine for quite some time, nearly ten years." *Has it been that long?* "And you recently are getting over another one?"

I nodded and added, "To be accurate, I think it was actually two. I had the first big attack at the office at the end of January and then a milder one came on the next day."

"Right, which is why you couldn't come in-person the last time. Well, how have things been since then?"

This would normally be the part where I tried to brush off the extreme exhaustion, unstable mobility and brain fog as normal and that I would be alright, given more time. Dr. W would then in turn, look over me and gently disagree with my own self-diagnosis, saying that what I was going through was far from normal. She would then proceed to explain how important it was for the brain to heal after being exposed to such trauma.

But this time was different. During this migraine's aftermath, I still experienced exhaustion, brain fog, and persistent tremors. I was still having issues with focus, feeling as though I was on the verge of collapse. I shared all this with Dr. Toule, unsure of what he would say or do.

"Hmm…how have your iron levels been?"

"They've always been on the low side."

"I see. Are you taking any supplements for it?"

"I have been taking Proferrin for some time."

"I'm going to write you a requisition to do some tests, including looking at your ferritin levels. In the meantime, did you say you work?"

"Yes…full-time and yesterday was my first day back."

"How did you feel after finishing work?"

"Exhausted and depleted. Couldn't think or do anything."

"Hmm…well that doesn't sound good. I think you still need time to recover. Hemiplegic migraines are no joke and if you've been going through them time and time again, it's likely that your body and brain needs more time to heal."

"Are you thinking that I have to be away from work for an even longer time?"

"Well, that's up to you. But I would suggest going to work part-time on a gradual basis to begin with would be the better way. You can't expect yourself to go back to immediately being at a hundred percent.. Two to three days in the office to start, would be my advice."

It was inevitable and there was no point in arguing. This was my body protesting to say it had enough and it was finally time that I listened. With an exasperated sigh, I agreed to working three days a week and we discussed being in the office from Mondays through Wednesdays where I would be off the remaining two days. Given the weekend, this schedule would allow me to rest for four straight days. I was to stick with this arrangement for at least four weeks and go back to Dr. W if there still wasn't an improvement. I was then finally released from the doctor's office with more top-ups of the usual medicinal cocktails: Verapamil, Metoclopramide, Cambia and Rizatriptan.

When I got back to the office later that day, Layla and the rest of my team were as understanding as ever. They assured me that I could take all the time needed and that I didn't have to worry about anything except focus on getting better. My mind then wondered had people not witnessed for themselves how debilitating the hemiplegia was, would they have been just as understanding; or would the natural instinct of human skepticism have permeated through leaving a pathway of suspicion and doubt behind my back?

***

Working part-time had its benefits and drawbacks. On the one hand, already feeling that I had once again abandoned my team when I was supposed to be leading it, there was a compelling desire to squeeze in five days' worth of work into three, which made for some of my most stressful weeks. But on the other hand, given the extra days to rest without the obligation to monitor emails and messages, gave me the release I needed to work on my recovery. I just had to get through the first three days of the week.

It was during this time when one of my good friends called to ask if I would be interested in seeing a TCM practitioner – one who prescribed herbs. While I was still seeing Livia once or twice a month, she wasn't trained in prescribing herbal remedies. I had been on Western drugs for so long and experienced more side effects than relief from my ailment, perhaps it was worth trying something different.

The TCM practitioner went by the name of Mr. Yu and he had set up his practice at home. I later learned that he came from a family that had generations worth of experience in TCM and natural remedies. My friend had thought I would be a good patient for him to see after her co-worker shared with her how Mr. Yu treated her for thyroid issues and how for nearly twenty-five years, she had had to rely on countless medications to keep things under control. But after seeing Mr. Yu for just over six months, all her hormone levels and blood tests miraculously went back to normal and she no longer needed to depend on her pills. It was by the good grace of my friend's co-worker (a stranger to me) where she initiated the connection with me and Mr. Yu and I found myself knocking on his doorstep within that same week.

Mr. Yu was originally from China and could only communicate in Mandarin. I was thankful to be somewhat fluent in my Chinese and even more grateful for Google translate whenever I needed to type out Chinese characters when texting him. Mr. Yu was a tall and slim middle-aged man with a sort of tranquility about him that was comforting and calm. He was a man of great wisdom and when he spoke you were at peace. It was as though you were in the presence of Buddha himself. He was someone you were naturally inclined to listen to.

My first visit with him took over two hours as he assessed and explained what he thought were my main issues. He first began asking where I was from and when my health problems first started to show itself. I explained what a typical hemiplegic migraine was like for me and what usually happened when the paralysis set in, including how much longer it now took for me to recover. Mr. Yu then examined the rest of my facial complexion and asked me to stick out my tongue to see its shape and color.

He quickly diagnosed a Qi and blood deficiency as the main source of my issues. In TCM, 'Qi' is like energy and is considered the powerhouse to all life beings – including humans. Its concept is often linked with blood and both together are looked upon as the drivers to what gives life. Without Qi, life could not be sustained and so for all our body parts to function properly, there must be sufficient amounts of both Qi and blood. For me, because I was seriously depleted of both these elements, essential nutrients from the foods I ate that should have been broken down and carried through the blood stream was not happening. It was because of this long-term deficiency where my numerous organs – spleen, stomach, heart, kidney, lungs and liver were all negatively impacted, leaving a great imbalance.

Given my constitution, he theorized that this deficiency must have started in my youth and had been neglected ever since. He correctly surmised that I had "lung issues" during my childhood with frequent coughing, a weak immune system and asthma – all due to the presence of not having enough Qi in the lungs. Then, we moved onto my spleen and stomach where he explained the spleen being responsible for holding blood in the places where they should and that if the Qi was lacking there, I was likely prone to frequent nosebleeds. While I don't remember when it actually started, by this time, it was common for me to have heavy nosebleeds every couple of days. There had been times the flow would get so heavy; I could only lean over the garbage can and let the blood pour out until it stopped on its own. When I had raised this with doctors, they blamed the climate and dismissed it as an inconvenience but was nothing to fret over. With both the spleen and stomach being paired as sources responsible for digestion, any Qi imbalance would give a multitude of digestive issues. Last but not least was the liver and kidney. The liver was the main organ of detoxification, getting rid of what we don't need while the kidney was where reserve Qi was kept; and if it was healthy, it would supply the energy to any organ low on Qi. Deficiencies in these body parts would render headaches, insomnia, fatigue, and irregular menstruation cycles to name a few symptoms; while the mind and heart would also be impacted creating negative emotions like irritability, anger, fear and sadness. I later learned that in TCM, even human emotions were linked to specific body parts and connected to how healthy you were.

Mr. Yu then asked if I had any children. I told him that I had one boy - twelve years ago. He commented that it must have been a very difficult pregnancy. He wasn't wrong. Being with child, meant in essence, growing another internal life source. Mr. Yu explained that the lack of Qi meant that my body likely had to work exponentially as hard to sustain both my and baby's life. He then went on to remark that it must have been nothing short of sheer willpower that I was able to deliver the child safely into this world. It was somewhat miraculous that I carried Isaac to term and that both of us emerged unharmed after childbirth. But sheer will could only go so far and he deduced that I must have had at least one miscarriage along the way, given that my body was likely further depleted of the Qi after Isaac; and it would have taken another miracle to bring a second baby to term. It was common knowledge that miracles rarely happened twice.

Mr. Yu's diagnosis for all my ailments – the ones I knew about and the ones I didn't – could all be attributed to a lack of Qi and blood. Without sufficient supply, my body had to ration out its reserves, first distributing the life source to the most critical – like the heart and lungs, at the expense of other parts of my body that would have benefited from my Qi, like my limbs. According to Mr. Yu, this was also the reason why it was always difficult for me to conserve heat; my hands and feet were always cold to the touch no matter how warm it was. There was not enough Qi and blood to go around rendering my extremities deprived of warmth because of the lack of blood. Without adequate Qi, my body could not function smoothly and would find itself "stuck" which then caused a build-up of excess mucous causing more bodily blockage which in turn triggered things like headaches and migraines. Why the migraine evolved into something like hemiplegia was likely an indication of how "blocked" my system was.

At this first session, Mr. Yu patiently and gently explained all the principles, logic and rationale that his diagnosis was based upon. A few days later when I returned to his place to pick up the herbs, I was given instructions on how to take in this new set of concoctions: The herbs needed to soak in water for two hours before boiling, along with ginger root slices and five pitted dates. After boiling the herbs, I would pour the water out into two servings and drink one in the morning and the other in the afternoon. Given my condition, this would be my routine every day for at least the next six months. I was to text Mr. Yu at the end of every week and send him a picture of my stuck-out tongue for him to monitor and gauge signs of improvement. The weekly picture of my tongue would help inform him of whether he was to continue making the same batch of herbs for the following week; or if he needed to make some adjustments to the ingredients, depending on my changed constitution. I was initially charged eighty dollars per week for these herbs. This later decreased to about fifty dollars per week once I no longer needed as potent a tonic. This was another experience where I gave thanks that I still had a job with a paycheque that made it possible for me to afford such expenses.

While it had been years ago, this wasn't the first time I had taken Chinese herbs, so I was already prepared for its bitter and unbearable taste. This was validated by my first few sips. *Yup, still tasted like dirt, mud and filth all mixed into one cocktail.* If it weren't for previous experience, I would have thought the man was trying to poison me!

Studies say that it takes a little over two months to form a habit. When it came to getting used to the routine of brewing the herbs, getting used to its taste and picking up a new batch every week, I would say that that would be accurate. Within eight weeks, not only did I get used to the routine of preparing the brew, but Luc also learned how to make this potion so I didn't have to stress over boiling a new batch for the next day once I went back to work full-time.

Within the first month of taking the herbal mixture, my nosebleeds stopped and my menstrual cycle near regular. I took a risk and made a personal executive decision to stop the Verapamil in place of taking in Mr. Yu's herbs and noticed improved focus and concentration. Though not a huge improvement, I have felt a slight difference in my energy level. Still tired when getting up in the morning, but not as depleted as before. I have had a few instances where the migraine headaches have come back. Instead of automatically reaching for drugs, I have instead gone to Mr. Yu to seek relief.

With his "press needles or seeds," Mr. Yu applies them to specific pressure points on my hands that are linked to the brain. At an initial glance, these types of needles looked like small surgical adhesive patches. But if you examined them closer, you would have seen miniature pointed needles attached to these small patches. I've learned that press needles can be left in for extended periods of time and because they are like tiny bandages on your pressure points, I wouldn't have to lie on a treatment bed like traditional acupuncture sessions. The patches would only need to be stuck to where I needed them to be and I would be on my way. The whole process usually took five minutes or less — and he never charged me for these quick treatments. The discovery of these mini-needles has been a lifesaver many a time, relieving me from excruciating pain so that I would be able to function for the rest of the day instead of being reduced to a curled-up quivering ball in bed.

Since starting these herbs, I haven't experienced hemiplegic episodes. It is a good sign for sure, but being paralysis-free for at least eighteen months would be the true test to discern whether this alternative treatment approach has been effective, given that my attacks typically come once or twice a year. I dare not say that I am hopeful, only that I am cautiously optimistic.

CHAPTER 21
ENOUGH

The first half of 2023 was a doozy and one I craved to be wiped clean from my slate if given the chance. From the dramatic hemiplegic episode at work to recovering at home to being a part-time employee, it was already late spring by the time I was able to switch back to full-time status at work. It felt as though five months' worth of time had been violently taken from me, but at least I was much more put together and felt less broken compared to how I was at the beginning of the year. At the office, my colleagues welcomed me back with open arms and suggested that I let my team know of my condition. While Layla, my direct reports and some of my closest peers knew, most people on the team that I led did not know my secret.

I had always been guarded in disclosing such personal information but given the number of times I had to leave work unexpectedly; I knew I couldn't keep it a secret any longer. While details weren't necessary, it was only right that I would tell them the reason for my sick leave so that the rest of my co-workers wouldn't have to speak on my behalf, if I ever had to be away again.

My heart hammered against my ribs, palms slick with fear, as I spilled the words: *'hemiplegic migraine.'* I went on to explain that this type of migraine was not your typical severe one-sided head pain. Instead, when an episode came on, it would cause paralysis on the one side of my body that would take upwards of three weeks to recover, re-learning all the basic life skills like walking, talking, and feeding myself. I skipped the parts of being, at times, completely catatonic, brain-fogged, and depressed that often accompanied the physical disabilities. At this point, people knew enough and didn't need to be burdened with the grisly details. The words tumbled out, each syllable a betrayal, as my voice, wavered in the sterile air of the conference room. My palms slicked with sweat, while I longed to disappear into the cracks of the table. In that moment, if a blackhole from space miraculously appeared in front of me, I would have jumped right in it to be willingly swallowed up whole. Once my confession was out, a hush fell over the room, thick and heavy with unspoken questions, their silence more deafening than any outburst. Some expressed their concern and others thanked me afterwards for sharing. I silently breathed a sigh of relief. My duty was done and wished that I would never have to make such a public announcement again.

If someone had asked me why I was uncomfortable in sharing my condition, I wouldn't know how to answer. It wasn't because having this ailment – or any ailment – was shameful. I *know* this wasn't my fault.; I *know* a hemiplegic migraine doesn't make me any less competent; I *know* this isn't something that defines me. But I also know it has been because of the hemiplegia that my closest loved ones have cried themselves to sleep in the darkness. In a way, the paralysis that has taken me hostage has also stealthily taken those around me as its captives too. Of my family and friends who have witnessed through the years the hemiplegia, I can tell they too have been conditioned to build a habit of surveying my every move out of the corner of their eye, in case my body gives way and I collapse.

Perhaps it has been more guilt than shame that has made me want to shove my head in the sand whenever the hemiplegia has been brought to light. I have wanted to be so many things, but being a burden has never been on the list; and is what I am now, despite the greatest protests of not wanting to be. It is this heavy weight that I carry into a battle I have been forced to wage against my will that has been made more challenging with my loved ones who have also been dragged into the fold like collateral damage.

To confess this hidden curse was to tear open the wound, to show the raw, fractured truth of who I'd become. That I have been a coward, too weak to admit that I am not enough for anything or anyone – not even for the ones I hold dearest and who are supposed to love me.

***

In the subsequent weeks that followed, I continued to recalibrate my mindset back to what I once recognized as a normal daily routine: morning exercise of running and weights (albeit, still only able to lift no more than five pounds); work at the office or at home; eat dinner; oversee Isaac's homework; sleep and repeat the next day. The weekend routine included running errands and driving Isaac to his extra-curricular activities with occasional social gatherings with friends or family.

While on Mr. Yu's herbs, I continued to keep with my vitamin regiment and made greater efforts to stay more in tune with my ageing body. To say I have now fully recovered and regained my strength in its entirety would be a lie. Each episode endured has chipped away at me, like waves eroding the shore, leaving me a fragmented version of my former self. Strength that once flowed easily feels like a distant memory, lost behind a veil of fatigue. My left arm remains a stubborn rebel, refusing to cooperate with simple tasks like lifting a frying pan to cook a meal. The end of my workdays – or any day - still leaves me thoroughly depleted and I am always tired, no matter what I do or don't do. But while fatigue is with me all the time, my mind is more focused and anchored. I don't feel as suppressed from reality as I did with the brain fog when ingesting all the pills that I had. I would like to think that that's a good thing.

Five months. The calendar page mockingly displays the countdown to another anniversary from my last hemiplegia, another reminder of the day my world had once again fractured. *Can I face it again, or will the weight crush me this time?* This could be a stressful waiting game, but I am grateful for the family and friends around me who pull me out of this heavyweight so that I can focus on living.

On my forty-third birthday, some of my dearest girlfriends – the ones whom I initially met when working at the optometry shop during my teen years, surprised me alongside my sister with a road trip to Calgary. When my girls popped out of the car which I thought would just be me and a friend for a weekend, gave me such gratitude and joy. Tears welled in my eyes as they piled out of the car, a chorus of familiar laughter. My girls, the ones who'd seen me at my weakest, were here to remind me I still mattered. Their embrace, warm and genuine, shattered the wall I'd built around myself. It has been because of people like them - with their thoughtfulness, their countless years of kindness, their undying support, and their love – that I have been brought back from the darkest despair and reminded that I am not alone. That despite my defects, there is still enough in me to live well. That despite everything, I am enough.

AFTERWARDS

When I was twenty-one, I took a couple semesters off from business school and embarked on an adventure to Singapore through a student practicum, working for a boutique executive search firm. It didn't take long for me to fall in love with the country's dizzying gleam of skyscrapers reaching for the humid sky, and myriad of hawker stalls that were always filled with the potent collage of chili oil, dragon fruit sweetness and jasmine whispers. I was there for just under a year and had the time of my life. I had the opportunity to learn so many things, become better acquainted with my extended family and had the good fortune of meeting such extraordinary people – some I am still in contact with today after twenty-two years. It was through this experience that I was able to prove to myself that I was capable of being an independent woman. Singapore uncaged me, a phoenix rising from the ashes of routine. Laughter painted the humid nights, and every sunrise felt like a fresh start, my independence a badge of honor I wore with pride. It was one of the best years of my young adult life.

I remember one night in Singapore when I was strolling along the pier at Clarke Quay with my cousin, a man at a small kiosk stopped us and asked if we wanted to have our fortunes read. Curious and amused, we took up the fortune-teller's offer and let him peer into our futures. Reading my palm like a roadmap after asking about the writing of my Chinese name, he prophesized that while I would never go hungry, my life would be fraught with obstacles and challenges. He insisted that if I changed the last character of my name to a different character (but one with the same tone), it would mitigate many of the hardships he foretold. Needless to say, I never followed his advice; and wonder after twenty-some years later if I should have.

Ten years. Ten autumns have surrendered to winter since the hemiplegia first painted its icy touch across my body, stealing my voice and twisting my reflection into a stranger's mask. Though not one to look back into the past often, Luc has commented on how he thought my life was "done for" when he found me paralyzed, unable to talk with a face so distorted, it was unrecognizable. For my child, the echo of my paralysis always hangs in the air, a phantom limb he can't quite grasp, like a bittersweet whisper that taunts him for not having a healthy mother.

In these last ten years of being stuck with this thing, I have continuously browsed through the myriad of articles exploring the mysteries of hemiplegic migraine in hopes that I would one day come across something signaling that a cure has been found. But there is still a long way yet for such a day to come.

Recently, as I have slowly come to terms with my condition, a friend suggested that I join *The International Hemiplegic Migraine Foundation Support Group* on Facebook. It has been both encouraging and disheartening to see so many people in the world go through what I am going through; and unable to find help. Hope flickers like a dying candle in their eyes, extinguished by the crushing weight of medical bills and the hollow echoes of misdiagnoses.

The hemiplegia wears a thousand masks, a chameleon slithering between diagnoses, leaving doctors bewildered and patients adrift in a sea of uncertainty. From the number of doctors and other health care providers that I've encountered, so many have never even heard of this type of migraine before, let alone knowing anything about it to treat. Many times, people who go into the ER with stroke symptoms but have test and scan results that come back inconclusive or normal, are often dismissed as being an anomaly case; or are given the wrong type of treatment that manifests into other issues later on – all without diagnosing the original problem which was the hemiplegic migraine. I believe the underlying problem is that still today, many in the medical community just don't see migraines as a serious condition. For them, migraines continue to be just really bad headaches. Patients who report on their challenges of migraines are looked upon as complainers who overthink things too much and are dismissed, all too quickly and carelessly. The ailments they have are all in their head and are more for psychologists or psychiatrists to treat instead.

On this front, I consider myself lucky to at least have had Dr. W who has been willing to listen, advocate and think of different ways to get me help when she couldn't provide it herself. If I got a dollar for every time people have told me how lucky I was to have Dr. W as a doctor, my family and I would already be super wealthy people. But getting treated for any ailment, especially in a place like Canada – a fully developed country – should not be based on luck. And even if you happen to be the lucky few who are diagnosed properly, without having your symptoms easily dismissed as a "psychological one," the medical community still isn't in agreement on how to treat this condition. For instance, there are some who are against using Triptans (like Rizatriptan) and others advocating their use as an effective approach. Even identifying triggers of what causes the hemiplegic migraine is varied and inconsistent. Hemiplegia's web ensnares each of us differently, a cruel puppeteer pulling invisible strings, leaving us dancing to the rhythm of unknown triggers. What is consistent is that once a hemiplegic migraine chooses you to invade, you will become completely paralyzed, your life entirely disrupted.

Here in Canada, there seems to be only one national support group – Migraine Canada™ – that can potentially offer a voice for people like me and I only just recently discovered their existence, by accident. There is still so much work to do in uncovering the mysteries of this evasive disorder; and yet, there does not seem to be the aggressive will that is often needed to tackle such a conundrum. I suspect it is an issue of funding due to its lack of publicity and awareness of the disease. It just isn't a sexy enough topic for people to notice, and it leaves those of us who have already been struck by the hemiplegia to continue to be at the mercy of doctors and specialists who also do not know what to do. It is like the blind treating the blind.

Some may think that with the sharing of my story, I have found my peace with the hemiplegic migraine. That I have somehow accepted it as a part of me, that it is a part of my life. This is not that kind of book.

Thanks to the migraine, I have learned that the most excruciating pain is the sort that is invisible and untouchable. But while the migraine has lashed out some of its cruelest evils, I have also experienced the greatest kind of love because of its curse. I have come to learn the importance of gratitude and know now that without health, there is nothing. But despite all this, I will *never* make peace with it. Though unable to prevent the hemiplegia from entering my body when it decides to come, I at least have the will and freedom to reject its presence. It is the only power I have left against the paralysis. At best, there have been times when I've shifted my mindset to think that the migraine is what my body uses to signal that I've overdone it. It is a beacon that warns me that I've been going too fast and in need of slowing down. But I will never accept it as an extension of me.

While my story is not about making peace, it is about raising and spreading awareness of something that may otherwise have been buried. It is my hope that with my voice, I would be giving those who are suffering like I have, validity. For those who are still searching for answers to what is afflicting them, I have given a palpable possibility to pursue.

There are still many nights where I have been unable to sleep, afraid that if I drift away, the paralysis will once again silently take over. From time to time, I still find myself fending away the dark thoughts that lurk in the corner of my mind, taunting me that another hemiplegic episode is coming for me soon.

But in these moments where I would have easily yielded to fear, anger, and guilt, I am instead learning to acknowledge these emotions and honor the pain that has been in my past, so that I can choose between two paths: to stay stagnant and let all bad things in until I wither away and disappear; or to fight for my place in the world to move on and explore what other possibilities are there for me. To date, I have chosen the path of moving forward with my loved ones every time. It hasn't always been easy and there have been countless days where everything in me refuses to even try. But just as I was chosen to carry the hemiplegic migraine, I was also given life, and so I must continue to live.

The hemiplegia may grip me, but it will never define me. On these two battered feet, I stand tall, my heart a patchwork of scars and hope. I am still breathing, still laughing, still daring to believe that being alright isn't just a dream. Instead, it's the horizon I walk towards, one sunlit step at a time, because I am still living. I am still here.

RESOURCES

Since the publication of my journey with hemiplegic migraine, in addition to the Migraine Canada™ webpage, I stumbled upon by accident another resource called The Canadian Migraine Society:

Website: *https://www.migrainesociety.ca/.*

I was especially impressed of the vast information this webpage provided not only for people like me who suffer from migraines, but also for those who may have to care for someone with this condition. There was one resource labelled as a "Primer for Friends and Family" that I found especially helpful and was able to solicit permission from the Canadian Migraine Society to share:

A Chronic Migraine Primer for Friends and Family

You have been given this guide because someone you care about lives with a debilitating, complex neurological disease called Chronic Migraine. There is surprisingly little public awareness and understanding of this disease. My firm belief is that what people living with migraine really want, and need, is respect, understanding and empathy. I hope this information is useful in moving us all toward that end.

— **Maya Carvalho**, founder of **Canadian Migraine Society** and **Chronic Migraine Support Group Canada**

WHAT EXACTLY IS MIGRAINE?

- Migraine is a clinical diagnosis based on symptoms and medical history. At present there are no tests such as bloodwork, MRIs or scans to diagnose migraine, however your physician may order tests to rule out other dis-eases. Migraine includes a severe, throbbing or solid, intense headache, typically on one side of the head (but not exclusively) that lasts from 4–72 hours and is often accompanied by other symptoms including nausea, vomiting, light and sound sensitivity. The pain is different for everyone, but many have described it as being more intense than childbirth — without the reward. Other migraine symptoms include dizziness, vertigo, brain fog, fatigue, neck pain, muscle pain, aphasia (loss of the ability to speak, comprehend language, read, write) and ataxia (loss of muscle coordination, unsteadiness of gait), visual symptoms, cold hands and feet, mood changes, sensitivity to smell, diarrhea, constipation, fever, and swelling. There are some forms of migraine which do not include headache.

- The World Health Organization states that the disabling effects of severe migraine are "comparable to dementia, quadriplegia and active psychosis" (*Shapiro RE and Goadsby PJ Cephalalgia 2007*). Furthermore, the WHO classified the constant nature of **chronic migraine as "more disabling than blindness, paraplegia, angina or rheumatoid arthritis."** (*Harwood RH et al. Bull World Health Org 2004*).

- **Chronic Migraine** means that the person experiences **15 (or more) migraine days a month**. Take a moment to imagine incessant, intense pain and symptoms taking over your life. Many people have four phases of each migraine attack: **Prodrome**, **Aura**, **Headache** and **Postdrome**. A full migraine cycle can take several days to experience. Given this frequency, and the length of the combined phases of each attack, people with chronic migraine **are very rarely symptom free** — even on their good days.

- Each person living with chronic migraine is different and their attacks can have very different symptoms. Some people do not have head pain but other symptoms which are equally debilitating. **Migraine is a spectrum disorder — each migraine varies**, some are more tolerable than others.

- **There is no cure for migraine at present.** Some people can go into a migraine remission for a few months or years. Some people are lucky enough to find one medication or treatment that works extremely well; but for most of us trying to reduce our migraine attacks involves a **long-term multi-modal approach**. It requires an ongoing commitment to the trial and error of numerous medications, treatments, procedures, lifestyle changes, physical therapies and more. All these things *in combination* can make a real difference but there is no magic bullet.

- Some people experience intractable migraine 365 days of their lives. This means that they never get a respite to recharge, reboot, and rally for the next attack — it is always with them. If your loved one has a constant intractable migraine, **you should give them a medal**. You should realize how strong they are and what a struggle it can be to simply make it to the next day.

- This constant cycle of debilitating symptoms and recovery from those symptoms creates enormous fatigue. This is not the same as being tired— it is a pervasive, serious depletion of energy. **Some people can manage a few activities on a good day, others can only ever manage one**. Talking on the phone can be hard. Socializing can be hard. Physical exertion can be hard. Everything that requires energy has a cost. We make those cost/benefit decisions every day of our lives in order to maintain relationships and some quality of life. If you can't imagine this, ask about it.

- Most people with chronic migraine have comorbid illnesses such as IBS, Fibromyalgia, Arthritis, PCOS and many others. Try to imagine navigating other illnesses, medications and treatments, on top of chronic migraine. It is a complicated challenge, and in Canada, we rarely encounter healthcare professionals who look at us holistically and coordinate all our medications and treatments. That burden is left to us. **It's a huge job, a complex job, and a job that requires endless patience and tenacity. Be proud of your loved one for doing this**.

Things to AVOID saying:

— *"You have a migraine... again?!"* Yes, we do. That is the definition of chronic migraine.

— *"Are you better now?"* No — we are not better. Migraine cannot be cured, but our symptoms might be more manageable on one day than another day. Some people are very lucky and can go into a remission from chronic migraine but this is still not the case for most people.

Things that are HELPFUL to say:

— "I'm sorry your attacks are so frequent, that must be exhausting, you are an incredibly strong person."

—"How are your symptoms today? How are your pain levels today?"

—"What would be the best way for me to support you through this?"

—"Thank you so much for coming — I know this will have a cost for you and I appreciate it."

WHAT CAUSES MIGRAINE?

- Migraine is a genetic neurological disease that affects 1 billion people worldwide. It is not the same as headache — **headache is only one symptom of migraine**. Although the causes are not fully understood, it is now believed that migraine attacks originate in the brainstem area and involve hyper-excitability of the nervous system. Basically, neurons misfire and unleash an electrochemical reaction that sends pain signals to the cortex and cause other migraine symptoms.

Things to AVOID saying:

— "My neighbour's daughter's best friend did X and she cured her migraines." There is *no cure* for migraine, and it *cannot* be conquered by a magic X, Y or Z. Yoga will not stop it, a vacation will not stop it, and drinking more water will not stop it. Some of these techniques may mitigate a few

triggers but again, managing chronic migraine requires an involved, multi-modal approach and these types of simplifications tend to diminish the seriousness of this disease.

— *"I had a migraine the other day and took two Tylenol and it went away."* If two Tylenol eliminated your mi-graine, it is likely that you had a bad headache and not a migraine. It's incredibly frustrating for a person with chronic migraine to constantly deal with a lack of validation.

— *"Why do you have to take so many pills?"* or *"You really need to stop taking so much medication."* Unless you are a neurologist, you have no expertise in how much medication is necessary to manage this illness. Some people need two pills a day and some need six. Be thankful you don't have to deal with the myriad side effects that we do — it is not fun.

— *"You look great — you don't* look *like you're in pain."* Most of us do everything we can to hide this disease from people and look like we are not in pain. This is not indicative of how we are feeling on the inside. It is simply a reflection of how hard we want to feel normal, for a few minutes, an hour, or a day. It is also a reflection of how much we value our time with you and how much we don't want to affect others by looking the way we actually *feel*. Be flattered rather than questioning our pain.

Things that are HELPFUL to say:

— "I'm so sorry you have such a serious disease. I hope you find some treatments and medications that can help you manage it."

— "You look amazing — you hide your pain so well."

WHAT ARE MIGRAINE TRIGGERS?

- **Triggers are not causes — the cause is genetic**. Triggers simply set off the electrochemical reactions in the brain that cause the symptoms. For people with chronic migraine, it is rarely a matter of one trigger, but rather **multiple triggers stacking up** that tip us over the threshold into a migraine attack.

- **Each person with migraine has different triggers**. By the time a person becomes chronic, **their triggers are often numerous**. Triggers can be environmental, physical, and psychological. Some common triggers are weather fluctuations, hormonal shifts, loud noises, bright lights, perfume, too much physical exertion, stress, anxiety, food (fermented, aged, high in histamine or tyramine), alcohol, dehydration, and sleep disturbances.

Things to AVOID saying:

— *"Wow you seem so delicate and sensitive to everything."*

— *"Come out with us anyway, you'll feel better."* The patient is the expert, if they are telling you they can't go out, listen and respect that.

— *"You just need to destress. You just need to relax. If you take a vacation, your migraines will go away."* No, they will not. It IS helpful to get stress under control as a general life goal, but stress is *not* a trigger for everyone and again — it is not a *cause* of migraine.

266

— *"Oh no — why did you do X? Now you've given yourself a migraine!"* Do not blame the person for not being able to control all their triggers. It is a maze of landmines you never want to experience. It is *never* the person's fault if they trigger a migraine. Remember, triggers are *not the cause* of the disease. **Things that are HELPFUL to say:**

— *"It must be so challenging to navigate all those triggers every day. Which triggers are the worst for you? I'll try to reduce them when we're together."*

— *"If doing X is too much for you, I totally understand. I know you would be there if you could. Please do what is best for your health."*

HOW YOU CAN HELP YOUR LOVED ONE WITH CHRONIC MIGRAINE:

- **Be flexible with your plans**. We are rarely symptom free so it is impossible to plan ahead. We do not know when a migraine attack will hit, how intense each one will be, and how debilitated we will be that day or even the next day. Please try to be understanding if we have to cancel plans. I guarantee we are more upset about cancelling than you are, and we are the ones living with the attack that caused us to cancel — not you.

- **Offer to visit with us on our terms.** Chronic migraine typically makes our lives shrink down until we have limited social interaction. This can be extremely isolating. Every single visit with a friend or family member *means more to us than you know*. You can offer to do it during the hours when our pain is usually lower (ask us), and start with something easy like a cup of coffee so that there isn't too much physical exertion.

- **Ask about our triggers and symptoms and try to pay attention to them**. If possible, modify the environment when we're together to make it as calming and quiet as possible. Do not wear perfume or light scented candles if you know that is a trigger for us. Try to keep loud noises away from us. If food or alcohol is a trigger, do not push any foods or drinks by saying, "Oh, just try it!" or "A drink will take the edge off." You do not live with the consequences, we do.

- **Be conscious of how much we must preserve our energy.** We must constantly be pacing ourselves to not push ourselves into an attack. For more information look up Spoon Theory. For most patients that means limiting the duration and number of activities in a day. For many people, one activity is all we can manage. Do not push people to do overdo it and *never suggest* we are lazy. People living with chronic migraine are pushing through 24/7 with pain levels and symptoms you can hardly imagine — try to have empathy.

- **Offer to accompany us to our neurology appointments or other doctors' appointments.** We need advocates with us who can pay attention, stand up for our needs and concerns, and be a second set of ears for the information being given to us. Appointments are typically very short and there can be a lot of stress about getting our questions answered. Having support in this area can make an *enormous difference*.

- **Offer to take care of simple errands** that might be far too physically demanding for a person with chronic mi-graine such as grocery shopping, pickups at the dry-cleaner, going to the pharmacy, online shopping, or even just dropping off a simple meal so we don't have to cook. Driving can be a trigger for many people, so offering pick-ups and drop-offs can also be helpful.